THE JUSTICER

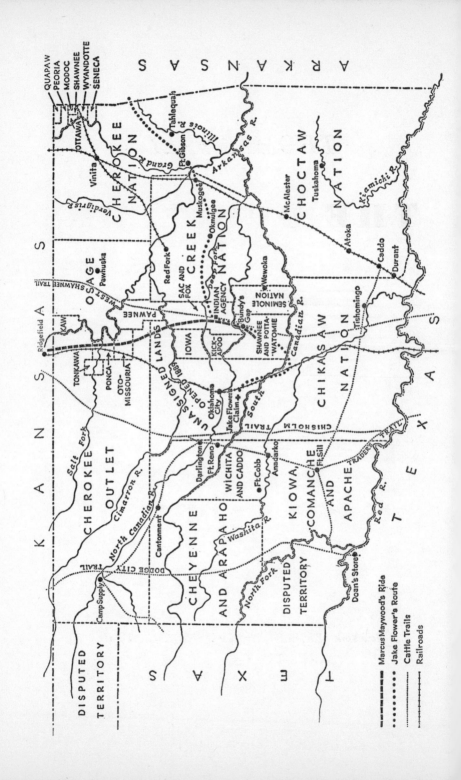

THOMAS FALL

THE JUSTICER

New York   RINEHART & COMPANY, INC.   Toronto

To my father and mother

Published simultaneously in Canada by
Clarke, Irwin & Company, Ltd., Toronto

FOREWORD

Neither the town of Ridgefield nor the court depicted in this story ever actually existed. However, certain courts with similar power and jurisdiction over government-owned lands and territories did exist during the post Civil War era. They were United States District Courts with special Circuit Court functions for cases of crimes committed where no state laws prevailed.

It is astonishing today for us to realize that these were criminal courts from which there was no appeal. Effective May 1, 1889, however, Congress enacted a law providing that "the final judgement of such court may be re-examined, reversed, or affirmed by the Supreme Court of the United States upon a writ of error. . . ." Thus the end of federal criminal courts of no appeal in America.

Public execution by federal courts came to an end a few years prior to the date of this story and the author pleads literary license (that happy institution) for setting a legal public hanging in the autumn of 1889. Ironically, no nation which practiced public execution later than the mid-1880's still has capital punishment in its criminal statutes. It almost seems a pity that the barbarism was stopped; for although the public enjoys its drink of blood, as a famous judge has recently pointed out, it also appears to have become disgusted with judicial execution in nations where it has been permitted to drink its fill.

Since the author had no intention of depicting or characterizing any actual historical individual or situation in connection with this period, he created Ridgefield and its court wholly out of his imagination. It would have been somewhere near the border of southern Kansas, overlooking the Cherokee Strip, if it had actually existed.

The Indian Territory was in a state of advanced chaos. It was a no man's land in the middle of a fast growing Southwestern civilization—a land where laws were confused and cultures in upheaval.

The Five Civilized Tribes (Cherokee, Creek, Seminole, Chickasaw and Choctaw) had been moved before the Civil War from their original homes in Eastern and Southern United States to the Indian Territory (now the state of Oklahoma). The removal treaties effecting this great migration of humanity engendered some of the bitterest controversy in American history outside the war itself. They had often been negotiated by ambitious and opportunistic government officials and signed by self-appointed groups of Indians whose authority was at least doubtful: but quickly ratified by the Senate and enforced by United States troops withal (the Cherokee Trail of Tears being a grisly example).

The Civilized Tribes, however, managed to build new nations for themselves in the West, with governments of an essentially elective and democratic nature providing for schools and even orphanages to be sustained by their national treasuries. But the war destroyed their civilization again. Naturally hostile to the United States, and goaded by influential Indians who previously had been slave owners, the Civilized Tribes joined the Confederacy, spending the war for the most part fighting among themselves over whether they should have done so.

The reconstruction period therefore found them beaten, starving, and in helpless violation of all their old inadequate treaties with the United States which, by then, had decided to place every Indian in America on a reservation somewhere and keep him there. New treaties were of course essential; and the Civilized Tribes were once again divested of their lands. The United States saw its chance to move yet dozens of other tribes and clans from the west and north. The new treaties promptly squeezed the Five Civilized Tribes into the eastern half of the Territory, making room in the western half for the removal of Cheyenne, Kiowa, Arapaho, Comanche, Apache, Wichita and Caddo groups. And many smaller clans from various parts of the nation were also singled out and literally stuffed into obscure corners of the Territory, frequently upon lands already designated, thus becoming additional sores upon the agonized body of Indian humanity.

And throughout all this unfortunate living arrangement, by 1889 (the year of the first run), had spread the ubiquitous renegade, black, white, mulatto, even Oriental, often wanted at home for one crime or another, sometimes merely opportunistic, usually willing to defraud and to plunder: a tragic backdrop against which the age of the American Indian would come to an end.

THE JUSTICER

"The truth is in all the things
that make men lie."

CHAPTER ONE

Although the people who knew him in Ridgefield were already forming a definite picture of him as a criminal lawyer, Angus DeWolfe had no precise image of himself. He was not on the verge of becoming rich, as many believed. He was certainly not cunning. And he did not feel mysterious simply because he preferred living quietly in a boardinghouse, occasionally playing rook in the evening, to carousing in saloons among extroverted bores. A lonely man, who enjoyed the law and believed in it, he was neither egotist enough to think of himself as fastidiously ethical nor cynic enough not to be.

His only close friend was his partner, Colonel John Beleau, who, he suspected and feared, had recently begun to share some of the unflattering appraisal of him. And he was hurt, for the Colonel had in fact been more father than friend. Angus's only specific enemy in town was Judge Willard Ring of the Federal District and Circuit Court. Judge Ring's attitude toward him had painted a part of the troubling portrait.

Angus had felt a distinct aversion to the Judge for years before he laid eyes on the man. The Judge, of course, had never heard of him prior to his practice in Ridgefield. Being highly moral men with different sets of moral values, the two had rubbed each other roughly from the beginning of their acquaintance.

The very bitter quality of their feeling was born on a hot summer night when the Judge hammered a deadlocked jury for a verdict in the murder trial of a half-breed Kiowa known down in the Indian Territory as Foxjaw.

"That jury takes a long time," the Indian said, looking at Angus stoically.

"They're afraid of the Judge," he replied. "But we're holding our own, or they wouldn't have stayed out this long."

He glanced around the restive courtroom, wondering if what he had said was true. Ben Procter, the prosecutor, was sitting at the opposite table with his assistant, Red Molloy. Angus knew they both still smarted from a defeat he had recently given them on a Supreme Court appeal involving the slavery laws. They were leaning toward each other in attitudes political and opportunistic. He grinned inwardly and shifted his gaze from them to the bench.

Judge Ring seemed dwarfed by the huge maple desk, but his head loomed large beneath thick hair, turning gray at the temples. His carefully trimmed mustache and whiskers were also touched with gray. His ears matched the size of his head, and nestled close underneath the shocks of hair. He was somehow neither handsome nor ugly, for the power of his personality always pushed through his physical semblance and created the man: fearsome, loyal, honest, cruel, insipid, depraved—depending upon the beholder's standards of measurement. To Angus, Judge Ring was a tragic failure: a modestly intelligent lawyer whose thwarted ambitions, agitated by a tinge of religious fanaticism, had so ensnarled his perspectives as to blind him to everything except the obvious.

When the jury finally came in again, Judge Ring leaned forward in the high-backed chair, his rich baritone vibrating into every corner of the room: "Mr. Foreman, have you reached a verdict?"

"Your Honor," said the foreman, "we have not. We're still deadlocked."

The spectators buzzed and the Judge rapped sharply with the gavel. He stared at the spectators through the silence he had induced, then turned to the jury.

"Gentlemen," he said urgently, "it is inconceivable that you could need more time. But I will give you more if you would like."

"It won't do any good, your Honor," the foreman said quickly. "We're not going to agree."

Angus watched the bench tensely. If the Judge kept pounding them, someone might yet break.

"The Court realizes," the Judge was saying, "that it is quite late. But we must bear in mind that it is our privilege as American citizens to lend ourselves tirelessly to the cause of justice. Are you certain, Mr. Foreman, that you won't be able to agree?"

"There's not a chance, Judge Ring. I'm certain."

"If you had a night of rest, and resumed your deliberations tomorrow, do you believe you might be able to reach a verdict?"

Even as the foreman answered, the individual jurors shook their heads vigorously.

"Very well," said the Judge. He leaned back in his chair and gazed wearily across the courtroom, his eyes returning at last to the jury. He said, in a soft, tremulous voice, "I will excuse you now, gentlemen, and declare a mistrial. The cause of justice is always strengthened when honest men debate an issue, whether they agree or not. Mr. Foreman, will you please approach the bench before you leave? The rest of you are now dismissed."

Angus sighed and looked at Foxjaw, whose face was a study in impassive brown. His long training as an Indian child never to show emotions to a white man now masked completely anything he may have been feeling.

This aspect of Indian behavior was to Angus the most curious thing he had learned about them. It was not really stoicism, despite its appearance, for Indians were emotional people; it was simply learned and studied silence, inevitably employed in the presence of whites.

"At least they did not hang me quickly," said Foxjaw.

"They're not going to hang you, either."

While the Judge conversed with the foreman, Angus exchanged glances with Ben Procter and Red Molloy, who were still sitting silently at the prosecution table. Procter was no fool; he most certainly knew that Foxjaw had not deserved a first-degree indictment. In asking for it, he had yielded to the Judge's righteous fury; and the Grand Jury had obliged merely because the prosecutor had made the request. Or could a man in Procter's position, goaded by ambition, praised by the local newspaper, bludgeoned by the pious friendship of Willard Ring, have much room left in his mind for reasonable consideration? Would there ever come a time in criminal jurisprudence when prosecutors in general might conceive of themselves as protectors of the innocent as well as pursuers of the guilty? As long as the office of prosecutor was a logical steppingstone to greater political opportunity, it seemed doubtful.

Judge Ring was pounding again.

Angus looked up and the Judge was staring at him. "The Court has decided to withhold its decision regarding another trial until nine o'clock next Thursday morning, Mr. DeWolfe. I would like to see you in chambers for a few minutes."

"Very well, your Honor," Angus said.

"And you, too, Mr. Procter."

"Of course, Judge," Ben Procter said.

"The Court will stand in recess." The Judge gave his gavel a cursory rap. He rose and strode from the courtroom through the back exit.

Angus turned to his client. "I'll come over to the jail later, Foxjaw."

"Tonight?"

"As soon as I've talked to the Judge."

He entered the private office behind the courtroom with some inner discretion warning him that hatred of the Judge could eat away his reasoning capacity if he were not able to control it.

The office was politely comfortable, even though its appointments were austere. The walls were paneled, and bore two large framed photographs— one of Abraham Lincoln, the other of U. S. Grant. The windows were curtained in gray velvet and the carpet was gray and red. The private desk was polished yellow maple, identical with the one in the courtroom.

"Have a chair, Mr. DeWolfe," said the Judge.

"Thank you."

"Sit over here, Mr. Procter."

"Thanks, Judge."

Ben Procter was a handsome, blond-haired man—lean and muscular. His countenance was stamped with alertness. Angus had never known a person more suited, from the mere standpoint of looks, to a public career. His smile was warm and easy, his manner considerate and not unduly considered—when he was off the courtroom stage. Yet he seemed always to be seizing the small opportunities. His mental vigilance was inevitably toward the next phase of his career; on the larger, more fundamental considerations of justice and punishment, he seemed unknowing.

Angus sat facing the desk, and the Judge frowned, not too unpleasantly.

"The vote was eight to four," he said.

"Is that right?" Both lawyers were surprised.

"The foreman told me that the first vote was six-six, and the second eight-four. It never changed after that."

Now the Judge paused, to let them consider.

"Surely," said Angus quickly, "there's no point in another trial under this indictment, Judge. It's obvious that——"

"Mr. Procter," the Judge cut in, ignoring Angus utterly, "the Court would entertain a motion by the government to reconsider the question of indictment."

Angus decided to hold his tongue and let them arrive at their conclusion. He thought that if he observed carefully, he would see Judge Ring making up Ben Procter's mind—and that the process would work as fast as Procter could figure out what the Judge wanted.

Procter said, "My office would hesitate, Judge, to burden the government with the time and expense of another trial if a satisfactory plea could be obtained without it. Molloy and I will work on your suggestion in the light of the Grand Jury investigation."

The Judge then turned to Angus. "How would your client plead to manslaughter, Mr. DeWolfe?"

"Guilty," Angus said steadily. "Mr. Procter knows——"

"I'm sure Mr. Procter knows whatever you have told him," the Judge cut in again, summarily showing his contempt. Angus worked to keep a rein on himself, but the back of his neck grew hot.

The Judge's expression did not change as he turned impassively to the prosecutor.

"The Court will consider whatever motion you put before it at nine o'clock Thursday morning." He cleared his throat, turning once more to Angus. The new wild flash in his eyes reflected a surge of bitterness. "Now I would like a word with you privately, Mr. DeWolfe."

"Certainly, Judge," Angus said thoughtfully.

He watched with curious amusement as Ben Procter awkwardly bowed out of Judge Ring's chambers—the functionary, observed in his pettiest function.

Judge Ring launched into him quickly.

"Mr. DeWolfe, you have been clever again. I am sure it gives you great satisfaction." His baritone had suddenly left and he was speaking in a high, tight voice. He paused, trying to regain control.

"I beg your pardon, Judge?" Angus said.

"You heard me, I am sure. Your trickery and your unflattering accusations of my motives in the courtroom bring me to the verge of tears. You accused me of prejudice, yet everyone knows that I am one of the best friends the Indians ever had. You told the jury that I would try to lead them into a conviction. I should remand you for contempt."

Angus stared at the Judge, and weighed his words.

"I am convinced," he said, "that Procter would have asked for manslaughter in the first place if left to his own thinking, Judge."

"Don't badger me," the Judge replied. "You know your man is guilty."

"He killed a man, no doubt about that. But——"

"There are few 'buts' that can be heard by the dead, Mr. DeWolfe. Your client, with a pine club, cold-bloodedly knocked a man's brains out. Now a fine woman is a widow, and three helpless children have no father."

"You explained that to the jury," Angus said heavily.

"It was my duty. I would be remiss if I did not guide the jury whenever it needed guidance."

The Judge paused again, and leaned back in his chair. He stared steadily, as though Angus might be capable of disappearing if his eyes were lifted for an instant.

"Mr. DeWolfe, I have been presiding Judge in this district for almost fifteen years. I believe I am respected by most of the people within my jurisdiction—respected even by the criminal element. It is my belief that you dislike me personally. I would like to ask you man to man whether my suspicion is correct."

"I simply don't believe in capital punishment," Angus replied evasively. "It keeps us medieval."

The Judge considered for a moment. Then he said, "The Lord spoke unto Moses, 'And if a man cause a blemish in his neighbor, so shall it be done to him; breach for breach, eye for eye, tooth for tooth: . . . and he that killeth a man, shall be put to death.' It's a harsh pronouncement, and it's probably the only Biblical directive to which I can't heartily subscribe. No man suffers more than I at the spectacle of men on the gallows. But I do not consider that I have ever killed a criminal. It is the law that kills them. Not Biblical law, but the law of this society, duly legislated by democratic process. I didn't make it, and I have no right to change it. Neither have you."

Now the Judge stared at him triumphantly, as though there were no conceivable rejoinder.

In Angus's mind was an epithet that had attached itself to Judge Ring months before—"The little man with the big gavel." He wondered what kind of person the Judge might have been if Nature had made him six inches taller. Certainly his gavel would have seemed smaller.

"Can we admit," he said slowly, "that the law is only an abstraction, Judge Ring? It changes as the hearts of men change."

"The hearts of men?" The Judge was bitterly sarcastic. "Have you any real concept of the men with whom this court must deal? During my tenure I have appointed a hundred and fifty-nine deputy marshals, who have risked their lives every minute of the day and night hunting down outlaws who know every trail and hide-out in the Territory. The Kiamichi and the Winding Stair are as familiar as the palms of their hands. Fanatic Confederate sympathizers will often aid a criminal simply because he is wanted by the United States. And you speak of the hearts of men. But let's not evade my question." The Judge interrupted himself, coloring slightly. "You bear me personal malice. I want to know why."

"I assure you," said Angus, believing a small, quieting lie more valorous than an unimportant troublemaking truth, "that I am only fighting for my clients' lives."

"Very well," Judge Ring said, a little sadly it seemed. "We will leave it at that." He got up from his chair and strode to the windows behind his desk. The draperies were drawn and he stood silhouetted against the gray velvet, a study in black and gray. "I have hesitated to call you down before now in the hope that, after you became familiar with my court, you'd temper your methods. You have been a disrupting influence ever since Colonel Beleau brought you here—how long is it? Almost two years? You have cast aspersions upon my integrity since the first case you defended before me. Nevertheless, I would like to be your friend. I would like to help you get back on the right road. That's all I have to say."

"Judge, I——"

"Good night, Mr. DeWolfe."

Angus stared at him, speechless.

The Judge took out his watch and began winding it with the large gold key which dangled from the chain on his chest.

By the time Angus had visited his client at the jail and returned to the street again, it was past eleven o'clock. He was still convulsed with anger.

Few lights were on except the row of new electric arcs which were the most recent development of Ridgefield. He remembered the time he had come through here twelve years ago, on his way from the Arizona Territory back to Maryland, determined to continue his education.

Ridgefield had been a rough and callow town then, of less than two thousand people—grown up with the help of the ever-expanding railroads from a cattle-trail watering stop. He remembered the way it came into view as he approached from the west—a burst of life on the dry prairie. He remembered the red and yellow clay-brick chimneys glistening in the sun, and, as he came nearer, the rush of wild excitement as crowds of people gathered to watch one of Judge Ring's mass executions. He remembered his first glimpse of the monstrous gallows: the high hewn beam stretched across a macabre scaffold fourteen feet high. Its victims—five of them—were hanged together that day. He could still hear their bootsteps on the planks. He could still see the dangling bodies and the thousands of gaping faces, and the vision made him ill.

CHAPTER TWO

Angus did not consider Sarah Borden unusually attractive, yet he watched her. Her feet were dainty and her face was clear and open. Her nose turned up at the very end. She was a trifle skinny, and her eyes darted when she talked.

This morning she was serving his breakfast at her mother's boarding-house table. She set out coffee and round brown biscuits, but refused to look at him.

"Thank you, Sarah," he said, pulling the coffee closer. "How are you this morning?"

Her nose seemed even more sharply turned on the end.

"Very well, thank you," she said, then disappeared with a rustle into the kitchen.

He would never marry this one, he thought. God forbid that he should want a wife that badly. Sarah should have been spanked by her father when she was younger.

Presently she came scowling with his plate of eggs.

"And here's the morning *Monograph*, Mr. DeWolfe," she said, placing the newspaper beside his plate. Then she disappeared again. He saw that the paper was neatly folded with an account of yesterday's court proceeding facing him.

He looked more closely. The item was more editorial than news. Judge Ring's powerful court was being traduced by the scurrilous tactics of an Eastern lawyer who obviously cared only for one thing: money. If this man continued, and there was no way to curb him, the incorruptible court would cease to function effectively. Criminals would thrive, no citizen would be safe. He could not help smiling at the inflammatory clichés.

He pushed aside his breakfast, only drinking the coffee. As he started to leave, Mrs. Borden, Sarah's plump and pleasant mother, appeared in the kitchen doorway.

"Aren't you going to eat, Mr. DeWolfe?" she asked.

"I'm not very hungry, Mother Borden," he said. "I enjoyed the coffee."

"You usually have a good appetite."

"Yes, I know. But not this morning."

"I feel sorry for you, my boy," she said, with pity swirling in her eyes.

"You do?" he asked.

But she had already disappeared into the kitchen.

He went unhappily to his room and dressed for work. Some people despised his mythical cunning, some even envied it; but he had not known that anyone pitied him for it. As he passed the front door, Sarah Borden spoke to him again.

"Mr. DeWolfe," she said, "my mother is too embarrassed to tell you, but we think you should find another place to live."

"Is that so, Sarah?"

"We aren't the kind of people who would protect criminals."

Then she fled to the kitchen.

Ugly thoughts confused his mind as he walked to his office on South Street above the bank. The Bordens were ordinary people with limited intelligences and there was no cause to hate them for the quality of their consciences. Yet he was greatly disturbed.

He paused before the glass-paneled door which bore his name:

Col. John Beleau——Angus DeWolfe
Attorneys-at-law

I hope you haven't turned on me, Colonel, he thought.

Later he realized that it had been a premonition. When he went inside, he could see through the door to Beleau's private office. The Colonel was obviously waiting for him.

"Good morning, Angus."

His partner was a mild-humored man, so blond of hair that its gray hardly showed. He would have been handsome if he had weighed thirty pounds less. He was everybody's friend, especially Angus DeWolfe's. He had given Angus his start in Ridgefield, with really no more recommendation than a letter from McCordle and Earnest in Washington, for whom Angus had apprenticed as clerk and librarian. The Colonel had been attracted by his previous acquaintance with the outlying western territories. Beleau was a gracious man, beset somehow with the permanent stamp of gentility, which made it impossible to view him as a figure of strength. But Angus loved him.

"I see you've read the paper," he said.

"My boy, you must be reasonable about this," the Colonel said, coming into the reception room to meet him. "You must temper your approach."

"You know, Colonel, on my way to the office this morning I searched my conscience, and so help me I came out clean. To hell with the Ridgefield *Monograph*."

"Angus, you can't take that attitude and get anywhere. You just can't do it."

"Get anywhere?"

"You know very well what I mean." The Colonel was breathing hard, his agitation greater than was characteristic of him. "I know you're sincere in your opposition to capital punishment, and you're a good lawyer, but——"

He broke off suddenly as footsteps approached the door. Two men entered together. They stood inside the door and waited for the Colonel to acknowledge them. Angus recognized them and understood immediately why his partner was so upset.

"Come in, gentlemen," the Colonel said. "I didn't expect you back so soon. Angus, you remember Mr. Hampton and Mr. Spencer from the railroad?"

"Yes, of course," he said, shaking hands, although he would have had trouble recalling their names. They were representatives of the company which retained Beleau and DeWolfe on an annual basis. Since the railroad had long been the Colonel's client, Angus did not know these men well. He had only met them perfunctorily on two or three occasions, a sense of discretion having prompted him to remain in the background.

"Mr. Hampton and Mr. Spencer were here earlier, Angus. We've been talking about you, and we've decided that you're making a mistake."

The man named Spencer was impatient.

"The railroad has the public feeling to consider, Mr. DeWolfe, as you must know. We are distressed with some of the publicity you've been getting."

"To be blunt," said the one named Hampton—and the ferret quality of his features magnified his sharply intoned voice—"the railroad simply can't tolerate your type of practice. There's no point in beating around the bush."

"I suppose not," Angus replied slowly. "No doubt you gentlemen have read the morning *Monograph*."

"Yes, we have," Spencer replied. "It expresses our own sentiments, Mr. DeWolfe."

"And yours, too, Colonel?" he asked, angered enough to put his partner on the spot.

The Colonel flushed. "Hoey Johnson wrote that piece, Angus. It's what old man Johnson wanted written. Most people will agree with it."

The Colonel was, of course, right. Most people liked being worked up a little, for agitation lessened the oppressiveness of routine living. Most people like to talk, and old man Johnson knew what all successful purveyors of conversation topics know—that most people will more readily agree with an argument that is easy, obvious and indignant, than with one that is thoughtful and forbearing.

He asked, "Am I being told that I can't associate with a firm that represents the railroad?"

"Precisely," said Hampton.

"Unless," said Spencer, "you decide to give up the criminal practice. I don't know how lucrative it is, but——"

"The retainers," said the Colonel quickly, "are not Angus's prime consideration, I assure you."

"Whatever the prime consideration is," Hampton went on, "the railroad must think about the public. We can't retain a man who defends the thugs who rob our trains. I'm sure you'll have something to say to us promptly, Colonel."

"I will," said Colonel Beleau.

Angus did not answer, but watched the two men leave the office in step, as though they were part of a well-drilled squadron.

Now he knew. The Colonel was in an impossible position, and Angus felt sorry for him. He wondered what he would do if the situation were reversed.

"My boy," said the Colonel gently, "you'll be ruined if you continue——"

"Fighting for my clients?" Angus asked.

Beleau thought for a moment, his face showing pain. "Don't be caustic with me," he said. "I make my living mainly off the railroads. My family depends upon my income—and the railroad's attitude has got to be important."

The Colonel was father of three children, the oldest being a young man of twenty-one, now studying medicine in Chicago. The other two were daughters, sixteen and thirteen, both still going to school in Ridgefield. The Beleaus were a substantial family, held together by the Colonel's successful pursuit of his chosen profession.

"Yes, I know," Angus said.

"Men learn," the Colonel went on, pulling at the skin which covered his Adam's apple, thereby giving himself a suggestion of triple chin, "that they simply can't oppose the trends and beliefs of the vast majority of people. That's a fact."

"I don't want to think you're being fatuous," Angus replied bitterly, "but aren't you advising me in the light of your own problems? I don't care what Hoey Johnson writes for his uncle. And I don't care what two pea-brains from the railroad think. But I do care what you think, Colonel—and I can't help wondering if you do actually believe I'm wrong."

The Colonel stopped pulling the skin on his neck and looked away. "I mean every word of it. Your remarks about the Judge yesterday, when you made your summation—people here love the Judge."

"So he told me last night. What I said to the jury was true, wasn't it?"

"Perhaps there was an element of truth in it. But you might have said it more carefully——"

"And have the jury misunderstand me? The Judge admits that he deliberately leads them. When I challenged him in chambers, he quoted the Bible."

"Why must you defend such criminals, anyway? Tell me the truth—is it for money?" The Colonel was looking straight at him now.

"I'm getting nothing from Foxjaw, and you know it. He isn't a killer. He hit a man when he was drunk, while they were scuffling half in fun. The other man might have killed him."

"But what about the others? Halley for instance, and that horrible Gunnysack McCloud?"

"You know about those fees, too," Angus snapped. "I haven't been holding out." He glared at the Colonel, now more shocked than hurt.

The Colonel's wide, childish eyes stared back. "Thank you, Angus," he said earnestly. "And please accept my apology for asking such a question. Everyone in town was shocked when you turned the trick for that monster Gunnysack. And everyone knows you were well paid. People want characters like that put away. They *should* be put away. Damn it, Angus, Judge Ring is right. He's dealing with cold-blooded killers and rapists, men who'd shoot you for a nickel. A civilized community has a right to want them done away with."

Angus pulled his tie loose and his shoulders sagged. He said, as much in colloquy with himself as with the Colonel, "Foxjaw isn't cold-blooded. He wouldn't shoot anyone. It's true that some of the felons coming through the district court are incorrigible—many of them are. But I see no point in killing them for the excitement and entertainment of the populace."

"What a way to talk," cried the Colonel. "A fellow with your youth—with your prospects."

"Oh, stop it," Angus said. "This is all because I'm not afraid of the Judge. And because you're worried about your railroad practice. Isn't it?"

"Partially, I suppose, but you put it so baldly as to magnify the truth. There is some element——"

"Christ," Angus said. "And you have the effrontery to accuse me of being mercenary."

The Colonel turned fiery red. The blush rose from his collar and suffused his face in scorching embarrassment.

"Let's let our tempers cool," he said. "We shouldn't talk this way to each other."

"I'm sorry, Colonel. We shouldn't."

The Colonel went into his private office and began puttering with things, moving papers about, self-consciously covering his hurt feelings with pretense.

Angus went into his own office and sat quietly, cast adrift in a new dimension of loneliness. He had leaned heavily on his partnership with the older lawyer. In this town, among people who were essentially alien to him, he had gone his lonely way from the boardinghouse to the office to the courtroom. Always the office, engendering as it did a sense of the Colonel's civilized character, felt warm and welcoming; and he welcomed the feeling. His greatest asset in this association was not the Colonel's intellect or legal knowledge, but the very unbarbaric quality of his partner's character.

Impulsively, he turned to the half-drawn map which lay on a table behind his desk. It was a map of the Indian Nations, which he had begun sketching several weeks earlier. He had traced in the rivers, railroads and cattle trails from an almanac map, and had begun finding the boundaries of the various tribes from what he knew of the removal treaties and from information he could pick up from the Indian Agents he knew. To forget for a moment his messy impasse with the best friend he'd ever had, he began studying the map again.

There had been bubbling for years in the back of his mind an ambition to write a treatise, perhaps a book, on the criminal problems among the Indians. He was certain there could be developed a meaningful correlation between the removal treaties, their enforcement, their impact on the changing cultures of the tribes, and the incidence of crime in the Indian Nations. He believed that only statehood could unify the laws and provide a proper legal jurisdiction for the entire Indian Territory.

These thoughts always absorbed him, and he chafed under the knowledge that he would never do the research, never make a survey or indeed publish a book, if he did not learn to control his mind and his energy. He wasted his off-duty time—dreaming. Until lately, dreaming of women. Or, rather, of a woman who did not exist. A woman who would help him with the study he would love to make. A woman who——

Shuffling feet at the door broke into his reverie.

Luke Sweeley, the lame old drayman who always met the train from St. Louis and carted the mailbag in his mule-drawn surrey to the post office on the main floor of the Federal Building, came through the reception room into his office. Luke grinned, depositing a bundle on Angus's desk.

"You're getting lots of mail lately," he said. "Business pretty good?"

"Yes, thank you, Luke. I'm beginning to need a secretary."

"You need a good wife, Angus. That's what made a man out of me."

"Thanks for the advice," Angus said, annoyed.

The old man winked, then asked, "Is that a map of the Nations?"

"Yes. I've been drawing it."

"Got it wrong here," Luke said, squinting at the map. "This east-west line between the Cherokees and Creeks crosses the Verdigris River south of the railroad, about right here. And down here, where the boundary runs into the Arkansas River, it's about fifteen-sixteen miles west of Fort Gibson. The line don't actually touch the Grand River at all."

"Thank you," Angus said, trying not to be impatient.

Luke was a garrulous character, much too spry for one his age with a game leg—a knee which was stiff with a slight bend in it. His eyes were faded blue, and the skin around his eye sockets was mottled with tiny white tumors. A cataract was encroaching upon the left eye, which gave it a wild look. His mustache was white and trimmed, and bore the only untidy aspect of his appearance; the center of it was stained from tobacco juice. Luke chewed incessantly, and could hold the juice in his mouth for interminable periods if he were caught with no place to spit. He had been known to swallow it surreptitiously in emergency; but he did not like to be observed swallowing, for he rather fancied his reputation for being able to hold it.

"Any time, Angus," he replied. "I could help you with the western part, too."

"I wish you would, Luke. Sometime."

Luke sniffed at the rebuff. Then he pushed the mail bundle closer. "These are all yours, Angus. I've got the Colonel's in another bundle. If you ever hire a secretary, I might apply for the job. I'd make a good detective, too. But I wouldn't want to work for crooks and killers, like you do. That'd be the only hitch in it." He looked coyly unconcerned and Angus was amused by the antic. This was the first touch of humor anyone had shown him recently.

"Are you trying to pick a fight with me, Luke?"

"This ain't really none of my business—but tell me, do you really think that Injun wasn't guilty last night? And wasn't that other fellow you got off, that Gunnysack nigger—wasn't he just about the worst killer Judge Ring ever dragged out of the Nations?"

Luke was considered half-witted by most people; not demented, in a strictly scientific evaluation, but simply short of practical brains.

"Luke," he said, "Foxjaw is guilty of killing, but not of murder. He is guilty of manslaughter."

"The man he hit with that pine knot was slaughtered, all right."

"Well, Foxjaw will go to prison. But he won't be hanged. And what we established in the Gunnysack case was that his conviction in Judge Ring's court was illegal. It was a complicated case, so we'd better not go into it now."

"Is that so?" said Luke Sweeley. He grew silent and backed away from the desk, glancing again at the mail.

Angus untied the bundle and thumbed through the envelopes absently, noticing the curious letter for the first time.

It attracted his attention because it was written on fine white stationery

[22]

in light blue ink, certainly a lady's handwriting. It bore no return address, but had been mailed in St. Louis.

It was quickly obvious that Luke Sweeley was hanging around to watch his reaction to that particular letter.

"What's so interesting about this? Have you already read it?"

"No, I haven't read it." Luke grinned. "I just read minds and signs, Angus. I guess she's going to fool her pappy, sending it from St. Louis."

"Who's going to fool her pappy?"

"Miss Ring," said Luke.

Chuckling, the old man hovered nearer the desk, but Angus pulled the letter out of his vision.

"How do you know who it's from?"

"It's Miss Janet Ring's handwriting. I've seen it many times. Her old daddy'd be in a fit if he knowed his girl was writing to you." Luke laughed heartily. "She knows it, too. So do you, and so do I."

"I suppose you want me to let you read it," Angus said.

Luke backed away.

"It's none of my business, except that I keep my eyes open around this town. Reckon I could guess what's in it, anyway."

The old man turned from the desk and limped through the reception room, descending the stairs to the street below with a clump at each step as his game leg reached it, out of control. There wasn't a sound from the Colonel's office, but Angus was certain his partner had been listening. He wished he were alone with the letter.

When he tore it open and saw that it was indeed from Janet Ring, he was not surprised only because Luke had taken the totally unexpected element away. Perhaps the last person from whom he would have expected a letter was Judge Ring's sheltered, plain-faced, old-maid daughter.

My Dear Mr. DeWolfe:

I am addressing this communication to you out of desperation. You must surely know that my father would summarily disown me if he should ever discover that I have corresponded with you.

I urge you, Mr. DeWolfe, to come to the defense of Marcus Maywood, who has been sentenced to hang on September fourteenth next. You are undoubtedly familiar with his recent conviction for the murder of the unfortunate Flower family. The counselor from St. Louis who defended him has since died of a heart condition.

Mr. DeWolfe, let me make clear that I am no hypocrite. My family holds you in disdain for the disturbance you have lately created in my father's court. But I do sincerely believe that you are the only person who could help this pathetic Indian boy, and he does not deserve to die. He has no money, but I will be responsible for your retainer. The defendant in question is a former student of mine.

I beg you, Mr. DeWolfe, to regard this letter in strictest confidence. And please do not communicate with me, for my father would surely discover it, and I would never be able to explain. It is a risk even for me to write to you.

Yours hopefully,
Miss Janet Ring

When he had finished reading it, he looked up and saw his partner standing at the door, watching him.

He said, "Want to see something curious, Colonel?"

Beleau took his spectacles from his shirt pocket and perched them on his nose, reading the letter slowly. Then he put it on Angus's desk, sorry he'd even touched it.

"You shouldn't have shown this to me. It's confidential."

"Judge Ring shouldn't have tried the case if his daughter was involved. There's grounds for appeal right there."

"You've got to fight with the Judge, haven't you, Angus? I suppose you remember the Maywood case."

"Doesn't everybody?"

"That Indian butchered four people. Four perfectly innocent human beings."

"Something must have been going on between him and his teacher, too."

"Angus, Janet Ring may be an old maid, but she's a person of rare and delicate character. She'd naturally be sympathetic to an unfortunate former student. But that Shawnee is a crazy killer, and you've got to keep out of it, for Christ's sake. Now—I'm going out to see Landsby this afternoon and won't be back in the office until tomorrow. I'll try to talk to Hampton and Spencer again, if you'll just give in a little. They'll be at the hotel for a couple of days."

"Colonel, if——"

"Don't say it, Angus. Let's don't talk about it any more until tomorrow morning."

The Colonel walked out of the office, covering up his sorrow with a blustering stride. Angus sat alone, unable or unwilling to think. He wasn't sure which.

He glanced at the letter again.

The image of Janet Ring riding in her father's buggy came to him. He had often seen them together on Sunday afternoons. He had always been amazed to note that the "girl" looked more like a little old lady. Was she delicate and rare? He laughed at the Colonel's pretty notion, even as a great sadness settled over him. He lit a cigar to keep from feeling completely alone.

CHAPTER THREE

The next morning he heard some talk about Janet Ring in the back of Phil Beckett's pharmacy.

Beckett's was a friendly place to congregate; there, among the fragrant soaps and medicinal candies, faintly touched with the smells of camphor, calomel and coal tar, one could always join an amiable conversation. On the table near the back lay Milwaukee, Chicago and Kansas City papers never more than a week old. Nobody ever made you feel more welcome than Phil Beckett.

"She looked like an old maid even as a girl," said Abe Heller, who was in from the dry goods store. "Some people were born not to get married, I guess. It's a tragedy when it happens to a girl."

"Her daddy wouldn't want her to get married," said someone else. "He's a great Judge, and a great man, but that's a fault it seems to me. You know, I've never seen her in his courtroom, not once in all these years."

"She was at the trial of that Shawnee Indian one day," said Phil Beckett. Angus listened, watching Beckett compound a pepsin elixir for one of Doc McKay's croupy patients.

"She was?" he asked. "I've never seen her in the courtroom."

"I was on that jury," said Phil Beckett. "She came to hear the verdict, and I remember she got up immediately and left."

"It'll be curious to see if she comes to his hanging, won't it?" said Sam Wilson, proprietor of the harness store next door.

A sudden silence fell over the little group. Angus felt that they had only then become conscious of his presence.

"If somebody like Angus don't get him off," said Sam Wilson. "I'd better get back to the store, boys."

One by one the others followed Wilson's move, nodding and grunting. Soon Angus was alone with Phil Beckett and Doc McKay. He stood quietly, watching Beckett finish the preparation, feeling strange and resentful. Earlier in his life it had been easy to have people gather around him.

"Phil usually makes me do my own work behind the prescription counter," Doc said. "The boys gave you the cold shoulder all of a sudden, didn't they, Angus?"

"I'm not the most popular man in town right now," he admitted.

Doc scratched the pink top of his balding head. "Don't let it worry you. You're doing all right. Don't let Phil here push you around, either, just because he was on a jury. He's only a country cough-syrup maker."

Doc laughed good-humoredly, and so did Phil Beckett.

"I'm not trying to practice law, Doc," said Phil. "Here's your bottle of swill. This stuff won't cure anything."

"Sometimes it makes folks think they're getting medicine, and it works," Doc said. "Goodbye, Angus. We ought to have a talk sometime. My business is keeping people from dying. Same as yours, in a way." He winked.

"Goodbye, Doc," he said.

Phil Beckett was a slender reed of a man, no bigger at the waist than a good gatepost. But his face, long and pleasant, was strong-looking. Angus had always thought of him as fairly intelligent. He leaned against the counter and watched Beckett casually.

"Tell me about that Maywood trial," he said at last.

Phil Beckett shook his head. "That Indian hasn't got any money, Angus."

"I defend people for nothing sometimes—if I think there is anything I can do."

Beckett looked skeptical. The vertical lines of his face were accented by his eyebrows which gradually arched.

"There isn't much to tell. Maywood killed that family that was crossing the Shawnee country to their claim. Then he tried to fake an alibi with the Quaker schoolmaster down there. When they caught him, he had Jake Flower's money sewed in his mattress. He murdered the whole family— father, mother and two little kids."

"Pretty grisly," Angus said.

"Folks in the courtroom got sick at their stomachs."

"What was the motive, Phil? Why is he supposed to have done it?"

Beckett flushed with sudden anger, his face admitting that talking about it had made him very tense.

"You say *supposed* as though there might be some doubt."

"Unless somebody saw him do it, he's convicted on circumstantial evidence. There's really nothing wrong with saying supposed. I didn't mean to offend you."

"Angus, I can't forget that you sprung that Gunnysack McCloud at the last minute. It was a clever trick, and you're a smart lawyer or you couldn't have pulled it out of the bag. But I don't quite know how you could sleep at night after doing it. Now I guess you're going to spring this Shawnee butcher boy."

Beckett had lost control of himself; he was consumed by raging contempt, and Angus realized that talking to him was useless.

"Phil," he said, "I hope you'll——"

"I've got a lot of work to do, if you'll excuse me." Beckett turned his back suddenly and busied himself with his bottles.

One man's reasonable doubt, Angus knew, was a second man's quibbling and a third man's virtual proof. Out of the domain of the exact sciences, a jury admonition might be expected to say, there is no absolute certainty. Guilt of the accused must therefore be deduced largely from a variety of circumstances leading to proof, not absolutely certain, but beyond a doubt for which a reason exists. If the jury could reconcile the evidence before it with any reasonable hypothesis consistent with the defendant's innocence, it should do so. No such hypothesis lived in Phil Beckett's mind. The Shawnee Indian, believed deserving of life by the Judge's old-maid daughter, who had not been a juror, was certainly deserving of death in the opinion of everybody's friend, Phil Beckett, who had.

Thinking about it, Angus walked down to the depot and sat on a wooden bench, watching heat shimmers rise from the railroad tracks until Luke Sweeley drove up in the wobbly surrey.

"Waiting for the train, Angus?" the old drayman asked, mopping his face with a blue bandana.

"No, I've been waiting for you."

Luke sat down on the bench. He took out a plug of tobacco and bit off a large portion, wallowing it cumbersomely in his mouth to get it soaking.

"Care for a chew?" he asked.

"I don't chew. Thanks, Luke."

Grinning, Luke stuffed the plug into his shirt. "Did you come to ask me about that Shawnee over in the jail?"

"How did you guess?"

"Miss Ring writes to you, a man that defends criminals. That's cipher number one. She went to the Indian's trial one day, first time she ever set foot in her pappy's court. Cipher number two. Add them together, she wrote to you about the Indian. Her pappy would skin her if he knew it."

Luke smiled pleasantly, pleased with his deduction. And Angus was surprised at the logic. Here was an old codger, long since reduced in status to the position of town clown by the people of Ridgefield, now significantly involved in an intrigue that few people knew about. Crazy old cripple, gimpy Luke, they called him. For the most part he was treated as though he had no feelings of his own, and Angus believed that he had been guilty of this himself. The town dumb-wit isn't supposed to have feelings, to say nothing of intelligence; every town knows that.

Luke pulled at his whiskers.

"I always believe in a fair exchange, Angus. I'll answer your questions and you answer mine." Now the old man balled up the tobacco with his tongue, tucked it deeply into his cheek, and squirted tobacco juice eight feet into the sun-baked ballast beside his surrey wheel. "That a fair exchange?"

"A lawyer can't talk about his clients, Luke. It's against legal ethics."

"Maywood ain't your client," Luke said.

"How do you know?"

"I hauled some lime down to the jail and while I was there, I asked him. That's how I know."

"You're pretty damn curious, it seems to me," Angus said.

Luke shrugged. "I'm asking questions, same as you are."

"I didn't mean to offend you this morning, Luke. I had a lot on my mind. I really will appreciate it if you'll tell me what you know——"

"I know he ain't your client. That's about all." Luke chewed contentedly, looking away toward the sun.

Angus mopped his face and tried again. "All right, I'll play it your way. Ask me a question."

Unblinking, the old man said, "Did you ever kill a man?"

He glared at Luke, who went on quickly to amplify his question: "I mean in cold blood. Not in the war and not prosecuting or anything like that, but shoot a man down?"

Luke's tone bore finality. We play, or we don't, he seemed to be saying.

"Yes," Angus replied, and a sickened feeling hit his stomach. "Once— about twelve years ago."

"An outlaw?"

"Yes."

"Must be why you don't believe in hanging. Some folks think maybe you're an outlaw yourself. Your turn."

Angus wondered vaguely if he would ever be completely free of the memory of shooting Drogan that day in the canyon below the waterfall— of turning red with human blood a serene pool of mountain water; of ending one life and in the process maiming another, his own. He knew that somehow he must never cease remembering altogether. Some part of his stability rested upon a continuous departure from that moment.

"Why did you ask me that?" he said.

Luke squirted tobacco juice at the surrey wheel again. "Thought you wanted to know about the Indian."

The old man's comic indifference brought Angus back from the past.

"All right. Here's my first question. What has Janet Ring ever had to do with Maywood that you know about?"

"Well, quite a bit." Luke grinned. "She used to slip off to see him, east of town. His cabin is on my place, you know. He paid me a dollar a month. It was just a shack that some niggers used to live in before I bought the place from the bank. Between quitting time at his office and dusk, was when she used to go out there. She always went home before her daddy left the court. You know how late he works all the time. I'll bet I'm the onlyest man in Ridgefield that knows she used to go visiting that Indian. I've been feeding his horse at my barn. I guess he'll be mine after they hang the kid, won't he?"

Angus laughed. Luke took on stature in his eyes. Dressed like a clown, with whimsical speech and a pretense of casual curiosity, he was involved up to his ears in the story of the Indian and the old maid. It seemed logical now to believe that Luke had known all along the content of Janet Ring's letter; that ciphers number one and number two had been deductions after the fact.

"Ask your next question, Luke," he said.

"All right. This one's been a puzzle to me. I've heard the boys around town arguing about it. The question is, do you ever sneak upstairs at the Red Handkerchief?"

He was amused as well as surprised by this one.

"Who's been saying I did?"

"You ain't married, you don't mix up much. Some says you probably go whoring on the sly."

"That's a fairly personal question, isn't it?"

"Yes, and I feel kinda bad about it, too. But I'm such a nosy old man— you know how it is." Luke shrugged, indicating that he could do no more about it than Angus could.

"I defended one of the Red Handkerchief girls before the magistrate last year, after that ordinance was passed that they couldn't be on the streets alone after dark. But it wasn't social. It was purely business."

Luke chuckled. "Other way around would have been business to her, Angus. I guess it's your turn again."

"All right. What did they do out there at his cabin, when she visited him? How did they spend their time?"

"In a little garden he built," Luke said. "Raised wildflowers they found in the woods. Read poetry. I don't know nothing about poetry myself. Sometimes they was silent and I don't know what they was doing then." Luke sniffed and rubbed his nose with the back of his hand. "You can go and see the garden. It's a right pretty spot. The cabin ain't locked, or anything."

"Well, I'll be damned."

"I sure was, when I discovered it."

Angus laughed heartily. "Do you think she was in love with him?"

"She was his teacher, that's all I know for sure. She's maybe nine, ten years older than he is."

"Do you think he's a killer?"

Luke blinked thoughtfully. "The jury said he was. Everybody seems to think he's as bloody as they come."

"That's not what I asked. I want to know whether, in your opinion, he seems like a person capable of murdering four people for money?"

"I ain't the best judge in the world, I don't guess. That Quaker man wouldn't have lied."

Angus said, "If there's any reason at all—no matter how ridiculous it may seem—if there's any reason at all to doubt that he's guilty, I'd like to know about it."

"He never acted like a bad sort to me. He thought I was doing him a favor to let him live in that old nigger shack. But I don't think the Quaker was lying about it."

Luke Sweeley, therefore, had doubts—but were they reasonable? If he had been a juror, could he have been morally certain? No one had had a reasonable doubt that the Quaker had told the truth; indeed, his being a Quaker would have made any doubt of his truthfulness unreasonable. And were the facts involved, in reality, facts at all? Surely science could easily say that what stood for facts in a court of law were only the remembrances and opinions of human beings under stress: that "facts" were calculated assumptions—but that death was absolutely certain, and permanent.

"I have a few more questions, Luke. After I'm through, you can ask me anything you like."

"Fair enough, Angus."

"What's your opinion of Judge Ring?"

"Well, now." Luke worked the tobacco around in his mouth. "He hurt my feelings one time, when he first came here to live. I wouldn't trust what I think about him."

"How did he hurt your feelings?"

"I brought a load of his stuff from the depot—books and boxes of stuff that was sent here on the freight cars. He'd had George Conlon over there turning the sun parlor into a library, and he already had his big desk sitting there. And I done a foolish thing, Angus."

"What happened?"

"I sat down at his desk, pretending I was up in front of the courtroom. He had a rack of pipes sitting on the desk, and I picked up the largest one he had. I pounded like it was a gavel, and I said out loud, 'This Court will come to order.' Well, by God, Angus, I glanced up and there he was.

Standing in the door looking at me like I was a chicken thief. He said, 'Pounding a gavel doesn't make a man a Judge.'"

"Maybe he was just kidding you."

"Like I said, I might have been a chicken thief."

He found it curious that Luke's interest in the case, like his own, was based partially at least on hatred of the Judge.

"Does Miss Ring know that you're aware of her visits out there?" he asked.

"No reason why she should. I just happened to find out about it while I was fishing on Big Creek above the garden. I never even seen her buggy go by. My house sets off a piece from the road, with a lane leading to it. You ought to come out and see me sometime. I got a right nice little place."

"Let's go now, Luke. I'd like to have a look at that cabin."

"Come on. I've got to throw these mail sacks inside the depot first."

Angus climbed in beside Luke who slapped the mule with the reins. The surrey wobbled out of town on the dirt road which led toward the southeast. They passed the corrals near the tracks, many of which were abandoned, for the railroad had already begun picking up cattle below the Red River.

The change was still a marvel to him. The gawky village was now full grown, with a gas system, concrete sidewalks, good cobblestone streets divided by streetcar tracks, wagon and furniture factories, an ice plant, four grain elevators, a beautiful new Opera House. Ridgefield was becoming the front door of the American Southwest. And making money was fast becoming the heavily trafficked back door of the American dream.

He remembered the way it had looked when he came through here after completing his mission for the cattle company, determined to return to the East and continue his education. He remembered what he had said to the detectives McCord and Westron that day.

It had happened in the old Ridge Hotel, upstairs off the back corridor. They'd been feeding him whiskey for an hour, bragging on the job he'd done, trying to persuade him to stay. He remembered that he got up from the table and walked to the window where he stood gazing across the lower end of the town. Everywhere could be seen and felt the atmosphere that was being created for the hanging. Groups of men gathered, families camped in wagons at the edge of town, children played—killer and hangman? And beyond, the rolling grassland stretched toward the horizon over the Osage and Cherokee lands and the Indian Territory, a lawless country made bloody because white men had pushed the Indians for a thousand miles and were trying to push even more.

McCord had said, "This country needs you, Angus. The new Judge here means business. His kind of law will spread. Together, we can clean up this place."

And he had whirled on McCord in uncontrollable fury. "Shut up," he had said. "Don't try to pressure me. I'll make my decisions according to my own mind. Judge Ring is a medieval-minded functionary. Maybe you don't know what that means. Well, I know what it means. I wasn't always a God damned tramp." And he had left them gaping in disbelief, feeling that he could no longer stomach the sound of people, that the only company he wanted was that of his horse and the clean, honest smell of straw.

"I'm going to get me a new rig," Luke said, pulling him out of the past again. "As soon as I can afford it."

"You are?"

"One of them little jump-seat wagons. Old Eubanks is going to be mighty proud pulling one of them little outfits. He knows we're talking about him. Look at his ears wiggle."

The mule wagged his ears, then laid them back against his head as he pulled.

They spent most of an hour at Maywood's cabin, and turned up nothing of particular interest. The cabin had been ransacked by the deputy marshals who had investigated Marcus for Ben Procter, but it appeared to have been kept orderly before that. It was a two-room log cabin, well chinked and tight at the roof line. Luke told Angus that the Indian had spent quite a lot of time fixing it up. He had split a pile of cedar shakes with which he had repaired the roof. The stone fireplace and chimney had been carefully patched with good mortar.

"I bought the cement, and he done the work," Luke said.

In the bedroom, Angus noticed a row of clothes pegs along one wall. Marcus's clothes had been dropped to the floor below the pegs, by the marshals, no doubt, as they went through them. A thick feather mattress had been pulled off the rope bed and cut to shreds. The place was floating in feathers.

"It's a mess in here, ain't it, Angus?"

"You can see that Marcus kept a neat house, though."

"He was a clean boy, far as living habits goes."

Near the hearth a basket of wood chips had been turned over and kicked around. Angus picked up the basket.

"Let's gather up his stuff and take it over to your place, Luke. Seems a shame to leave it like this."

"I didn't know if I should or not. I didn't want anybody to say I'd been meddling."

They shook Marcus's clothes free of feathers and collected into the basket all the loose objects which lay around—a set of rawhide horse hobbles, a pair of Mexican spurs and some silvered horse trappings, a pair of old boots and a bootjack, a dirt-caked buckskin pouch and a fancy beaded calfskin poke, an old pair of soft leather gauntlets, and a small coal-oil hand lamp.

"Someone might steal this stuff," Angus said.

"Reckon it'd be all right if I cleaned the place up. I mean the feathers and all?"

"Have you got some bags we could put them in?"

"How about some gunny sacks?"

"Fine. Let's go through the feathers carefully."

But they found nothing. They filled three gunny sacks with the feathers, then swept the wood chips into the fireplace.

"Here's an old charcoal foot warmer, Angus. Want to take it, too?"

"We might as well."

They loaded everything into the surrey, then drove around the bend and through the lane to Luke's place.

Angus was amazed.

He didn't know why he should have expected to find Luke living in a hovel. But he was greatly surprised when they drew up in front of a tidy little house, painted yellow, with brown shutters and flower lattices with morning-glories.

Luke was grinning proudly.

"Told you I had a nice little place, Angus. Come on inside. I've got some good cool cider in my storm cellar, as hard as old Eubanks's head."

"I'd better go easy on it, then," Angus said.

The house was as neat inside as you'd have expected from the way it looked outside. It was furnished with comfortable factory-made furniture with strong springy seats and sturdy upholstery. Luke was particularly proud of the wallpaper which had been manufactured in Baltimore in five distinct shades of bronze. "Know how they get them gold colors to stick on, Angus? They mix it up with potato starch. That's what the drummer told me. Ain't it fantastic what they're doing these days?"

Luke's kitchen was orderly, but did not appear to have been used recently. "I like to eat in town as much as I can, Angus. It ain't much fun to eat alone."

They passed through the house into the back yard. While Luke went below, Angus looked over an intricately designed flower bed near the cellar. A rectangular planting of green bushes stood in the middle of the plot. At one end of the rectangle stood a huge egg-shaped sandstone boulder, at least four feet high.

"That's my wife's grave," Luke said, returning with a pitcher of cider. "Them bushes is white haws. Maggie was always partial to haws."

They sat on the porch, behind the morning-glories, and drank the cool cider, and Angus felt aware of the presence of Maggie Sweeley: strangely, Luke was not living in the past with her; she was living in the present with him.

"Angus, explain to me about that sonofabitch Gunnysack McCloud. I've been thinking about him ever since we sacked up them feathers. How come you was able to get him off the gallows by claiming that he's an Indian, when everybody knows he's a nigger and always was."

Angus had to laugh, and Luke bristled.

"Now, God damn it, I've got sense enough to understand it. He ain't no Indian and you know it."

"Under our laws, a man accused of a crime can't be tried by just any court, Luke. Sometimes a case gets tried in the wrong court, and if you can show that the court had no jurisdiction, you can get the conviction overthrown on appeal. Do you follow me?"

"Of course I follow you. You ain't got all the brains in town."

"Judge Ring's court has jurisdiction over the crimes down in a certain part of the Nations because it's a federal court and the Indian country is federal territory. But the agreements between the tribes and the United States say that only crimes between Indians and non-Indians will be tried by our federal courts. Any crime just among Indians remains under the jurisdiction of the tribal courts down there. Gunnysack was on trial for killing an Indian, if you remember."

"Now I get it," Luke said, with a gleam of awful mischief in his eyes. "So you claimed Gunnysack was an Indian. And since he killed an Indian, he should have been tried in the Indian courts."

"That's right," Angus grinned. "You're doing fine. The Supreme Court reversed his conviction on the contention that Judge Ring had no jurisdiction."

"That's pretty God damned clever of you, boy. But it ain't very honest, is it? I don't see how you could pull the wool over their eyes like that. Didn't the Judge put up a squawk? He knows Gunnysack ain't no Indian."

"That's the interesting part of the case, Luke. Gunnysack was a slave before the war. He was born to an Indian slaveholder, back in Mississippi —before the Chics and Chocs came to the Nations. After the war, there was a certain treaty that freed the Indians' slaves, just as the war itself had freed the white men's slaves. The white men's slaves became citizens of the United States, and the Indians' slaves became citizens of the Indian tribe to which they had belonged. So you can see that, legally, Gunnysack became an Indian. That's the point that won our appeal."

Suddenly Luke broke into a fit of laughter. "I'll bet that little Judge busted his beans on that one, didn't he?"

"That's what some people call a technicality, Luke. But I believe that even Gunnysack McCloud has a right to be tried legally. Especially if he's going to be hung."

"Are the Indians going to try him in their courts, Angus?"

"I don't know. Whatever they do is no business of the United States."

"Suppose they turn him loose down there. He'll go on another killing spree. He's already killed eight or ten."

"How do you know?"

"That's what they say."

"Are you one of those people who always listens to what they say?"

Luke's face clouded. "You're a puzzle to me," he said.

He got up suddenly and went inside the house. When he returned, he brought a bag of tobacco and some cigarette papers. He sat down again for a moment before offering Angus a smoke. Then he held out the tobacco bag.

"Want one?"

"I don't mind. I've just about got time for a smoke. Then I've got to get back to my office. I didn't think you ever smoked, Luke."

"I only chew in town," Luke said. "Maggie never did like for me to spit in the yard."

CHAPTER FOUR

The next day Angus made it a point to be extremely busy, and he suspected that the Colonel was doing the same thing. But his future had to be discussed, and on the second morning he knew the time had come.

Feeling uncomfortable at the boardinghouse, he left home without breakfast. He ate in the New Ridge dining room and because he dreaded seeing his partner, he lingered over Hoey Johnson's favorite newspaper and a cigar. He realized at last that he was merely stalling and decided to get it over with. The Colonel's habitual need for a night alone to think out the implications of a new idea before committing himself had now been stretched an extra day.

All the way up South Street, he had a feeling the Colonel would be waiting for him. But when he mounted the wooden stairs to his office he found instead, sitting nervously in the reception room, Miss Janet Ring.

He realized later that he had been more surprised by her looks than that she had come.

"Good morning," she said. "I'm Janet Ring."

"I know who you are, although we've never met," he said, trying to hide his reaction. "Are you here to see me or the Colonel?"

"You, Mr. DeWolfe. Colonel Beleau just stepped out for a few minutes. He said you'd be here presently." Her voice had a quiet, pleasing quality.

"Won't you come in?" he asked, opening the door to his private office.

He had expected her to be simply a dour-faced replica of her father, but she was not unpleasant-looking. She appeared younger than she had from a distance—but that might have been expected, if he had thought about it, for she could be no more than thirty.

Her face was flushed and she was quite nervous. She wore a dowdy pink dress, long white gloves with lace at the tops near the elbows, and carried a sun parasol. Her shoes were black and pointed, the latest St. Louis fashion. She was not heavy, but amply filled out. Her shoulders drooped a bit. The tight knot, into which her hair was tied, visible underneath the black brim of a small, prim hat, seemed to draw the skin at the sides of her face. She looked lonely, and he felt a trifle sorry for her.

"I'm sure you must have received my letter, Mr. DeWolfe."

"Yes. It was mailed from St. Louis, I noticed."

She said quickly, "I happened to be in St. Louis when I decided to communicate with you. I am a teacher in a Friends' school on the Shawnee reservation, and I have little opportunity to shop for my wardrobe except once a year with my mother when we visit St. Louis."

He had hoped, without really thinking about it, that she would be more straightforward. As he watched, it occurred to him that her manner was perhaps not coy, but fearful.

"I see," he said.

"I gather that you haven't been to visit Mr. Maywood yet, as I had hoped."

"No, but I have inquired into the case a little."

"You will take it, then? And file the appeal for him?"

Her face was suddenly hopeful, which made her rather attractive, despite the dowdy cut of her dress and the way she carried her shoulders. He wondered if this little woman could actually be in love with the convicted Indian.

"Maywood hasn't asked me to prepare his appeal. There isn't anything I can do unless he asks me to represent him."

"If you would visit him at the jail, I'm sure he'd ask you. I shall be responsible for your retainer myself. I am prepared to pay your . . . price."

He watched her closely. "Tell me why you are sufficiently interested in this man's defense to pay my *price*, Miss Ring. There's really no point in our talking about it until I know what connection you have with the case."

"He's a former student of mine," she replied evenly. "I would like to be sure that he is represented by competent criminal counsel."

He drummed his chin with his fingers, then realized that he was doing it and stopped. He didn't want to appear tense about this. He put his hand in his lap. It felt awkward there, and he would have moved it again if he could have decided where to put it.

"Miss Ring," he said at last, "do you believe he is guilty?"

Now she waited for several moments. He thought she was trying to calculate an answer that would be satisfactory to him. He was annoyed.

"Frankly," she said, "I don't know what to think. From our knowledge of him at the school, Friend Sparkman and I both thought it impossible for such a person to have committed a crime like that. But the trial was convincing."

"Is Sparkman the head of the school?"

"Yes."

"And is he helping you pay my price, Miss Ring?"

"Yes," she said steadily. "We both contributed before."

"Did you follow the trial closely?"

"It was much discussed in my home."

[37]

"And you thought it was convincing?"

"Everyone thought so."

"But you have some doubt about it now?"

"I didn't say that, Mr. DeWolfe."

He considered her for a moment in silence. He had been prepared to dislike her immediately. Yet there was nothing about her for him to dislike—at least, nothing quickly observable. The vision of her riding stiffly beside her father in the buggy came to him. He had seen them many times on Sunday afternoons, always assuming them to have a great feeling for each other. But if she were greatly like her father, would she not already have shown it?

"Miss Ring, I don't want to make you uncomfortable, but I'm sure we'll come to understand each other much better if we speak directly. The jury found Maywood guilty beyond a reasonable doubt. I wonder if you will tell me, off the record and in confidence, if you can honestly say that you believe him guilty beyond a reasonable doubt. Or do you have doubts?"

Her face flushed suddenly, and her eyes blazed. She was staring at him with vitality, a quality that he realized had been conspicuously missing until now. For the first time since entering his office she interested him as an individual.

She said, "Really, Mr. DeWolfe, I couldn't set myself above the jury in a criminal proceeding. But I do feel that he deserves a better fate than . . . execution. I know from having taught him that he is a tragic victim of a difficult time. If he committed the crimes, I'm sure he doesn't know why he did it himself."

"Then you do have doubt. You said 'If he committed the crimes.'"

She stared back at him. He was surprised that she could show so little of what she was thinking.

"I do not believe he would have been convicted," she said, "if he were innocent."

"Because your father's court is incapable of error?"

His bluntness was calculated. He wanted to sting her into a show of feeling, to bludgeon, if necessary, her self-control. He wanted her to tell him the truth about her relationship with the Indian.

"That's an unfair question," she said steadily.

"Now, Miss Ring, examine what you're doing for a moment. You come in here making insinuations about my price. You ask for everything to be kept secret. And you refuse to tell me the truth."

"Mr. DeWolfe," she said, and her lips drew thin, "you have no right to try to put me in the position of disagreeing with a jury verdict."

"All right, if you haven't got the courage to disagree with a jury," he said shortly, "I'll withdraw the question. But you must tell me the truth——"

"I've been telling you the truth!" At last genuine anger burst in her. "I'm not accustomed to being called a liar, Mr. DeWolfe." Her face was now quite pale, and her mouth quivered despite her obvious effort to prevent it.

He decided to let her sit in silence for a few moments on the chance that she might agitate herself a little more.

He took a cigar from his desk. "Do you mind if I smoke, Miss Ring?"

She looked away and he puffed on the cigar until it was burning nicely. Watching her, he rather admired her ability to pretend. Could she be pretending even to herself? he wondered.

"Now," he began again, "I am prepared to believe that you haven't told me anything that was untrue. But you've been telling only part of the truth, and it doesn't give a true picture."

"Why do you assume that I've been telling only a part of the truth, Mr. DeWolfe?"

Threatened, her self-control quickly returned. She was staring at him coldly again, and he was annoyed that he had miscalculated his maneuver.

"I'm going to answer your question," he said, "and if you don't start answering mine, this interview will terminate abruptly. I happen to know that you had secret rendezvous with your Indian at his cabin. You took books out there and read poetry with him in a garden of wildflowers."

He thought for a moment that she might faint. She grasped the edge of his desk for stability.

He went on quickly, "Just what do you want of me? Secret games? Or do you want me to save that boy from the gallows?"

Tears came into her eyes. She stared at him helplessly. He realized that she couldn't speak.

"There's something rotten about this," he said. "Obviously he shouldn't have been tried in your father's court."

Again he paused, but she could not speak. Her expression, however, didn't beg him to stop. She appeared to be transfixed by what he was saying, impaled upon his thrusts.

He said, in a gentler voice, "Now, Miss Ring, if I accept this case, I'll accept the retainer from you. It won't be a large amount, for I'm not trying to get as rich as you think. But I'll pull no punches, and there'll be no secrets. If I undertake it, somehow I'll keep him off the gallows. That will be my only concern. Do you understand?"

She continued staring. It seemed questionable now whether she had even been hearing what he had said.

"Miss Ring, does your father know that you were involved with this boy?"

He was amazed at the look that now came into her face. Instead of answering, she rose from her chair. Her lips parted in an apparent effort to speak; and then they closed.

She turned from his desk and walked across the room. She picked up her parasol and moved toward the door. She had her hand on the doorknob when she broke into tears.

She sank into a chair beside the door, and her parasol fell to the floor. He went to her, but she could not stop crying.

Her entire body shook. He gave her his handkerchief, then sat in a chair beside her and waited for her to cry it out.

Crying women had always irked him. The quick burst of tears seemed a cheap and easy way of turning a difficult situation to the benefit of the weeper. But this particular burst of tears had not been quick, and it had manifestly not been easy. His questions had put her in great pain, but it was clear that she had not cried for sympathy.

Or was it? he asked himself. Could it be that as a weeper she was simply cleverer than most? Somehow, "clever" was not a word that quite applied to her.

Watching her, he heard the Colonel pass through the reception room. He could always recognize the Colonel's heavy, yet somehow mincing, footsteps. The irony of Janet Ring's coming on this particular morning was not lost on him.

He smiled at her and said, "I suppose I should feel like a brute."

"You are not a brute, Mr. DeWolfe." It was the first time he had seen her actually smile. "I must apologize. Of course I was trying to make a game of this. I feel foolish."

"Would you rather we continued some other time? Tomorrow, after you've thought about it longer?"

"No, we can continue now. I shan't lose control of myself again."

He wondered how she would look if her hair were let out of the severe knot. She had an interesting face and he could imagine that, less controlled and admitting its natural vigor, it might even be pretty.

"Good," he said. "Why don't you just tell me about it, in your own way? The whole story, how and why you're involved with Maywood."

"Of course. I will."

"And you must understand that I'll do anything with the story that I think will be needed. If I don't accept the case, of course, everything you tell me now will be in confidence."

"I understand," she said, and he could see her bracing herself. "I'm astonished that you know of my visits to his cabin. There were several, last spring and the previous fall. I always return to Ridgefield during school intermissions. He came to visit me at home once, to inquire about some books I had mentioned two or three years earlier. I was gratified that his interest in books had grown, and I wanted to encourage him. I gave him the books, and then I took others out to his cabin, because—Mr. DeWolfe, this is very difficult for me."

"Please go on, Miss Ring," he said. "I think I can guess that you feared having him call at your home."

"Yes, that's it."

"Because of your father?"

"I was afraid my father might misunderstand."

"Because the boy is Indian?"

"No, only because he's a man, I'm afraid." He remembered the remark he'd heard about her in the pharmacy. Some people were born not to get married . . . a tragedy when it happened to a girl. He watched her with growing fascination. "At least," she said, "I thought it best to take the books to him, rather than let him call at my home. Certainly I wanted to kindle his interest in reading."

A touch of amusement reached him. Did she actually believe this to be an accurate estimate of her interest in the Indian? He was almost persuaded that she did.

"And the flower garden?" he asked.

Her face stiffened with embarrassment.

"I'm afraid Marcus got the wrong idea himself. Before I knew what was happening, he began doing little things. He found that I was interested in flowers, and he made the garden. I was gullible for quite a while. Then I realized that . . . he . . ."

"Was in love with you?"

"I'm afraid so. Or thought he was. I didn't want to hurt him. He was so youthful and enthusiastic. Soon, however, I realized that I had to discourage him. He had begun writing poems to me."

He could well imagine that it might have become awkward for her. He wondered what kind of poem would have been written by a love-torn Indian, capable of committing mass murder, to his teacher, who came into his garden with her hair tied tightly.

"You did eventually tell him, however, didn't you?"

"Yes. I told him that I was too old for him, and I was not in love with him. He said I was a coward, afraid to be seen with an Indian, which was why I always came quietly to his cabin. Of course I denied that."

"Go on, Miss Ring. Did he believe you?"

"No. He was angry. He thought I wouldn't consent to a romance with him because he was poor. Everything I said seemed to make him worse."

"In what way?"

"He grew almost violent. He said he would get some money and find out if that would make any difference in my feeling. It was horrible, Mr. DeWolfe."

"And you fear that he may have been keeping that promise when he killed the Flower family?"

"I can't describe the sickened sensations I have when I think of it," she said. "That I may have provoked such a thing is . . . horrible."

Her use of the word "provoke" attracted his attention. He could imagine a slightly different picture that would be more plausible—a picture that contained an additional element. To what extent might she have actually provoked the boy? Certainly, in the beginning, she had not gone to the flower garden out of a purely innocent interest in books. Why should she suspect that her father would think the Indian her beau unless she suspected or perhaps desired him to be? And, suspecting such, could she possibly have continued going there if the chance for romance had not aroused her? He could imagine that she might indeed have provoked the lonely Indian.

Was it possible, he also wondered, that she secretly struggled with a problem similar to his own? And if she suffered with the curiously uncontrollable tendency to view every male who crossed her path as a possible suitor, what had she thought of Angus DeWolfe? He shifted uncomfortably in his chair, irritated with the whole implausible idiocy of manless women and womanless men.

She was watching him intently when he glanced up.

"You mustn't let it play so dramatically in your mind," he said. "Whatever Marcus did was no fault of yours."

"I've told myself that," she replied, "but it is small consolation. At any rate, that's pretty much the story, Mr. DeWolfe. He wanted us to go back East, where he would find employment in Washington as an interpreter for the government. He knows a dozen tribal languages."

"Did he tell you where he planned to get the money?"

"No. I didn't ask him. I may have been afraid to ask—I'm not really sure. Anyway, he urged me to go with him. He had an idea that he was freeing me from a kind of bondage, I think. He was quite obsessed."

"Did he say he was trying to free you from bondage?"

"Not exactly. But I knew he felt something of the sort."

Again her choice of a word attracted him. Was it possible, he wondered, that she felt a bondage in her life and therefore assumed the Indian to have been trying to free her from it? In the name of filial devotion, could she have been living a kind of servitude? A manless thralldom?

He said, "How much of this does your father know?"

She looked down at her hands. "Somehow I felt that Marcus would be acquitted, and I wouldn't have to tell him."

Curiously, he did not want her to say any more about it. He needed to protect her dignity.

"Have you seen Marcus since the trial?" he asked.

"No. I didn't think he would talk to me."

He sat in silence for a while, considering his next move with her. He got up from the chair and walked to the window, looking down at the street below. One of Judge Ring's prison wagons lumbered from the direction of the Courthouse, inevitably on its way into the Nations again.

He turned from the window and faced her. She was quite composed. He noted with satisfaction that she was neither the stuffy old maid he had supposed her to be or the utterly delicate innocent lady Colonel Beleau had described. She was intelligent, honest and irrationally frightened—a condition, in a sense, similar to the Colonel's.

"Miss Ring, I would suggest that you contact the Quaker. If he agrees that I should take over this defense, then he'll probably be glad to see the boy about it."

"I'm very grateful, Mr. DeWolfe."

"And you must tell your father."

"About knowing Marcus?"

"Yes. We may have to ask for a reversal on the argument that your father was incompetent to conduct an impartial trial."

"Because his daughter was involved with the defendant?"

"Yes. I hope it can be avoided, because bringing you into it would tend to strengthen the case against the boy in a second trial. His need for money is weak as it now stands. Once you are on the scene, his need for money is a strong force. If we have to use you to get a new trial, we automatically build a tougher case."

"I understand. Do I also have to tell my father that I've seen you?"

"That's your business, Miss Ring."

After a pause, she said, "All right. I'll tell him about Marcus, but not that I've been here. And I will write to Paul Sparkman immediately. I'm sure he'll come to see you."

"Good."

She held out her hand, which he found sturdy and not too small. Then he opened his private door and watched her go through the reception room and disappear into the hall. She hurried, half on tiptoe, as though she were slipping away. He realized that he was already eager to see her again.

He knew, too, that the Colonel's door had been left ajar—deliberately, no doubt. He turned slowly. Beleau stared from behind his own desk, watching with sadly accepting eyes.

"Good morning, Angus," he said.

"Good morning, Colonel." He went to the Colonel's door, leaning against it casually. "She's a rather nice person. I don't know why I hadn't expected her to be."

"She was crying in there, wasn't she?"

"I had to be caustic with her at first."

"Are you going to take over the Shawnee's case?"

"Colonel," he said quickly, beating his partner to the inevitable truth, "we can separate. That will take the curse off you."

The Colonel's eyes widened. They wanted to disbelieve.

"Damn!" he said suddenly. "I just don't understand. You've got great prospects in this country, my boy. But you must spend your time defending the worst criminals in history."

Angus frowned, meeting the Colonel's gaze. Beleau had never accepted a criminal client himself. Naturally he couldn't understand. The Colonel could appreciate only those things which were cloaked with euphemism and gentle pretense; he could never grasp anything directly simple—a condition Angus believed to be universally true of the sentimental mind.

"I remember, Colonel, that you thought it was a good idea for me to join you and take criminal cases. It would make a nicely balanced practice, you said." He paused and smiled ruefully.

"But you go too far, Angus. You're letting these monstrous cases absorb you completely."

"They fascinate me," he said. "Public execution is a barbaric practice any way you look at it, to say nothing of the barbarism in judicial murder. I want to fight it because it seems important to me to fight it. What else can I say?"

The Colonel pretended not to be particularly struck; but his eyes narrowed, as they did when a point had been driven home. "Tell me why you have selected yourself to correct this thing. Is it because you killed a man one time out in New Mexico? Are you trying to square something with your conscience?"

"Perhaps," said Angus. His mind felt suddenly dull.

"My boy," cried the Colonel, "I had a hunch that was behind all this. Because you were forced to kill a man once in the course of duty——"

"I didn't say that," Angus replied, a little dazed. "The war made killing easy, Colonel . . . surely you remember. Indians and hide dealers slaughtered the herds of buffalo, and sportsmen from the East came out to shoot them just to watch them fall. Mustangers slaughtered the magnificent wild horses. Soldiers killed Indians, thieves killed ranchers, sheriffs killed thieves, cattlemen killed fence builders, plowmen killed trail bosses, Indians killed homesteaders. On top of all that, braggarts and bullies slaughtered each other. My brother was one of them. He was finally killed, and then I put on a badge and shot the man who did it. The decent impulses are finally beginning to emerge again—and one of the last of the sorry sights is that God damned gallows in the courtyard."

He paused, but his mind went on. If personal experience were directly responsible for his decision, why question it? Wasn't personal experience creating the Colonel's doubt? What else was there upon which, after all, to build a point of view?

"All this," the Colonel said, shaking his head, "because you killed a man one time."

"If you insist on putting it that way."

The Colonel's face turned red. "I guess there isn't much more for us to say, is there?"

"We know each other's feelings, at least. I'll always be grateful for the help you've given me."

"This depresses me, Angus."

"We'll both regret it at times—but it's clear that we'll be happier working apart."

"I won't consider it a break in friendship. Just a change in working habits. I hope that doesn't sound too much like euphemism." The Colonel tried to smile. "I know how you hate euphemism."

"I'll want to use your books for a while," Angus said.

"Of course," the Colonel replied. "And I wish you'd do something. Go with me to see the Judge, and then attend a public hanging with me. You'll see that Willard is trying to bring about the very civilization you want. You'll see what an impression it makes on people. His job would be impossible without the gallows. I wish you'd let me help you get to know each other better——"

"He *enjoys* hanging men, Colonel! I'm convinced that he loves to weep and contemplate his tragic responsibility while the bodies swing. . . ."

The Colonel suddenly looked into the reception room, and Angus turned to face Judge Ring, who was standing as stiff as a miniature statue dressed in a long, black coat.

Somehow, through his surprise, he said, "Hello, Judge."

The Colonel leaped from his chair and greeted the Judge with transparent embarrassment. Angus could see the comic aspect, for he was not particularly chagrined that the Judge had heard him.

"Come in, Willard, it's an honor to have you in the office," the Colonel said.

"Good morning, John," said the Judge.

Angus knew vaguely that they had belonged to a club together, but he was under the impression that Judge Ring was not an active member. He hadn't realized that they were on a first-name basis with each other.

The Judge closed the outside door, then lowered his voice. "Why was my daughter here, Mr. DeWolfe?" he asked steadily.

Angus did not answer. The Colonel was plainly wishing he were in South America.

The Judge went on, his words precisely clipped. "Let us speak to each other without subterfuge. I know she was here."

"Will you have a cigar, Judge?" Angus managed to say. "We may as well sit——"

"Mr. DeWolfe, I have just been through the ordeal of sentencing a man to death. The tragic responsibility of which you were speaking when I walked in has tired my mind and made my heart profoundly heavy. I ask your forbearance of my lack of patience with hypocritical amenities. Why did my daughter come to your office?"

Deliberately, Angus stepped through the door to his own desk and took a cigar from his drawer, but decided not to light it. He was almost dizzy with rage, but worked hard to remain civil. He said at last, "You must be mistaken, Judge——"

Judge Ring's face twitched barely enough to wiggle one side of his whiskers.

"Mr. DeWolfe, you are a liar," he said, glaring with hatred.

Angus forced a thin smile to his face, even as he felt himself redden. "I'm not a liar," he replied as pleasantly as he could. "I'm a counselor at law. There's a difference."

"Very little," said the Judge. "Are you trying to imply that my daughter is your client, and that your conversation with her is therefore privileged?"

"Not at all, Judge. I'm——"

"Rubbish." The Judge turned to Colonel Beleau. "I'll ask you, John. Do you know why she came here?"

Angus had never seen the poor Colonel so miserable.

"Frankly, Willard—the truth is, that I have been out of the office all morning. I walked in only before you did."

Judge Ring didn't actually accuse the Colonel of lying. But his eyes were accusing. He turned to Angus again, his large, sad face aflame. "I want to know why she was here, young man!"

"I said you must be mistaken," he answered steadily. "Is there anything else we can do for you, Judge?"

"Nothing," the Judge said. "Good day, sir."

He turned and left the office, shrunken with rage.

Suddenly Angus was so amused that he could afford himself the luxury of not being angry.

CHAPTER FIVE

When Janet Ring left the office of Angus DeWolfe and hurried downstairs to the street, her only urgent feeling was a desire for no one to see her who might mention it to her father. After she had walked a block up South Street past the bank corner, she began to relax. If she had not been seen until now, she was out of danger.

She decided to go immediately to her father's office and get it over with. Somehow, she would tell him.

Walking slowly toward the Federal Building, she recalled a bitter denunciation of DeWolfe her father had recently made at home—during the Foxjaw trial.

Her father had been eating his breakfast in a silence made dreadful by the fact that he was usually buoyant in the morning. He practiced morning buoyancy like calisthenics.

Because of his agitation over the trial, her mother had prepared one of his favorite breakfasts—a slice of boiled mutton, a hot muffin with a spoonful of jam, and heavily creamed coffee. And he had been eating it in silence, preoccupied and tormented.

Suddenly he looked up and said, "Have either of you heard of a lawyer named DeWolfe?"

Janet and her mother carefully refrained from looking at each other. They had had many discussions of a lawyer named DeWolfe.

"I've heard of him," said Janet hastily, to fill the threatening silence. "He defends criminals, doesn't he?"

Her pretense of innocence gave her no qualms. She had found life as her father's daughter simpler and smoother if she lied to him when the occasion called for it. Over the years she had learned to do it easily.

"He's an Easterner," said her father. "John Beleau brought him here a year or so ago. The most insolent man I've ever known."

"Is something wrong, dear?" her mother asked.

"Wrong?" Her father's face puffed with anger. "I'm going to have trouble with him. A real pettifogger. He's a dangerous man. But I shouldn't bring my troubles to the breakfast table." Then he continued eating in martyred silence, eating as though he were alone. . . .

Reaching the Federal Building, Janet went up the stairway toward the main corridor outside her father's courtroom. She felt a certain exhilaration. She liked what she had seen of DeWolfe. A pettifogger, was he? She didn't think so. She was mortified that she had made a fool of herself in the beginning. She wondered what he must think about her.

Sam Doolan, the crier, was not outside on his bench this morning, for the Court was in session.

She paused at the main entrance. A hushed expectancy hung in the hot, stale air. She heard her father's voice: "The defendant will rise."

She peered into the courtroom. The large audience grew instantly quiet. The defendant stood up before the bar. He was a broad-shouldered man, his hair hanging long around his bull-thick neck. He was breathing heavily.

Her father sat behind the bench on the raised platform above the well of the court. His eyes were fierce as he gazed down steadily at the defendant. His cheeks were hollow and his face no more than a ghostly imitation of the face she knew to be his.

Looking directly at the prisoner, he said, "Jason Sampson, you are known throughout this country as Oak Tree Sampson because, it is said, you are as tough as an oak tree. In the course of your recent life, you have terrorized one community after another. Drunken and bragging of your prowess, you have shot up people's property with your dispicable guns. And at last, in the village of Smithpeter, Chickasaw Nation, on the afternoon of May twenty-eighth, even while millions of citizens all over the civilized world conducted themselves with propriety and humanity, living together in peace and good feeling, in accordance with Divine direction, you found it in your warped and twisted heart wantonly to murder one Marvin Smith, proprietor of a general store. Only our Savior can now pardon your sin. I beg you to pray to Him for that mercy that no mortal man could have expected from you. Let me entreat you to consider your conduct and to reflect upon the helpless condition of the widow Smith and her infant fatherless daughter. Think of the dying groans of your murdered victim. Weigh your monstrous act against the mortal pain inflicted by it. And, finally, raise your bloody hands in humble petition before the judgment of almighty God, that salvation may somehow yet be extended even to you. I now sentence you, on the day of September fourteenth next, in a manner to be determined by the chief deputy marshal of this court, to hang by the neck until you are dead!"

Dazed, Janet backed out of the courtroom and stood, mercifully unrecognized, as people emerged into the corridor. The spectators were buzzing, a mesmerized and thrill-shocked audience for her father's grandiloquence. His oratory still thundered in her ears.

She felt sick.

She turned and fled down the stairway, hurrying home. She lived on a pleasant, tree-lined street with flagstone walks and square frame bungalows. The morning was bright and sunnily hot—a day created for lazy drifting clouds and warblers' songs, and for good feeling. But nausea hung inside her and she tried to steady her step.

When she reached home, she hurried up to her room, put away her parasol, and pulled off her hat and gloves. Then she sat on her chaise longue before the open windows. There was no breeze to stir the ivy which grew up the sides of the brick house and around the windows. She had planted the ivy herself, when she first came here, believing that it would cool her room. And sometimes the sound of it, rustling gently in a breath of air, did make the room seem cooler.

Her mother came upstairs, eyes childish with anticipation. "Tell me about it, darling."

"I just had to sit down for a bit first," she said.

"Is anything wrong? Are you ill?"

"No. I'm all right."

"Will Mr. DeWolfe take the case?"

"Yes, I think so."

"Is he terribly severe, Janet?"

"He's an interesting man, Mother. Just give me a moment."

"Then Luke was right about him."

Alice Ring—always polite and soft-spoken, even to members of her family—was quite excited. Janet liked her, but did not understand her. Sometimes she felt it almost inhuman of her mother not to show more evidence of the anguish and turmoil of her life. The secret drinking during execution times somehow seemed outlet enough—or was it shame of drunkenness that kept her outwardly self-contained the rest of the time? Janet often marveled at it. For whatever loneliness lived in Alice Ring's small frame, lived quietly. When she should have been excited about something, she was usually calm; when she should have been angry, she was polite; and when she should have been harsh and stern, she was gentle. Her animation right now was greater than Janet had seen in weeks.

She smiled ruefully. "He knew all about the flower garden—I haven't the faintest idea how."

"Has he seen Marcus?"

"No. He wants Paul Sparkman to arrange it."

"Splendid," Alice Ring said. "Did you like him at all, Janet? Is he nice?"

"I don't know what I think about him. He's a very serious man. Too serious, maybe, for his own good."

"He's defended several cases without fee. Shysters don't do that."

"He says I must tell Father about Marcus . . . and the garden."

"Good heavens!" Alice Ring cried.

Janet smiled to herself. She had always told her mother the details of her visits with Marcus, and her mother had pointed out his virtues in a campaign so obvious that it had been a little embarrassing—desperate, it almost seemed, to match her daughter off with any man.

"Darling," she said, "I know you can do it. I'm dreadfully sorry. . . ." Tears were in her eyes. "You're a wonderful daughter. I love you." Then she turned away to hide her feelings. "I'd better go down now."

"I'll be right down to help you, Mother."

"Perhaps you'd change the napkins."

Janet felt a great warmth. She knew that her mother wanted good things to happen to her, and the knowledge was comforting. Whatever else might be said of her home, she believed deeply that her mother had deserved a happier life.

Presently she heard her father below. She hurried to freshen herself at her basin. When she got downstairs, she took napkins from the buffet drawer and put them in the rings beside the plates, then disposed of the soiled ones.

Her father came into the dining room. If she had not seen it in the courtroom this morning, she would never have known that he had delivered a death sentence.

He was standing erect, as usual, his face impassive. His greeting was perfunctory. Then he turned to his wife.

"I'd like my lunch in the library today, Alice, if you don't mind. I need to search out some references."

He took his watch from his waistcoat pocket, withdrawing it by the large gold chain that hung across his chest. He stared at the watch, then wound it absently with the key which hung from the middle of the chain.

"I'll bring a tray," said Alice Ring.

"Thank you." He turned to Janet, looking up at her, for she was taller than he. Their eyes met and she felt herself cringe but tried not to show it. She wondered whether he could possibly be aware of the feeling that engulfed her when he looked at her in such a calculated way. "Janet, I'd like to see you in the library for a moment, if you don't mind."

"Yes, Father," she said. Her pulses were pounding.

"Thank you."

Then he turned and strode briskly from the dining room and disappeared into the library, closing the door behind him.

Janet's earliest, vague remembrance of her father was his glowing description of the kind of little girl he had always hoped God would someday send to him. Even in her childish mind, she had made fun of the little girl Father always dreamed of getting so easily, delighting sometimes in being as different as possible. *That* little girl would be a simpleton, she thought.

When she was older, if her offense was particularly painful to her father, he sometimes prayed for her in her presence. And his prayer might implore God to put the blame on him for having been an inadequate parent. Sometimes this would make her cry, and she would try for a while to be the kind of girl he had always wanted.

Barely seventeen when the family moved to Ridgefield, she was of healthy, rosy complexion, and her dark brown hair glistened with a burnished look when she was in the sunlight. Her body was lithe and handsomely made. Her eyes, brown and large behind long lashes, bore a hopefully expectant expression, as though they were constantly beholding things in her new world which were a delight.

But a sadness consumed her when her father destroyed her first romance in the West. She met a boy at church and was excited when he asked her out with him one afternoon.

"Me and Joe Bell are going to run some trotlines down at the river, and we thought you and Kate Cotter might as well come along."

His name was Floyd Green and his smile suited the size of his teeth. He was husky and timid, and his indirection tickled her. She went eagerly, although her father scorned her for wanting to go with such a bumpkin. And she had a good time. She stood on the bank and clapped her hands as each fish came off the hooks. She had never seen catfish before and her companions laughed at her ignorance. But they were not offensive and she could even laugh with them as she learned the things they knew.

"Your daddy is quite a man, isn't he?" Floyd Green said. "He already gave that Henry Henkin the death sentence. That must have took guts."

"Floyd," said Kate Cotter, "you ought to say courage. That other word isn't very nice."

"Pardon me," Floyd said. "Courage."

Janet was greatly amused. "You don't have to be so proper around me. I'm not *that* silly."

"I saw you driving your new rig the other day, Janet," said Joe Bell. "You handled the gelding all right."

"What's a gelding?" she asked.

The three giggled, then smothered their giggles. Kate Cotter whispered that she'd explain it to Janet sometime when they were alone; and Janet understood that she had made a blunder.

"We'd better be getting over to my place," Floyd said, red with embarrassment.

The Greens' farm was to her a place of gentle miracles. The windmill squeaked and squawked and the smokehouse smelled wonderfully of hanging hams and red-pepper strings and hands of tobacco and bags of garden sage. The farmhouse was redolent of sauerkraut and buttermilk, odors which stung her nostrils pleasantly. And it was plain that these prosperous farm people felt honored to be entertaining Judge Ring's daughter.

After refreshments, Janet took her cue from Kate and helped in the kitchen. Then Mrs. Green left them alone to wash up on the back porch.

"Kate," Janet said, "what on earth is a gelding? I felt like a simpleton this afternoon, in front of the boys."

"Don't you truly know, Janet? It's a horse that's been—you know. Cut."

"Cut?" Janet said.

"You know—like a steer. Had his cods cut."

"What?" Janet said. And then she understood. "Good heavens!" she cried. "Why do they do that?"

"Makes a better work animal. They say it takes their minds off—you know—everything but work. Like oxen."

Janet considered the revolting new information. "But that's awful, Kate —to make eunuchs out of them, just so they'll work better."

"To make *what* out of them?" Kate Cotter said.

"Eunuchs. You've heard of eunuchs, haven't you? They're men who have been—you know—cut like that."

"Good grief!" cried Kate, horrified. "Do they do that to men? In New York City?"

Janet giggled and explained what eunuchs were, and Kate looked a little sick and said she'd just as leave not hear any more.

Floyd's father cleaned the fish and sent a nice mess home with her. But her father laughed scornfully after Floyd had gone; and he buried the fish in the back of the garden.

"Catfish aren't fit to eat, my dear. If I don't bury them, we'll have all the stray animals in town holding convention here."

She found that afterward she planned her meetings with Floyd more quietly. If he had not indeed been as "country" as her father said he was, she might have been seriously tempted when he asked her to marry him that winter. Joe Bell and Kate Cotter got married on Christmas Eve. Janet caught the wedding bouquet and the irony of therefore becoming the next in line for the altar sent a tremor of pain through her heart. She had jumped as high as she could to catch the bouquet and in her eagerness had ripped her dress at the bodice; but she had paid no attention, for she had been instantly overcome with self-pity. The awful idea bolted through her mind that she would never marry.

Floyd drove her home from the church in his father's rig, and stopped between Gray's barn and her house. He drew a small present from his coat pocket and put it in her lap.

"Oh, Floyd!"

"It's not worth much, but I thought you might like it."

He grabbed her and kissed her fiercely. Aroused and deeply turbulent, she pulled the shawl loose from her head and wrapped it around his head, too.

"Where would you like to go, Janet, if you ever went on a honeymoon?"

"I wouldn't care. I used to think I wanted to go away on a boat somewhere."

"Gosh," he said, "you can dream, can't you?"

They sat absorbing each other's warmth, knowing the painful pleasure of young restricted urges; she felt the quickening of his pulse and he, the hot sweetness of her breath. Propriety held them there, suspended desperately.

"Floyd."

"Yes?" he said.

"Merry Christmas, Floyd. . . . Kiss me again, please. . . ."

"Do you know what you are, Miss?" he said, his voice suddenly shrill. "You're a doggone little monkey!"

She flung herself into his embrace. A wild thought struck her mind: she would make a real man of him—by the sheer force of her femaleness, she would make of him the male she desired!—by a kind of love-osmosis, she would transform every bumptiously grinning aspect of him into overpowering, articulate manhood, letting him now touch her body, kissing him again and again. . . .

A sudden sharp rapping on the front of the surrey brought her abruptly out of the ecstasy. Floyd turned her loose as though he had been shot. She whirled and saw her father standing beside the surrey. His eyes were at the point of popping out of his head. He had taken the whip from its socket and had cracked it sharply against the dash of the rig.

He said, "I was worried about you. I see that I was not worried enough."

"We were just coming home, Father," she said, too frightened to feel humiliation.

He walked to the front of the rig and took the mare by the bridle. He led them to the front of the house.

"Go inside," he said. "You too, Floyd."

"Father . . ." she said.

He whacked at the rig again with the whip.

"Inside. Both of you!"

It was always difficult for her to remember the details of what transpired when they got inside the house. She never forgot the picture of her mother, standing helplessly in the doorway to the dining room; she often thought her mother might have done something, but she never knew quite what. Her father noticed immediately that her dress had been torn, and she was terrified for a moment that he would hit Floyd with the whip. She protested that she had torn the dress while catching the wedding bouquet—she remembered that.

"Don't lie to me, young woman! I've had enough lying from you for one day!"

She remembered that her father seemed to hate her when he said that. The deepest possible contempt had curled on his face.

"I swear to you, Father——!"

But he whacked the back of the sofa to silence her. Dust flew and a sharp line remained where the whip had struck.

Then he told Floyd to come into the library with him and when they came out again Floyd left the house at once. He tried to smile secretly at her. She always remembered that he tried to smile. And he disappeared from town the following week. She had not seen nor heard from him since.

Many times, as she later viewed herself and the mystery of her life, she wondered whether that first afternoon with Floyd Green had not marked the beginning of her decline. She did, indeed, often think of her life as a mystery. She had never suspected that she would be a person who would eventually grow into a dowdy schoolmarm—a worker among the Indians. In her mind, and in her heart, the future had always presented itself as a parade of normalcy: courtship; marriage to a fine, strong man; children. Those ordinary developments would be her romantic adventures.

Were they too much to have asked? She even wondered at times if she had asked too little. Perhaps she should have tried to become a poetess or a musician—or an artist. But such possibilities were never considered in her truest dreams. She had written some poems, but they did not deceive her: they were only girlish rhymes, devoted to the proposition that the best of all possible worlds was the world of husband and children—several children. What happened, what happened? her heart had cried repeatedly during the years after the direction of her life in the West had taken definite, observable shape. And always her thoughts pointed back to her father and she could not think about it any more.

Janet didn't like to go into her father's library. In a sense, it symbolized the sternest part of him, although she had never known exactly why. Every book was always in its place, and the papers and files were carefully labeled and the writing secretary was orderly. She had only to step inside the room to feel that she was disturbing it.

No criminal ever walked upon the platform of the courtyard gallows with a greater constriction in his stomach. She reached for the doorknob.

"Come in, Janet," he said.

She turned the knob, prepared to die.

"Will you have a seat for a moment?" he asked without looking up.

"I could come back later, Father, if——"

"Not at all, my dear. Sit for a moment, please."

She sat in his leather guest chair. He continued peering at a large law volume. The only unorderly aspect of the room was the hole in the row of books from which the volume had been taken. She had always assumed that her father knew everything that was in all those books and was therefore a kind of giant.

Presently he looked up.

"Thank you for waiting," he said. His face was pale and he seemed to wonder just where to begin. "I found time last night to go over the bills from your shopping trip. I must say, my dear, that we are not poor. You should have spent more. I wanted you to have a good time."

"Thank you, Father," she managed to say.

"You shouldn't try so hard to cover your expenses with your small salary. There's really no need to be so thrifty."

"Thank you, Father," she said again, helplessly inadequate to respond. She gathered her strength to smile. She might have been trying to pick up something extraordinarily heavy. As she struggled with it, his eyes fixed on her mechanically.

"That's all I wanted to say. Now I must return to my work. If you'll excuse me."

She was astounded.

And she was unable to put away her thoughts about the death sentence. Whatever impact it had had on him did not show. Could it be possible that there had been no effect at all?

She stood before him, struggling for words. She would tell him now. Somehow, with a great effort desperately derived from an understanding of its necessity, she would take command of herself and tell him. In the back of her mind lay a fierce desire to be able to show Angus DeWolfe that she was something more (much more) than a frightened ninny.

"Father," she said. "I need to talk to you about something."

He peered at her from underneath his massive eyebrows. They had remained rather dark as his hair and whiskers had turned gray. He always seemed able to strike any attitude with them. Now they were holding her at a quiet, speculative distance.

"Concerning Marcus Maywood," she went on quickly. "I used to see him occasionally at his cabin. Out on Luke Sweeley's place. I ordered several books for him from New York publishers." Her pounding pulses made her lightheaded.

"Go on," he said, staring at her in a curiously conjecturing way. Could she be amusing him? she wondered.

"I should have told you this before the trial. I feel terrible about it."

"Is that all? That you took books out to his cabin on a few occasions?"

"No—there's more. Marcus got the wrong idea, Father. He thought he was—that perhaps I——" She paused and swallowed. Then she blurted it out: "He wanted to marry me. It was perfectly absurd, but he asked me, and when I refused, he said it was because he was poor. And that he'd get some money. That was just——"

Her father said, "Just before he committed the crimes?"

"I'm afraid so."

Her father got up from his chair and paced the room. He said calmly, "Thank heaven you weren't harmed, my child. Thank God for that."

He stood before a bank of bookcases. She sat silently, believing she had said enough.

"What prompts you to tell me this now, Janet?"

"I don't know, Father. My conscience, I suppose."

The skin around his mouth drew into a bloodless smile. "Have you anything else to tell me?"

"No, Father."

"I hope you won't come here in a few weeks, saying your conscience has driven you to tell me something else that might better be said right now. I knew about your visits to that cabin while they were going on, supposedly behind my back. I knew about the ridiculous flower garden at the edge of the woods. I went out there once and looked it over myself. I did not know about the proposal of marriage—but I'm not surprised. I'm only revolted, I think."

She looked at him, astounded.

"You knew about it, Father?"

"If I'd confronted you with it, you'd have lied to me. I have always tried to minimize your lying, by avoiding the possibility for it whenever I could."

Anger gathered in her, giving her some strength.

"You would never tolerate the truth from me, Father," she said. "It was never satisfactory to you."

"How true," he said, almost gently. The pain that rose into his voice seemed to cascade over the room, flooding it with unyielding misery. He said, "I would never, never have tolerated the spectacle of having my daughter consort with such a creature."

"He wasn't a murderer then," she said. "You couldn't have thought such a thing."

"Janet, I have been dealing with criminals for many years. I have learned something about their character, I think. The very depraved ones are always weak—always willing to sneak around. I could have told you the kind of man he was. But the prospect of having you lie to me was even more painful. You would have lied to me, wouldn't you?"

She stared at him.

"Did you think it was fair for you to conduct his trial, Father? Shouldn't he have been tried in some other court?"

"Rubbish. Nobody ever accused me of unfairness. Facts speak for themselves. Now," he said, "I suggest that you ask God's forgiveness. I have already forgiven you."

She looked down at the floor, speechless. It would have been difficult for her to decide who was the more depraved—her father, or herself.

Although for years she had been feeling middle-aged, Janet was only twenty-nine years old. Her face was pale, her graying hair combed severely to the back of her head much in the manner of her mother's. She usually kept her eyes averted in the hope of hiding her sadness, for she did not want to be pitied. Fierce remembrance of Floyd Green and what she had done to him was a living malaise in her heart.

She sat before her mirror, staring at herself with distaste. It was something she had come to do out of habit: she rather considered herself deserving of unattractive appearance. She thought of Floyd Green, and of Marcus Maywood. And she said to herself: "Getting involved with me may be your downfall, Mr. DeWolfe. Something awful will surely happen to you."

She did not realize that she was smiling. Her mouth was naturally her most attractive feature: full and sensitive, delicately responsive to her feelings. But years ago it had set into an attitude of bitterness which, in time, had softened with the rest of her face into a permanent look of incurious detachment: the look calculated to suit her role and help her to pretend that she liked being an old maid.

Impulsively, she loosened her hair and combed a wave into it, letting it fall below her shoulders in a carefree manner. She straightened up her shoulders, setting them at a jaunty angle. She felt as foolish as a young girl. Lifting her shoulders had miraculously taken the middle-aged look away from her body, and she enjoyed the spectacle.

Her mother spoke from the doorway and she was startled. "Your hair looks wonderful, darling."

"I was just putting it up."

"Don't put it up yet. I haven't seen you with it combed out in the longest time."

"Father wasn't surprised when I told him I'd been seeing Marcus. Some-times I wish I'd never told him a lie in my life, Mother. He treats me as though it would be ridiculous for me to have an opinion of my own."

She turned back to face the mirror. Alice Ring watched intently. Their eyes met for an instant. Janet realized that she and her mother looked like sisters.

The idea spun in her imagination, causing her to wonder what people in Ridgefield probably thought of her—a lonely old maid who seldom went about the town. She had been an eager, vivacious girl when the family came here. Wouldn't people remember, and be curious about the spinster who had taken that young girl's place under the name of Janet Ring? Wouldn't they have speculated on the disappearance of Floyd Green—or did everyone in town except her know all about it?

"Mother," she said, "I've just been thinking about Floyd Green. Do you ever wonder what happened to him?"

"I've wondered many times."

"He gave me a Christmas present that night, just before Father found us. I must have left it on the seat of his surrey. Do you think Father made him leave Ridgefield because of me?"

"Try not to imagine such things, darling," her mother said.

"You *do* think so, don't you?"

"I don't know. Honestly I don't. But you must not be bitter about it. Whatever happened was a long time ago."

Curiously, Paul and Mary Sparkman had told her the same thing. Bitter-ness, Paul Sparkman had said, was the deadly enemy of hope.

She smiled a little.

"Mother—I'm going to do something brazen."

"You are?"

"I'm going to try to get Mr. DeWolfe to take me out sometime."

Her mother's face was a sudden confusion of apprehension and delight. "Good heavens, Janet!"

"He's one man Father couldn't push around." A look of relish crept over her face. "It wouldn't be very fair to Mr. DeWolfe to use him that way."

"Everything is fair, Janet!" her mother cried, quite bowled over with the idea. "Your father will be furious. I'm sure Mr. DeWolfe can take care of himself."

"He can stand his ground. There aren't many bachelors his age."

"He can be enticed, darling. All men can——"

They heard a clatter below in the street and Janet went to the window. "It's Luke," she said.

"I'll go down and let him in," Alice Ring said.

Luke Sweeley had never been a silly clown to Janet, perhaps because

Ridgefield had always seemed full of clowns to her and Luke had never particularly emerged as unique among them. He had spaded the garden for her mother many times, and Janet always felt that a lame man should not have to spade—but Luke had been able to do it with no apparent difficulty. He had described to her mother the way his wife had grown certain flowers back in Kentucky before the war (Luke called it the Rebellion), and he had always made special trips out to deliver parcels that he thought either Janet or her mother might be especially interested in.

It was Luke who had suggested to them that Angus DeWolfe be retained for Marcus. Both Janet and her mother had at first thought the idea preposterous. That her mother had felt so free to discuss this with Luke had suggested to Janet that Luke was probably the source of her mother's secret liquor supply.

Luke was already inside the front door when Janet got downstairs. His wrinkled old face was humorously casual, but she knew that he was bursting to hear about her visit to the lawyer's office.

That evening at the table her father smiled, but only with the muscles of his face, and spoke of Angus DeWolfe.

"Do you remember that lawyer I was telling you about not long ago?" he asked. He was looking at his wife, and then swept his gaze around to Janet. "The one who was making so much trouble for me?"

"Yes, Father," she said. "I think I remember."

"The man Colonel Beleau brought here from the East?" her mother asked, as blandly as if Luke Sweeley had coached her.

"That's the man. His name is DeWolfe. The Colonel has finally kicked him out." He was still looking at Janet, not observing her so much as shining the light of his knowledge upon her.

"Oh, that's nice," chattered Alice Ring. "Perhaps we'll soon be rid of him completely."

Janet lifted her fork as though she were interested in food.

CHAPTER SIX

Along the cobblestone streets which enclosed the Ridgefield court-yard moved a steady traffic flow of jump-seat wagons, surreys, rockaways, buckboards and buggies, drawn by animals whose steaming dung provided at once a banquet for hungry birds and full-time cleanup employment for eleven men in the street-sweeping department.

Angus stood on the sidewalk in front of the harness store, talking to Sam Wilson, the proprietor. Two prospective landlords had already turned him down.

"Sure, Angus," Sam Wilson was saying. He was a ruddy, deep-chested man with arms like a blacksmith's. "You can put your office up there if you want to. I'll have to get ten dollars a month for it." He grinned sheepishly. He had felt it necessary to search his conscience carefully before admitting Angus to tenancy in his loft.

"Fine, Sam," Angus said.

"Glad to have you," said Sam Wilson, but he did not seem particularly glad. He seemed rather to be pleased that his broad-mindedness had overcome his prejudice, perhaps proving that he was not as bad as he thought he was. "Here's the key. Let me know if I can help you get set up."

"I will. Thanks, Sam."

The next afternoon Paul Sparkman called on him.

The Quaker was large-boned and muscular. Although he was dressed in black from head to foot and held a large black hat conspicuously on his knee, his attitude did not suggest fanaticism. His thick brown-gray hair and square face gave him the look Angus felt a Quaker should have. His physique bespoke the gentleness of strength, and his countenance the strength of gentleness. As Angus talked to him, he understood why everyone had believed the man's testimony. Paul Sparkman was the kind of man you believed.

"And then, as I understand it, Marcus came to you and asked you to fabricate an alibi for him."

"Thee's quite correct, unfortunately. I had not yet heard about the tragedy. The lad was curiously unpredictable at school. He feared his absence from Ridgefield might seem suspicious."

"And he had not been with you at all during that time?"

The Quaker shook his head. His face was troubled and his eyes grew sad behind the bushy brows.

"At the trial I was cross-examined on that point. The counselor thought it astonishing that I had not delved more carefully into where the lad had been."

"I understand that later he claimed to have spent those days with his mother down in the Shawnee country."

"That's what he said, after I confirmed that he had asked me to alibi for him. Since it was the second story he had told, no one was likely to believe him."

"Do you think he killed those people?" Angus asked abruptly.

"Friend," Paul Sparkman said, "I was certain at the end of the trial that he was guilty. It was the most crushing experience of my humble life. My heart can not abide the thought of this lad hanging in the courtyard. Whatever evil ruled his hand, I knew him always as a fine lad. An interesting lad. I pray thee will try to save him."

"I'll do my best. Let's go to his cell together, and after a while I hope you'll leave on some pretext and let me talk to him alone."

"The other lawyer found him so unco-operative that he cared not much what happened."

"I'll go to St. Louis in a few days and get whatever information his associates have on the case."

"Does thee feel hopeful, Friend DeWolfe? I would like to feel hopeful myself."

Angus rose from his desk and took his coat from the tree in the corner.

"The Judge is his own most successful adversary. He leads his juries, in one way or another, and the Supreme Court will never tolerate it."

"I have mixed feelings about Friend Ring," the Quaker said, frowning.

"My feelings are not mixed at all," said Angus.

"Thee will admit that he's a good man, though."

"All men are good until the devil gains a foothold in their hearts. And then they are apt to do mischief."

"Thee's surely jesting. I'm certain thee's not so orthodox as that."

"I apologize," Angus laughed. "Is it correct for me to call you Reverend, or should I say Mister?"

"Please call me Friend. I *am* thy friend," the Quaker smiled.

"Very well, Friend Sparkman—I wish you'd tell me a little about Miss Ring. What sort of person is she?"

Sparkman seemed surprised.

"A splendid person, I think. I'm not quite sure what thee desires to know."

"How long has she been working for you?"

"Five years. She'll start the sixth this autumn. I consider her a splendid teacher."

"Has she lived in your home all the time she's been down there?"

"Yes. Mary Sparkman, my wife, and I admire her very much. The lad was her pupil for three years. He speaks English fluently and he's had a fair introduction to literature and history. Thanks to Janet Ring."

Angus paused, wondering if the Quaker was deliberately avoiding his essential question.

"What I'm really interested in," he said, "is the—shall we say—personal side of her."

"Personal?"

"She's young, obviously intelligent, and she could be quite attractive. How do you account for it?"

Sparkman considered the question. "Thy query is curious, Friend. I don't know how fairly I could answer. I recognize that what thee say is true, but"—he glanced at Angus narrowly—"it does not seem related to the Maywood instance."

"She's a puzzle to me," he grinned. "Did her father arrange for her to come down there?"

"No," said Sparkman slowly. "Friend Jasper Binder, pastor of the Christian Church, wrote to me about her. She had inquired of him about becoming a teacher on one of the reservations."

"She seems rather a tragic person to me. It must have been difficult to be Judge Ring's daughter."

"It must be difficult to be Judge of the court here," Paul Sparkman said. "My heart goes out to him. To every judge."

They moved toward the door together.

"My heart doesn't go out to him," Angus said. "My criterion of value is life, really—rather than people. A man is no deader if he is killed by a bandit than if he is killed by judicial order."

The Quaker was looking at him now with quizzical interest.

"What about natural death? Does thee hate that, too?"

"Natural death, in a sense, seems to be the final part of life, doesn't it? It belongs in the order of things. I don't think it's natural for men to kill."

"Is thee a vegetarian, Friend?"

"I mean, of course, except for food and clothing. All the carnivorous mammals of nature kill for food."

"And do animals not kill for protection?" asked the Quaker, curiously enjoying himself. "Willard Ring would explain that the gallows is for society's protection from those few who are out of control."

"But we are capable of protecting ourselves without killing. Therefore, it seems to me, we must do it—or surrender our claim to distinction among the living creatures."

"Thee's a singular and forthright man," said Sparkman cryptically. They walked downstairs and onto the street together.

The jail in the cellar beneath the Courthouse was in reality a dungeon. Its floor was flagstone and its walls were cut stone, thick, massive, cold. It crawled with vermin.

The only ventilation came from tiny windows near the ceiling, which opened to the ground level outside. Bathtubs were whiskey barrels, cut in half, which were filled and emptied occasionally by Negro attendants employed by the court. Toilet pails were also emptied by the attendants from time to time. The perfunctory treatment of lime and whitewash was to little avail; the stench was permanent.

Judge Ring hated the jail. Angus knew that the Judge had repeatedly requested an appropriation for the construction of a new federal jail; the Judge, of course, recognized that the county could not build a jail to be used almost exclusively by the United States. But there had been no success. Judge Ring had prevailed upon the county authorities to brick up the inside walls of one of the double cells for the use of women prisoners, and to inaugurate a regular Sunday-morning religious service, now conducted by a Protestant minister and a Catholic priest.

Angus was discussing the Judge's attempts to improve the conditions of the jail with Sparkman as they walked toward the Courthouse.

"Thee's sure to find," said the Quaker, "that in many ways Friend Ring is a very progressive man."

"It makes him all the more incredible to me."

Together they mounted the front steps and walked around the corridor to the stairway which led down to the dungeon. The jailer greeted them.

"Good afternoon, Mr. DeWolfe. Good afternoon, Parson."

"Call me Friend," Sparkman said with a smile. "May we see the lad again?"

"So Mr. DeWolfe is taking over the case for the Shawnee."

"That is correct," Angus replied.

The jailer looked him over contemptuously, then shrugged. "Do you want to talk to him privately?"

"If thee please," said the Quaker.

"All right, I'll have a cell emptied. We're pretty full down there right now. After the fourteenth there'll be more room."

"How many are being executed then?" Angus asked.

"Six, counting your man. Only five if you get him off." The jailer's face reddened as he turned away. "Have a seat. I'll put your Indian into a cell in the back."

The Shawnee Indian boys and men never wore long braided hair, as was common with so many of the tribes. They bobbed their hair, cutting it just below the level of the ears. Marcus Maywood, however, did not have an Indian haircut. He was groomed in the manner of the average white man. After seeing him, Angus knew that he had encountered the boy before, but had not known who he was. Marcus's eyes were soft brown and solemn. His hair was black; his skin the swarthy, reddish-brown color of the medium-dark Indians. The thin, straight-lined features of his face gave no trace of deep feeling; only his eyes suggested his attitude, and that was doubt and distrust. His lips were on the verge of a smile, a tight smile with a cynical touch in it.

Angus and the Quaker sat on the bench in the cell and listened as Marcus told essentially the same story that he had told in the trial. He had gone to visit his mother, and upon his return had discovered that he was wanted for questioning in regard to the Flower family murders. He stated, as he had testified, that his mother had given him the money that had been found in his mattress. Presently Sparkman made an excuse and left them alone.

"Marcus," Angus said, hoping to begin reassuringly, "Friend Sparkman has told me that you were reluctant to have me for your counsel."

"Does it matter?" the boy asked bitterly.

"Of course it matters. I don't want to undertake your defense if you don't want me. I'm here at the insistence of Sparkman. He is your friend."

"He testified against me," said Marcus Maywood.

"He was subpoenaed by the district attorney. He had to tell the truth— he had affirmed an oath to God."

"Why should I talk to you?"

"Let's get this straight right now. I won't be a witness if you get a new trial, and I won't have to tell anybody anything. If your conviction is set aside, you'll automatically have another trial. And Sparkman will have to testify again, just as he did before. Many people believe you're guilty, Marcus."

"Do you believe it, Mr. DeWolfe?"

"To be honest with you, I haven't decided yet."

"And what if you decide that I'm guilty?"

"I'll try to keep you off the gallows."

"For life in prison?" The boy's facial muscles scarcely moved. "I would rather be hanged."

"Marcus," he said, hoping to kindle some show of feeling, "did you have anything to do with the Flower family at all?"

The Indian stared at him. "I never saw any of those people in my life."

"If you're lying to me, you will go to the gallows."

"I will go anyway." The boy's face now twisted and contempt visibly touched his lips. "Among my people belief is in the heart, not in the head. If you don't believe me now, you never will."

The dark brown eyes were blazing, and Angus watched him closely. "If you never saw the Flowers in your life, why do you think you were convicted?"

"The Quaker convicted me."

"His testimony that you asked him to lie for you?"

"Yes."

"Was he telling the truth?"

"Yes."

"Why did you try to frame such an alibi, anyway?"

"Because nobody would have believed me. They were looking for me when I got back to Ridgefield. I thought they'd believe a Quaker. And I thought I could trust him to help me."

Marcus's mouth closed tightly and he sat in silence. It was clear that his reason for asking Sparkman to lie for him was indeed fear—but fear for having been involved with Janet Ring, not that an Indian would be summarily dispatched to the gallows.

"Let's go back a bit," Angus said. "Why did you visit your mother in the first place?"

"I asked her to come to Ridgefield to live with me."

"Did she plan to come here?"

"No. She refused."

"Marcus, when she was first questioned, she didn't know anything about the money. Then, after she learned that you'd been picked up with three hundred dollars in your possession, she claimed she gave it to you. Naturally, she didn't convince anybody. I have to know where you got that money."

The boy's nostrils flared like a frightened mustang's, but he said nothing.

Angus tried again. "Maybe the Flowers were dead when you came upon them. Maybe you happened along and took the money off dead bodies— that would make a logical story. Maybe we could prove it somehow, if it's true."

The Indian looked down at his shoes, refusing to answer.

"But it isn't true, is it?"

"No."

"Then where did you get the money?"

"I told you." The hatred in his voice was like a stench in his tiny cell.

Angus said gently, "Do you know how I first came to be interested in your case? Janet Ring wrote me a letter."

Now the boy looked up.

"She told me about her visits to your cabin. She told me you wanted to marry her. Isn't that why you went down to see your mother? Isn't that why you needed money?"

"Mr. DeWolfe," the boy said finally, "I won't have her brought into this. No matter what you do, I won't have it——"

"Maybe it won't be necessary," Angus said. "But we've got to explain why you asked the Quaker to lie for you. Nobody will ever believe your mother gave you that money."

"Not even if it's true?"

"How *could* it be true? She's living down there now with your kinfolks in a log hut, obviously very poor. Where would she get three hundred dollars to give you?"

"That is none of your business," Marcus said. "It has nothing to do with this case, and——"

"She testified that it was wrapped up in a piece of buckskin. Everyone in the courtroom laughed. Where could she have gotten it, Marcus?"

"I don't know!" His eyes still blazed, and his jaws made angry knots at his cheeks.

"This is our problem," Angus said. "We're going to file an appeal to the Supreme Court. In order to ask for a new trial, we must present a clear, logical reason why the conviction was either prejudiced or illegal. Do you follow me?"

"Yes."

"We can ask for a change of venue and a new trial on the contention that Judge Ring couldn't have given you an impartial hearing, since it was his own daughter you were courting when you got the money——"

"Mr. DeWolfe," said the boy grimly, "if you do that, I will try to kill you. I'll deny everything you have said."

"I won't do anything you don't agree to. Don't worry about that. I'm telling you that the sure way is——"

"No!"

"Are you willing to be tried in this court again?"

Marcus's mouth twisted downward.

"Do white people only think of their skins, Mr. DeWolfe?"

"All right," Angus said wearily. "Leave it at that for the present. But once more, before I go. Where did you get the money? I know your mother didn't give it to you. Let me see *your* sense of honor——"

Suddenly the boy leaped from the bench and lunged toward him. His strong young hands grabbed at Angus's throat with all the fury of his sad and angry heart.

Angus shoved him back with a quick thrust of his elbows, then slapped him with his open palm. He grabbed the boy's shirt front and slapped him again. The attack subsided almost as suddenly as it had begun. Now Marcus stood mutely before him. His eyes were averted, and he looked ashamed.

Finally he said, "I am sorry, Mr. DeWolfe. I know you're trying to help me."

"It's all right," Angus said. "I understand why you did it. You know that somehow I'm going to find out where you got that money."

"I doubt if you will," said the boy.

"Now you're admitting that your mother didn't give it to you, aren't you?"

"No," he answered in a softly trembling voice. Defiant tears swam in his eyes.

"If we don't give an explanation for the money, there isn't much chance."

"I understand." Marcus paused and turned away, staring at the cell wall. "Paul Sparkman could have kept me out of all this."

"If he'd been willing to lie."

"I don't feel like talking to you any more today, Mr. DeWolfe."

"Very well, Marcus. I'll see you again later in the week."

The boy did not answer.

Angus stood for a moment at the door of the cell, then went through it and across the main room of the prison. The smell of urine split his nostrils. He stared at the miserable creatures who were sitting around in little clusters, on benches, on the flagstones, some chained to the walls, some hobbled with their feet chained together.

They were all watching him. He knew that many of them considered him a man who could work miracles with the Supreme Court. Once, a few weeks earlier, the wife of a convicted killer had come to him and said, "Please, Mr. DeWolfe, I want to buy from you one of those Supreme Court reversals for my man. He's over at the jail now."

He crossed the prison rooms, toward the stairway. The stinking air and the oppressive atmosphere of the jail had given him a fierce headache.

Assuming Marcus guilty, the real tragedy, he felt, lay in the boy's own feelings toward white people. It seemed that the Indian might never have killed had he not been twisted out of reason by his desire to claim a white girl for his wife. He hated white people—had been taught to hate them—yet he wanted one for his own. And if he were innocent? Then a subtler guilt had made him prefer the chance of death to any further revelation of himself.

Back in his office, Angus went over the case again with Sparkman—telling him everything except the part that Janet Ring had played in Marcus's life. Apparently Miss Ring had not told Sparkman about it, either.

He suspected that the purest sentimentality lay behind the clinging hope

[67]

of the boy's innocence. Who were the people who held that hope? The Quaker, the old-maid teacher, the reform-minded lawyer, the town clown who had a personal axe to grind—all gentle-hearted by nature, all prone to sympathize with the unfortunate for one reason or another. Would that be an observable common denominator, he wondered, if he could line up together all the people whose hearts bore hope for Marcus Maywood? Were the clowns, the reformers, the hopers and dreamers by nature, also the sentimental rejectors of obvious truth? Had their own hurts made them sensitive? Or had their sensitivity made them hurt more than most?

He said, "In what way was Marcus 'curiously unpredictable' when he was in your school? I believe those were your words."

Sparkman considered the question, dredging his memory.

"He was a moody lad—from the beginning. He feared white people unreasonably. After his father was killed, his fears were turned to hate. Sometimes he would be absent from school for days. But he read his books even when he was absent. After Janet Ring came to work with us, she was able to coax him out of his moods. By 'unpredictable,' I meant that he was erratic in attendance and in classroom participation. He was never unruly."

"Tell me about his father. You said he was killed."

Sparkman frowned. "His father was a bitter, frightened man, repelled by the idea of education for the Indian children. He had been close to starvation several times in his life. . . ."

Marcus's father, as the Quaker told it, had at first urged peace between the Shawnees and the Pottawatomies when they found themselves living on the same land. Both tribes had been awarded the unoccupied space between the north and south branches of the Canadian River in the central part of the Territory.

Indian resentment of the many removals had excluded the white man from any consideration within their codes of honesty. By the time they reached the Territory, they could lie to white men with impunity: doing so had become manifestly the right thing to do.

Then, as living proved to be more difficult, the tribes began to dishonor each other. The Shawnees and the Pottawatomies, competing for survival, became bitter enemies, united only in their hatred of the whites.

"At least," said Sparkman, "that's the way I see it. The Shawnees and Pottawatomies are not warlike—they have never been murderous as groups. Sometimes, in the intensity of their anguish, they have burned each other's houses. They have thieved each other's horses so often that I doubt if even the horses know to whom they belong."

Angus laughed at the Quaker's picture.

"Are Marcus's people actually hungry down there?"

"Some years, yes. Very hungry. They have hunted out their territory already. They kill many animals and birds for their spring Bread Dance—ill considering that it's the time for nesting and borning the young. They believe their seeds will rot in the ground if they do not have their Bread Dance before they plant. The lad's father died during a horse-thieving episode that happened to coincide with a cattle drive coming up the West Shawnee Trail. . . ."

The Quaker went on to explain: Clayt Mosley, with twelve cowboys, a chuck wagon, and a wrangler, was driving fifteen hundred head of mixed cattle—steers, bulls, cows, yearlings—to the Osage Reservation, under contract with the Osage Indian Agent. He had started with only ten men, but had taken on two more before he reached the Texas line because his herd had gone crazy, running night after night. The two extra hands proved to be the bad ones. Clayt liked to have cows along, dropping calves from time to time, because the cows would bawl for their calves which, he believed, had a soothing effect upon the entire herd. A practical man, he always shot the calves immediately, for in the process of birth they had served their purpose of motivating their mothers' bawling and if allowed to live would only slow him down. As he crossed the Nations, however, instead of killing them he gave the new calves to any Indians who happened to be near.

Marcas Maywood's mother had, in fact, that year accumulated several head of cattle by begging the newborn calves from drovers who came up the West Shawnee Trail.

By the time Clayt Mosley reached the Shawnee-Pottawatomie country, his herd had diminished to no more than thirteen hundred head. They had stampeded six times already. His men were edgy and exhausted. He was bedding his critters down carefully, trying to discover the cause of their running; he could have shot the Indians himself, he said, for riding wildly into his sleeping herd that night, sending them off again on a five-hour moonlight rampage.

The Shawnees and Pottawatomies, quite unaware of the existence of Clayt Mosley's jumpy trail herd, had been quarrelling over horses for a week. A group of Shawnees, including Marcus's father, whose Indian name was Ho-lah-go-nah, had taken twenty-five saddle horses from the Pottawatomies by slipping a rail fence corral gate while the Pottawatomies were celebrating their own successful theft. They drove the horses quietly for a mile or two, then ran them hard in order to get a good start, in the hope of possibly eluding the Pottawatomies entirely. In their flight, they rode, stolen horses and all, into Clayt Mosley's herd in the flat below Bundy's Gap.

Pete Ritter and Handy McClain, Clayt's two new cowboys, were night-riding the herd when it happened. They weren't ever convinced that these

Shawnees weren't trying to cause a stampede. The two cowboys simply yelled, "Injuns!"—drew their Colts and emptied them right into the redskins' faces.

Ho-lah-go-nah fell off his horse, killed instantly.

"And, of course," said Angus, "it was considered just one of those things."

"Thee cannot imagine the suffering it caused," said the Quaker indignantly. "Everyone was sorry—except possibly the two that fired the guns. They fled before daybreak. By the time the incident was over, Clayt Mosley had purchased those horses from the Shawnees. He told me he wanted to make them feel better—and he could use the horses in Texas. He picked them up on his way back south after delivering his herd. Marcus and his poor mother moved into a cabin with his uncle's family, and finally, when he returned to school, he was morose. But he never seemed to lose interest in his books. It was the next year that Janet Ring came to work with us. She was able to perk the lad up a bit. Mary Sparkman and I thought she worked miracles with him."

"You assigned him the name Maywood, I suppose."

"Yes. We give all students Anglo-American names when they enter school. It is recommended by the Indian Office. Marcus is the only member of his family who has been to school."

"What kind of person is his mother?"

"She plowed and planted, built her home with her own hands, cut wood and butchered animals for food, and wanted no part of white civilization. I think she would have been pleased if her son had decided to kill as many as he could before they got him. She might have suggested these murders to him, even after all these years. I do not know."

"I'm going down there and talk to her," Angus said. "I'd like for you to interpret for me, if you will."

"Thee'll be most welcome. And I'll take responsibility for thy retainer myself. Several people contributed before, and I'm sure I can handle it again in a similar way."

"However you and Miss Ring want to work it out," Angus said.

"What do thee think, now that thee's seen the lad?"

"I haven't a guess. He talks convincingly—about the wrong things. Maybe he'll open up a little more next time."

"Miss Ring might be able to give thee help. I am certain that he was fond of her at school."

"I'll keep it in mind," said Angus. "I'll write you soon."

"Splendid," said the Quaker, lifting his black hat from his knee. "Mary Sparkman and I will be eager to hear from thee."

CHAPTER SEVEN

Angus quickly became attached to his barren, creaky-floored office above the harness store. He liked being spread out; he savored the sense of freedom in being entirely on his own.

The Colonel called on him shortly after he returned from St. Louis where he had learned exactly nothing from the associates of the lawyer Caulfield, who had come down to defend Marcus the previous spring. Although he wanted to maintain Beleau's friendship, which he would always value highly, he was relieved that the partnership had ended. He knew already that the Colonel's mild geniality had influenced his own judgments ever since he had been in Ridgefield.

"This will make a fine office, Angus," the Colonel said after looking around. "You'll get on with Sam Wilson, I think."

"I hope so. A couple of people turned me down. But I'll have to get used to that, I suppose."

"You will if you stay in criminal practice. And Angus, if you should need any money—if things go slow for you——"

"Thanks, I'll yell if I do."

He wondered with amusement if any words spoken by one human being to another could possibly be more comforting than if-you-need-any-money. There was I-love-you, of course, but those words reflected a different problem. Warmed by the Colonel's gesture, he surrendered himself completely to good feeling and even walked downstairs after his former partner had left and loafed for a few minutes in the back of the pharmacy.

When Angus needed to move around the Ridgefield area, he sometimes hired a saddle horse at Slattery's livery stable. One afternoon he had been out to see a farmer whose son had got into trouble at a barn dance the previous Saturday night, and was leaving the stable after returning the horse, when Janet Ring pulled up beside him in her father's fancy buggy. It was a trim, high-wheeled rig with transverse springs, tufted leather seats, and a black folding calash that, when extended, reached out almost as far as the whip socket.

She was smiling at him.

He did not know that Luke Sweeley had told her this was the best place to meet him casually and inconspicuously. He knew only that she hardly resembled the girl who had come to his office a few days earlier. He could not quickly determine the exact difference, but he was happily surprised.

"Good afternoon, Mr. DeWolfe," she said, holding the reins pertly. "I saw you leaving the stable and thought I might save you the walk home."

"That's wonderful," he said, climbing into the seat beside her. She offered him the reins.

"Ladies don't really like to drive buggies, especially if there is a man available." Her laughter bubbled, coquettishly out of character. Taking the reins, he looked at her again and noticed that her cheeks were tinged with a self-conscious blush.

"If your father saw me in his rig, he'd have me up in court, Miss Ring. There must be some law I'm violating."

"I doubt if there is," she said. "I'm so glad to run into you, because I have been anxious to ask you about the Maywood case."

"You could have come to my office any time you wanted to. I have a new place now, above Wilson's. The Colonel and I are no longer together."

"So I have heard," she said, and did not seem to know how to continue her lighthearted sociability. He knew that she was stricken with inadequacy —that she had begun a conversational gambit alien to her character; and he was flattered that she had been sufficiently attracted to behave this way.

"Of course," he said quickly, "I understand why you didn't."

"Paul Sparkman told me of his visit with you."

"He's a remarkable man, isn't he? I haven't known many Quakers. Does he talk Plain Language in school? I should think it would confuse the pupils."

Janet Ring laughed. He liked her laughter—especially when it was unself-conscious.

"Mary doesn't speak Plain—and Paul tries not to in the classroom. But it's such a part of him! Most Quakers who teach have abandoned it, I understand. It does confuse some of the pupils at times. But not Marcus. How is he, Mr. DeWolfe?"

"He still won't talk about the money," Angus said. "I'm working on the appeal, but I don't know where we're going if we get a new trial. I didn't learn a thing in St. Louis."

"Am I correct," she asked, "in assuming that you will base the appeal upon courtroom irregularities, and not upon a contention that he may be innocent?"

"That's essentially correct, Miss Ring. I can't find any new evidence. Have you any further ideas about that?"

"No," she said, and seemed suddenly to withdraw from lightheartedness entirely. And just as suddenly his mind shifted from the puzzle that had been with him for days.

He had been trying to draw a picture of the convicted Indian, trying to reconcile the disparate character elements he had discovered: sensitive lad who read books of poetry, wildflower gardener in love with his white teacher, efficient worker in the Indian Office, convicted murderer of an entire innocent family.

Now he was wondering about the teacher. He knew that she had been educated in New York and had come to the West for the first time when her father was appointed to the bench out here. She could not always have been so retiring and fearful. There was vitality in her that showed despite her efforts to keep it hidden. He felt that her true personality, her capacity for human warmth and joy, was buried somewhere inside her as though clamped tightly in a box underneath a heavy lid, and that her father (or perhaps her fear of him) was sitting on the lid, ruthlessly denying her the right to be alive as a woman.

"Did you tell the Judge about your friendship with Marcus?" he asked.

"Yes, but it wasn't necessary. He already knew."

"Did you tell him you'd been to see me?"

"No," she said, "but he probably knows that, too. He seems to know everything I do."

"Then you're not as afraid of him as you were when you wrote to me. You said he would disown you."

"No," she said, trying to smile, "I'm not as afraid, Mr. DeWolfe."

But her face told him that she was not fooling herself about this. Her lips were tight and her mouth was drained of color. She was Judge Ring's old-maid daughter again.

"Then I'm sure you'll let me drive you home," he said.

"You'll what?"

"I must protect my dignity, Miss Ring. Your father keeps the rig at Gray's Barn, doesn't he? I'll drive you there, see you to your porch, then walk to Mrs. Borden's. Anyone who sees us will have a better impression of me than if I let you deliver me to the boardinghouse and go home alone." He smiled at her. "I wouldn't want to appear unchivalrous."

"I suppose not," she said, staring straight ahead. "All right, Mr. DeWolfe. You may drive me home."

"If you'd rather I didn't——"

"No. Please drive me home," she said urgently. But she would not look at him.

He wheeled the buggy around and drove in the direction of Judge Ring's residence north of the square.

Early evening dusk was closing in when they reached the horse barn which was only a block from her home. It had been in the outskirts when the Rings moved there, but was now quite surrounded by the growing town. He pulled through the gate and helped her to the ground. The stableboy was astounded when he saw them, but took the rig away in bug-eyed silence. Angus couldn't resist a smile.

"It's not likely that your father is at home now, is it?" he asked as they walked away from the barn.

"He usually comes home late," she said.

"Would it be so terrible if he should see us together?"

"I don't know, Mr. DeWolfe. I think it would."

"I would like to take my chances some Saturday afternoon and call on you again."

She considered the idea and he knew that she liked it. He knew also that it was essentially unfathomable to her—an abyss of improbability.

"When Father is at home?" she asked.

"Whether he's at home or not." She didn't answer and he said, "Perhaps we could go riding."

"Perhaps," she said.

"I understand you went to school in New York."

"At Miss Gibson's Academy." Her voice now bore a strange sound, as though they weren't really her words at all, and he marveled at her.

"I lived in Washington for a few years. Do you miss the East?"

"I've almost forgotten what the East was like," she said, and sadness seemed to live in the simple statement.

They had reached her front porch and she stood before the steps, plainly terrified.

He said, "Miss Ring, I wouldn't like to be a nuisance about this. But I'm serious about calling on you sometime. Would you let me?"

"May I think about it?" she asked. "I would like you to, I think—but may I have some time before I answer?"

"Why, of course."

"I will write you a letter if I decide that it would be all right."

"Splendid. I'll haunt Luke Sweeley until he delivers it."

"Mr. DeWolfe, you must think me terribly backward, being so inconclusive about everything. You are very kind to me."

"Good night, Miss Ring," he said.

She disappeared inside the house and he walked down the street feeling wonderfully lightheaded.

As he approached the square he met her father, who had just emerged from the Federal Building. When they were face to face on the sidewalk, Angus bowed in recognition.

"Good evening, Judge," he said sociably.

The little man paused, staring at him, then glanced up the street toward his home.

"Good evening," he said, his face mirroring with disbelief the suspicion in his mind.

Angus kept walking. When his back was to the Judge, a happy grin burst over his face.

He worked prodigiously on his case, absorbed and determined. The letter from Janet Ring did not come.

He searched for reversible errors. He analyzed the original indictment, picking it for inconsistencies with the verdict. He organized a damning summary of remarks from the bench which would have tended to lead the jury. Agitation grew in him as the presentation took shape—heightened, no doubt, by his increasing awareness that he could see no substantially stronger defense than had been offered at the trial. And by the fact that still he had received no letter. He thought about Janet, enchanted by the notion that behind her fright was an interesting girl who was probably very attractive.

When the appeal was prepared, he felt a little better about the case. The Judge's windy admonition alone seemed sufficiently demanding to assure the conviction of scrutiny before the Supreme Court. The Maywood jury had gone into deliberation with a savage picture in Judge Ring's Bible-pounding words of the once hopeful but now dead Flower family—father, mother, and two helpless little children. . . .

Six days before the scheduled execution, which was to have seen Marcus Maywood walk with five other convicted killers across the trap on the high scaffold in the courtyard, Judge Ring summoned Angus to his chambers. He informed the lawyer that he had issued a stay of execution, pending the Supreme Court's action on the appeal.

His massive eyebrows arched contemptuously. "Mr. DeWolfe," he said, in a high voice, "your bill of general exceptions is a clever document. I have no doubt that the Supreme Court will reverse me, stuffed as it is with ignorance and self-satisfaction."

He peered over his glasses, his face contorted. Threatened, his sense of power was now aroused and maddened. His diminutive body seemed to swell with anger.

Angus straightened himself to a height which loomed gigantically, and looked down at the little man with confidence.

"I expect it to," he said.

Judge Ring's face turned a shade grayer.

"I have learned," he said, "that some time ago, in the vicinity of Slattery's livery stable, my daughter offered you a ride in her buggy. I have further learned that you took the reins from her and drove her home, openly inviting the public to gaze at the spectacle. She is deeply distressed that she permitted you to make a fool of her. She has led a sheltered life, and is not in the least capable of handling the advances of men with disreputable backgrounds. Leave her alone. Good day, sir."

Angus stood in silence, looking down at the Judge. The enormity of their antagonism toward each other staggered him. The stolid dignity of the gray-draped chambers became suddenly saturated with the smallness of hatred, and humanity was for the instant sucked out of both men.

Angus turned abruptly and left the room, realizing that he would not get the letter he had been waiting for.

The next morning, Sarah Borden, thin-faced and nervous, served his breakfast and coffee as usual. Although no further mention had been made of his leaving the boardinghouse, the tacit assumption seemed to be that he would leave as soon as he could find a place. He hoped every day to see signs that they were relenting, but no such sign was visible on Sarah.

When she served his breakfast, she placed the morning *Monograph* beside his plate. She had begun to make a practice of thrusting the paper on him when he was unfavorably discussed in the prints.

"Have they torn me to bits again?" he asked.

Sarah did not answer, but moved to the kitchen door and stood barely inside with an air of perverse satisfaction on her face. He found it curious that she could be a fairly attractive girl despite the cold meanness that was in her. Her attitude seemed to suggest a fear that if Gunnysack McCloud didn't get her, Angus DeWolfe would.

Taking pleasure in disappointing her, he ignored the paper and ate heartily, asking for a second cup of coffee. He left the table without looking at the newspaper, not even glancing back at her as he departed the house to walk toward his office on South Street.

But he hurried, conscious of the stares he attracted from everyone who saw him. Most of them, it was plain, had read the morning paper.

He read it when he reached his office above the harness store. His copy was waiting, half underneath the door.

JUDGE RING CRITICIZES SUPREME COURT, the headline screamed.

He pulled off his coat and hung it in the corner before opening the paper. Then he read Hoey Johnson's journalism.

In an unprecedented action, Judge Willard P. Ring of the U.S. District Court called in reporters from this newspaper yesterday afternoon for the purpose of lodging an official complaint against the Supreme Court of the United States. Judge Ring made it clear that he believed such a complaint should be lodged through the medium of a newspaper, because of the importance of the subject matter to the citizens of this community. He told this reporter that he had communicated with the Supreme Court in Washington by letter, but his pleas and explanations had fallen on deaf ears; and he felt that now, in consideration of his friends and neighbors, he must speak out publicly. Then he read the following statement, a copy of which he gave us so that there would be no mistake in reporting exactly what he had said. . . .

Angus paused, frowned in astonishment, and fumbled in his desk for a cigar before continuing to read the story. Then he read Judge Ring's incredible statement.

"Heinous crime is on the increase in the area of my jurisdiction. The Supreme Court of the United States is aiding the crime wave. One wonders how long nine indifferent men can sit in Washington and believe they understand the conditions with which we are faced out here. This shilly-shallying with justice must cease if we are to stay chaos from our doors!

"I want to make clear once again to my fellow countrymen that the only objective of my court is to establish a certainty of punishment for the guilty and a rigid protection for the innocent. Criminals no longer know they will pay with their lives for murder committed. There is a growing probability that the Supreme Court will seize upon some flimsy technicality and thwart the justice of our jury system.

"I feel it my duty to God, to my country, and to my own conscience to make this clear to the very public which is placed in jeopardy."

Angus put down the newspaper. He puffed thoughtfully on the cigar, blowing smoke with a growing feeling of delight. He knew that the Judge was in trouble now—a wounded miniature bull, fighting blindly. A smile spread over his face.

CHAPTER EIGHT

Heartened as he was by the stay of execution, Angus was none-theless aware that the defense of Maywood at the new trial would be an-other matter.

He began preparations by constructing in his mind the strongest possible case against the Indian. He assumed the role of prosecutor and pursued every conceivable line of argument and evidence that could lead toward the appearance or probability of guilt. He outlined the case, step by step, as he would present it to the jury if he were the district attorney. Then he be-gan tearing it down, systematically searching for evidence to cast doubt upon every aspect of adverse testimony. And there was always the gap. A boy without money suddenly had a large sum in his possession, and had tried to arrange an alibi. How could doubt be thrown on that?

Curiously, when he became depressed, his quandary over the boy would shift subtly and he would find himself trying to understand the riddle of Janet Ring. In his mind he would stand unseen near the wildflower garden where Janet and Marcus Maywood had supposedly shared an interest in poetry. He would listen to what might have been conversations between them, letting come to life in his imagination a little drama of a love-torn Indian and his white schoolteacher.

The puzzle of Judge Ring's daughter consumed him. How could a woman, nearing thirty, be so terrified of her father? Had she ever been out with a man in her life? How could she possibly have reached that age and still be gentle and sensitive if love had never touched her? What would her father do if a gentleman should one evening rap at the door and an-nounce that he had come to take her to the Opera House? And what would be the look on Judge Ring's face if that man should happen to be Angus DeWolfe?

He was severely annoyed with himself. He jammed his cigar into his mouth and tried to study the trial record before him. He realized that he had a headache. And he felt so lonely that he was stricken with an urge to go down to the Red Handkerchief Saloon and drink himself stupid. The romantic notion of an evening of debauchery, followed by sudden clarity and new wisdom, seemed inviting and logical.

There was a rap at his door and Luke Sweeley came inside.

"Saw your lamp burning, Angus," the old man said.

"I always have it on when I'm working at night," he replied, astonished at his sarcasm.

Luke blinked, but did not retreat.

"Saw it last night and the night before, too."

"And you decided to come up and see what you could find out?"

"Angus. . . . I thought we'd become friends finally. You've got no call to be nasty to me, boy."

Angus was contrite. Talking to Luke sometimes required a lot of energy.

"You're right," he said. "I'm sorry."

Luke grinned, fidgeting with his hat, which he was holding with both hands. "Already forgave and forgot." Now the old man's eyes were narrow speculative splits in his leathery face. He leaned against the desk, still turning the hat in his hands. "You been getting enough sleep? You look tuckered out to me."

"What makes you think so?"

"Oh, little things. You passed me by this morning, down near the hide house. Doc McKay said you didn't speak to him the other day. I heard him telling some of the boys about it. They're making bets you won't be able to clear the Shawnee."

"Is that why you came up here, to tell me that?"

"Not particularly."

"Then what's on your mind?"

"Just nosing around. Like you thought."

Angus laughed heartily and reached into the desk for cigars.

"Have one, Luke," he said. "You might as well sit down awhile. We haven't had a visit in a long time."

"Why . . . thanks, Angus."

Luke took a cigar and sat in the chair opposite the desk. He tossed his hat to the floor beside his chair.

"This thing feels as big as a gourd handle," he said. "Wonder how it would chew?"

"I wouldn't want to try it."

"I'll smoke it awhile, and see if I can stand it."

As soon as they had fired up pleasantly, Luke reached into his pocket and drew out a bottle of whiskey. It was a beautiful amber sight in the lamplight.

"Just happened to have this with me."

"Are you peddling whiskey, too?" Angus asked.

"You know better'n that, boy. Now stop picking on me and have a drink."

"Let me pull the shades first. Folks have got a bad enough opinion of me in this town."

Angus drew the shades which covered the two windows that opened toward the street. Then he took the bottle and held it up to the light, reflecting upon the varied forms of beauty.

"Looks pretty good, Luke. Make it yourself?"

"You know, Angus," the drayman said, "you're a puzzle of a man. Afraid of what folks'll think, and yet passing them on the street without speaking. You don't ever go down to the saloon when it's written all over you lately you needed a drink."

Angus turned up the bottle and drank freely from it, then handed it to Luke.

"It *is* good. I'm much obliged, Luke. Funny . . . I was telling myself before you came in that I might go down to the Red Handkerchief and get drunk."

The old man took a drink, replacing the bottle on the table between them, chuckling.

"I can just see you down at the Red Handkerchief. You're standing there getting tighter than Dixie's hatband, and whooping and hollering and then pretty soon you're upstairs messing around the girls. Wilder'n a coot, eh, Angus?" Luke threw back his head and laughed. Then his old face sobered and he said, "You're the strangest fellow I ever bumped into, Angus. Ain't anybody around here ever saw a man quite like you."

"I don't think I'm such a freak," Angus said.

"You live over there at them nice people's house and play rook cards at night, when all the he-men are down at the saloons gambling and cussing and drinking and looking for women. You'd be took for a real city slick, except everybody knows you've been all over the Territories out west. Can't nobody figure you out, including me." Luke laughed again, and pushed over the bottle. "Here, have another drink."

"How do folks know I've been all over the Territories? I've never told anybody, that I can remember."

"Fellow came through town a few months ago. Got to talking to people in the lobby over at the hotel. Somebody mentioned your name and he perked up his ears and asked a lot of questions. Said he used to be a cattle detective, and he knew you when you was a kid, just out of the war. First I ever knew you was in the war—I wouldn't have thought you was old enough."

"Well, I'll be damned. Do you remember his name?"

"Mac—something. Way he told it you used to be pretty good with a gun. Maybe he was laying it on a little, but he had folks listening."

"It was McCord, I guess."

"Was that when you killed that man?" Luke asked.

Angus nodded and continued drinking. The liquor warmed him and loosened the knots between his shoulder blades. Yes, he thought, he had killed a man one time. Jim Drogan had been one of those who could kill purely for pleasure. Angus suppressed a shudder and put it out of his mind. That was the way he had learned to handle the depressing subject. He could refuse to think about it, and then, for the period of refusal at least, it might never have happened.

As he drank with Luke, his reflections mellowed. He felt like standing on his desk and quoting from the *Rubaiyat*—the part about wine playing the infidel. He smiled at himself and the absurd notion.

"Are you laughing at me, boy?" Luke asked suddenly.

"Don't be so touchy. I was laughing at myself. There are some verses, written six or seven hundred years ago by a Persian tentmaker named Omar Khayyam. I just happened to think about them."

"Let's hear some of them. Can you remember any?"

"No . . . they're kid stuff, anyway. All about living today and letting tomorrow go hang."

"Sounds kind of shortsighted, don't it?"

"I used to think they were great."

"Do you know anything by Shakespeare and all those folks? I'll bet you do."

"All what folks?"

"Damn it, if I knew I wouldn't be asking you, would I?"

"No. I'm sorry to say I don't know much about Shakespeare, Luke. Or any of the great poets and thinkers." He felt sad that he had to say that—drunkenly sad and disgusted with himself. "I'm afraid I got started too late in life," he went on, talking less to Luke than to his own feeling of inadequacy. "I wasted my time. Instead of following Nat after the war, I should have gone on back to school. I didn't have much sense——"

"You ain't got much now, if you ask me. That kind of talk stinks worse than this cigar. Who is Nat?"

"My brother who was killed. Out in Arizona."

"Who killed him?"

"A man named Drogan."

"Is that the fellow you shot, Angus?"

"That's the fellow."

Luke pursed his lips thoughtfully. "Let's finish off this damned bottle. It's just sitting here evaporating."

They emptied the bottle, and then, as magically as if he had been performing a show before an audience, Luke produced a second bottle from another pocket. They laughed riotously as Angus opened it and took a drink to test it against the first bottle.

"Yep," he said. "It came out of the same horse, Luke."

"Shame on you. That ain't no way to talk."

"What's wrong? There's no women here."

"Don't matter. It ain't like you and I don't want to hear you talking that way."

Angus stared at the old man, a little flattered. Behind the whiskery, leather face and the gimp leg, Luke Sweeley was a warming character. You might get impatient with him, but you always went away from him feeling pretty good.

"I don't like to be daddied," Angus said. "You'd better cut it out."

"You ought to get married. It'd make a man out of you."

"What makes you think I'm not a man?" The effect of the second bottle was evident now.

Luke glared at him. "Sitting up here dreaming of going visiting upstairs at the Red Handkerchief ain't no way for a man to think. Them punks that strut around packing guns and playing poker, they're the ones that go upstairs. They ain't men."

"I didn't say anything about going upstairs."

"You was thinking it, though." Luke shook his head, puzzled. "If you was my boy, I'd of kicked your butt long before now if you hadn't gone and found yourself a good wife."

"If you don't shut up, I'm going to throw you out of here, Luke. Right on your old tin bucket."

"Just try it, and you won't ever find out what I know about the money that Indian had in his mattress."

Angus jumped out of his chair.

"What did you say?"

"You heard me. Now, you just behave yourself. I told you I was a good detective."

"What have you found out, Luke?"

The old man stared at him silently. His narrow eyes watered and he blinked. His chin quivered.

"I'm sorry. I guess I *was* trying to daddy you."

Impatient of drunken sentiment, Angus went around the desk and grabbed Luke's shoulder.

"What about it? What have you found out?"

"Maggie had me a son, a dandy little boy," Luke said. "He rolled off the edge of the porch and hit his head on a rock before he was a month old. It killed him. We lived out in Kaintuk then——"

"Luke, for Christ's sake, tell me what you've found."

"You've got to promise me something, first."

"What?"

"You've got to go see Janet Ring."

"I've tried to see her. But she's scared of her old man. She doesn't want me around there."

"Pick a time when the Judge ain't home. I've been watching her, and I know she's hurting."

"What am I supposed to do if she hasn't got the guts to stand up to him? She's a——"

"Just go to see her. It might frighten her, but it'd tickle her, too, Angus. She don't know nothing but book stuff, but she's a nice girl and she's worried about this thing."

"All right. I'll go to see her. Now, tell me what you've discovered. Do you know where Marcus got the money?"

"I believe I do, Angus."

Luke leaned back and lifted his feet to the top of Angus's desk. He struggled with his lame left leg, for it would not straighten out completely.

"See that red clay on my boots?"

"What about it?"

"Notice the white streaks?"

"Yes, Luke?"

"Well, there's your answer. You can use these boots as evidence in your trial, if you want to. I'm a better detective than you ever thought, young fellow."

Angus listened intently as the old drayman explained it to him.

Luke had laid out on his sofa all the things they had taken from Maywood's cabin that day. Like a row of exhibits, he said. He kept looking at them, every time he went through the parlor. And his eyes always came back to the round buckskin pouch with the single drawstring in its opening.

Finally, he knew why. It was dry and cracked from weather, and it was stained with dried clay. He examined it thoughtfully, recognizing it at last as a sacred tobacco bag, the type frequently used by certain Indians in burial ceremonies.

When a Shawnee was buried, the mourners always passed by the grave and took a pinch of sacred tobacco from the pouch which was held at the gravesite by some elderly member of the tribe who was a special family friend of the deceased. After the mourners had all dropped a bit of tobacco upon the remains of their departed loved one, the holder of the bag would then kneel and speak to his dead friend, imploring him not to permit the great sadness of his family to impede his journey to the happy life beyond the earth. It was intended by their Grandmother, Kuh-koom-they-nah, that Her grandchildren come to Her serenely after death. When the rite was concluded, the old man would drop the bag upon the feet of the deceased, and the grave would be closed.

Luke had examined the bag they had found in Marcus's cabin and had known from its condition that it had been buried. It was more than a hunch, he said, that had caused him to make a trip down to the Shawnee country to visit the burial grounds. As he had expected, Marcus's father's grave had been recently opened.

"That's why he won't talk, Angus," Luke said. "That boy robbed his father's grave, and he's ashamed of it."

"It sounds logical, Luke. He always closed up when I asked what his mother meant when she claimed to have had the money wrapped in a piece of buckskin. Could you go down there again right away?"

"Sure." Luke grinned happily. "This red clay on my boots, with the white streaks in it, came from that graveyard. It's on a long shelf above Owl Creek, right there in the Shawnee country. And that pair of boots we took from the kid's cabin had clay just like it on the heels. I can show it to you."

Angus stared at Luke in amazement. This man was supposed to be senile; his mind was thought to be twisted off at a tangent—harmlessly, even humorously, away from established norms.

"I'm in your debt," he said.

Luke glanced away, gazing out the windows as though the shades weren't drawn.

CHAPTER NINE

Mid-September brightened with a cooler sun as Ridgefield began glancing morbidly over its shoulder at the scaffold in the Courthouse square.

"Only five this time," said a janitor, who was pushing a broom at the Opera House. "We'll have a better show right here on the stage tomorrow night."

"Lawyer DeWolfe got one of them off," said a blackjack dealer at the Red Handkerchief Saloon. "He's got tricks, that DeWolfe."

"Judge Ring will get that God damned Shawnee yet," said a farmer, who was buying a length of rope at Sam Wilson's harness store below Angus's office. He fashioned the end of the rope into a noose and everybody laughed nervously at the sight of it.

The Ridgefield *Monograph* quickly put into words what many people felt:

> The Shawnee Indian, Marcus Maywood, will not be hanged tomorrow because his conviction has been "appealed" to the Supreme Court under certain legal technicalities. For those who do not already understand, technicalities are little quirks of law employed by clever legal minds to defeat the cause of justice. As the Judge himself recently pointed out, this review technique has become the stumbling block in our path of progress. How long, oh, Lord, how long . . . ?

Jacob Lotz, the hangman, was a lanky, thin-limbed Dutchman, who had migrated west from Pennsylvania a year after the war; he had ridden the cattle trails from the *brasada* below the Nueces to Dodge City, St. Joseph, and once as far north as Quincy, Illinois. His first experience in killing human beings came about when he was pressed into action as a quickly deputized sheriff in chase of cattle thieves along the Red River at Doan's Crossing on the hub of the Apache reservation. Later, as a deputy sheriff, he became acquainted with the prison problems and was so impressed with the dramatic change Judge Ring had wrought in the federal court that he applied for the official hangman's position. Whoever heard of a Judge holding night sessions in order to speed up the prosecution of criminals?

This was a fresh approach to law and order, and Jacob Lotz wanted to be a part of it. He was hired, and had personally designed the huge gallows in the courtyard. His extra pay, as hangman, was a hundred dollars per criminal hanged, out of which he had to buy a suit of clothes for each to wear and a blanket and a pine box for each unclaimed body.

Lotz laid out his ropes the night before the hanging to let them relax from their coiled shapes. He arose early on the morning of the hanging and carefully oiled them, rubbing the oil deep into the fibers by hand. He made the nooses and strung them to the scaffold an hour after daybreak. Then he attached sandbags and dropped them from the trap again and again until he was certain that all the stretch was gone from the ropes. He liked to break the necks instantly. So expert was he now, that the bodies only twitched.

From the jail, Marcus Maywood could see one end of the gallows through the tiny window near the ceiling of his cell. The sound of the sandbags dropping through the trap, creaking the newly oiled ropes less and less each time, had been the only thing he could hear. The snores and sleep-mutterings of the prisoners, which usually annoyed his thoughts, were now monstrously drowned by the sounds of Jacob Lotz's activities.

Marcus lay on his cot, shuddering with hatred as he caught glimpses of the dour Dutchman with the deep-set eyes and the darkened countenance going about his careful preparations.

In Marcus's mind, an image formed of the chain of circumstances which had propelled him to this near proximity to the ugly Jacob Lotz's macabre efficiency. It had begun the day, years ago, above the Poteau River with his father, when he had encountered a white man for the first time in his life. He had longed that day to be white, and the uncomfortable feeling came to him now that the gods of irony would be properly served if he should yet die for that sin at the end of a white man's rope.

He could remember when his family trekked south from Kansas, camping along streams and in the woods, progressing nearer the land between the North and South Canadian Rivers. And he remembered now the season of planting and building and the joyous hunt which celebrated the new home-making of the Shawnees. His mother built their we-gi-wa of elm bark and hickory poles, and he was taught by his father to hunt for prairie chickens as the first endurance test of his manhood.

He remembered running home, carrying his proud kill.

"Look, Father!" he cried as he approached.

Then he stopped.

A group of strange Indians were in his village, and he knew from the excited voices and the vigorous gestures that trouble was facing his clan—that a new disaster had come upon the Shawnees.

"What is it, Father? Are those men the Pottawatomie?"

"Yes," his father said.

"What do they want?"

"They say the white men have given them our land."

"But it has already been given to us. It is ours forever!"

"They say it is not true. They say their chief has been to Washington, and has been given the land below the North Fork and above the South Fork for *his* people. Our chief, John Warrior, says we must fight the Pottawatomie. We must fight for our land."

"Someone should kill the white men!" cried the boy.

Marcus remembered years later, when he was describing the trouble between the Shawnees and the Pottawatomies to Janet Ring, that time and distance had blurred none of the images. And the resentment, although tempered now by his feeling for his teacher and the Quaker, still raged in him.

"It must have been difficult," Janet Ring said. "Did your people and the Pottawatomies come to actual warfare, Marcus?"

"It was more like a feud," he said. "We thought they were responsible for our troubles, and they thought we were responsible for theirs. The hatred was deep."

"I can imagine," said Janet Ring thoughtfully.

They were sitting on a large gray limestone outcropping in the wildflower garden Marcus had made by slashing a winding path through blackjack thickets into the secluded glade.

Along the mossy bank of the creek grew pink knotweeds and touch-me-nots, and Marcus had planted mallows and adder's-tongues in the wet bog at the water's edge. Higher, in the shade of the woods, were wild geraniums and Solomon's-seals and sprightly doll-eyed baneberries. Here and there fringed milkwort nestled like clusters of purple butterflies.

It had been a labor of great love. Marcus had been filled with pride as Janet's interest and enthusiasm grew and as her knowledge of the plants began to match his own. They had read together the books she had brought, and she had told him of her former life in New York. And he had been in love with her. He had been in love with his fairy land of ferns and plants, and with every thrush and warbler in the sky-reaching trees and with every high-tailed squirrel in the woods and with every hawk that soared in the skies; he had been in love with the harmonies of nature, and nature had not cared that he was reddish-brown and Janet Ring was white.

"How did you finally settle the dispute?" she asked.

"The Quakers took our problems to Washington," he said. "It developed that our treaty had never been ratified by the Senate. The Pottawatomies' claim to the land between the rivers was legal. The government finally settled it by allotting them twice as many acres per person as we were given."

"Did the fighting stop then?"

"It still goes on, but less vigorously. There has never been enough to eat since both tribes came into the area."

"It makes me ashamed to be white," she said.

"You must never be ashamed to be white!" Marcus Maywood cried. He stared at her in astonishment. And she blushed hotly.

"Your people have been mistreated," she said.

"I love you, Janet. Don't ever feel ashamed of your color."

He paused, watching her with wonder, amazed at himself for having spoken of love. He had told himself that he would never say it—that he would somehow kill the impossible feeling in his heart.

Her blush deepened and he thought she was altogether beautiful—as delicate and rare as any flower that had ever blossomed, and she would prevail in nature, as the wildflowers prevailed.

"It is true, Janet. What I said."

"Marcus . . ."

"Yes?"

Now the excess of color was leaving her face. Her eyes suddenly bore a sadness that revealed her heart and crushed his. He knew instantly. He knew what he refused to admit until much, much later. Perhaps he never quite admitted it to himself until after he had been imprisoned—but he knew as he sat beside her on the moss-covered stone, surrounded by the green fronds of maidenhair and the tall pink dragonheads, that she could never return his love.

But hope obscured the truth. Merciful hope flung itself between his pride and his broken heart, letting his dignity preserve itself before her.

"Yes?" he said again.

"You were going to tell me about the first time you ever saw a white person," she said.

"Yes, I was. I got sidetracked, Janet."

Their self-conscious laughter was nonetheless gentle, and they lingered over it—stability's way of gaining time.

"My father took me over beyond the Poteau River the following fall. We were going to haul some lumber from a sawmill," he said, a little shaken.

"How old were you then?"

"About nine. The Agent had given the Quakers permission to build a school near our village. The first white man I ever saw was Paul Sparkman. He was at the sawmill."

"Were you surprised at the way he looked?"

Marcus laughed. He got up from the stone and walked to the edge of the woods where he plucked from deep in the leaf mold a slender white-stemmed plant. Its blossom was also white, and shaped like a delicate bowl.

"Do you remember when we found this growing last spring?" he asked.

"Yes. It's the pinesap."

"This particular one is what we call 'corpse flower.' It has no chlorophyl. It is a parasite that lives off the rotting tree roots below. Paul Sparkman explained it to me. He said that his people, back in Pennsylvania, call it 'Indian Pipe.' "

They both laughed.

"But you call it 'corpse flower'?" she asked.

"Yes. It is so white, it looks watery. I used to believe that white men would be the color of the corpse flower. I think I expected white skin to be bloodless. You can imagine my surprise when I met Paul Sparkman."

"Indeed I can," she laughed. "Did you tell him what you had expected?"

"Later . . . much later. After I knew him well."

"How did your people feel about the school?"

"They knew their own civilization was coming to an end when the school began. And they were right. . . ."

Marcus lay on the horror cot in his cell, remembering. Morning light streamed warnings through the window. The hangman had finished preparing his death devices and the dungeon jail was a silent sewer. He turned himself to stir circulation into his legs.

He did not hate her. He knew now that his feeling was something else. He burned with shame to remember the spectacle he had made of himself when, no longer able to maintain his pose of dignity, his mask of quiet stoicism unmasked of its own casual pretenses, he had broken, and boylike blurted out his torrential feelings again and again. It must have been trying for her. She had been gentle, always gentle. And she had been gently firm. His puerile thrusts, proclaiming agonies of love, must have torn her soft, sweet nature.

"It's because I am Indian!" he had said bitterly. "Why don't you admit it, Janet!"

And again he had slashed at her:

"I'm poor!" he had cried. "You are rich and white—and I am poor and Indian."

"No," she had replied. Her face had paled, and truth, like clear cool drowning light, had spoken through her lips: "I am too old for you, Marcus. I am only a symbol. You are not in love with me, you are in love with your teacher."

His mind, tormented and diseased with the morbid pain of rejection, had begun to justify, to plan—to scheme. She would go away with him, if he had enough money to take her. She must be miserable living in Ridgefield

[89]

where her dwarfed and cruel father controlled her every movement. She could not but loathe the ugly brick house near the square where her mother, frightened and aged beyond her years, continually shrank from sight—where her father, always the presiding judge, forever judging, hateful and fraudulent with piety, sternly commanded her weary heart and mind. She would go away—if she were not afraid!

He would get money.

Where?

He knew where . . .

He saddled his pony and rode through the moonless night across the Cherokee grazing lands. Whispers of whipped tall grass were drowned in the thud of his pony's hoofs as they beat the soft earth. He rested at the Salt Fork of the Arkansas, in the lands of the Ponca, and let his pony graze. Then he pushed on throughout the following day, avoiding the villages, skirting the herdsmen, crossing the country of the Oto-Missouria, toward the Cimarron. His mind kept pushing the scheme, the dream—enlarging, filling in, hoping, believing. First, money—then joyous flight with the girl . . . to the East, to Washington, to New York. It was a sleeping dream and a waking dream; an excited, convulsive fusion of a boy's scheme and a man's desire.

He crossed the sprawling red lands of the Sac and Fox and plunged his sweat-lathered pony into the Deep Fork and up the clay bank and through the scrubby post oak flats where as a youngster he had dreamed the dream of one day growing wise enough to pray the prayer to Kuh-koom-they-nah at the Bread Dance of his people. He rode past the stage stop known as Bundy's Gap, where his father had died six years before: when the grisly finger of a white man's hand had wantonly pulled the trigger of a Brisley Model hogleg Colt. "Injuns!" they had cried. "He-devils!"

He did not go immediately to the Shawnee burial grounds on the clay shelf above Owl Creek. He went first to the cabin of his cousins, where his mother, now bent, dispirited and old, was living out her days in bitter reflection.

Wah-che-nah was her name. Little Bright Feather.

The cabin was made of logs and chinked with stones and clay. His mother sat in a corner, with a buffalo robe pulled around her linsey dress. She was cold, and drawn in against the drafts on the tamped earth floor of the cabin. A coarsely woven shawl was around her head and neck, and on her feet were old buckskin shoes and leggings which had been cast off by some child of the Shawnee village.

Her face, deeply creased with age, turned toward him. Her eyes strove to see.

"Ni quetha," she said at last. "My son."

He knelt at her side.

"How are you, Mother? Are you well?"

"I am well."

And then she was silent. She closed her eyes and composed herself.

"Why did you come?" she asked.

"To take you with me to my cabin near Ridgefield. My cabin is warm and there is much food."

"No. I will not go."

"I could care for you there. I earn a salary at the government office."

"No. I will not live among the white people."

"I have plans," he said, "that will take me far away. But I will change them if you will come with me."

"No," she said with finality.

"I am deeply sorry," he said, and he wondered if he had told a lie. So hot was his desire for the girl—for the dream—that he felt no shame, nor even ingratitude.

"Then I must tell you what I am going to do," he said.

Now her eyes watched him narrowly, flashing suspicion. They told him that fear was in her heart.

"What will you do?" she asked.

"I need money desperately," he began.

"Are you in trouble?"

"I am in love."

"With a white girl?"

"Yes."

She closed her eyes. She did not move, but something in her seemed to shrink.

"She is unhappy," he said. "I want to take her to Washington where I will work for the government. I can be a translator and work for my people there."

His mother opened her eyes again. "Is it the teacher from the school?"

"Yes. I am going to take the money from my father's grave."

"Ni quetha. Ni quetha!"

"I must do it! I came to ask your permission."

"You will do it anyway?"

"Yes, Mother. There is no other way. I must do this thing. Money does no good when it is buried in the ground."

"It is evil money," she said. "It will destroy you."

"I must have it."

"And you must have the white girl?"

"Yes, Mother."

"Go away," she said. "You are not my son."

[91]

He fought the tears which filled his eyes. He rose from her side at last, and turned away. He walked outside the cabin and stood beside his pony. He put his face against the saddle and wept.

And then he rode to the Shawnee burial grounds and began digging into the clay shelf above Owl Creek. . . .

On his cot in the cell of the fetid prison, he wept again.

Shame and degradation for having opened his father's grave flooded him, and his body shook. It was only fair, it seemed, that he should die for a crime he had not committed; for the crime he *had* committed was worse, even though it was not against the white man's law.

"Indian!" said a voice from above him. "Hey, Indian!" His cellmate was leaning over the edge of the upper bunk. He was a thick-shouldered man, whiskered and bloated, grinning evilly as he looked down. "What's the matter? What're you bawling about?"

He refused to answer.

"Dry your eyes," the outlaw said. "You ain't going to swing. You've got DeWolfe. He'll spring you."

Marcus rolled far back on his cot, out of sight.

CHAPTER TEN

Angus walked toward the square on the morning of the executions, remembering with disgust the mob at the first public hanging he had witnessed here. What had been learned by the repeated spectacle of death?

From the appearance of things, five or six thousand people would be watching today. The wagon yards were full and the hotels were crowded. Café proprietors had advanced their prices in anticipation of a sellout. One enterpriser had installed a booth on the sidewalk to sell miniature nooses for souvenirs. Crowds were converging from every street.

He lingered near the square until he saw Judge Ring walking from the direction of his home, quick-striding in his black boots, immaculate in his cutaway coat, tall hat, and huge gold chain stretched across his middle. People stepped back to give him easy passing room.

Angus watched the Judge turn into the Federal Building. Then he skirted the crowd and went toward the Judge's home.

He stepped up the two brick steps and rapped the large brass knocker at the Rings' front door. He waited for several moments, then rapped again.

Janet Ring opened the door.

"Oh," she said, startled.

"Good morning," he said.

"Mr. DeWolfe. . . ."

She had straightened her shoulders and lifted her chin, not defiantly, but in a conscious hope to look her best. She was quite pretty, he thought, in a pale blue cotton dress which came up high at the throat. Her gray-tinged hair was wavy and nestled down around her shoulders in a most becoming manner. It was the first time he had seen her without the severe knot at the back of her head, and the intimate glimpse excited him.

"I hope you'll forgive my calling without an appointment, Miss Ring."

"Why . . . it's all right," she said. "I suppose."

She glanced over her shoulder, in a furtive gesture, then back at him.

"I saw your father pass the square half an hour ago," he said. "I'm sure he won't know that I have come here."

"Did you want to speak to me about Marcus? Perhaps I could come to your office."

"I would like to see you now, if possible."

She had a trapped look, and he wondered if he should insist. He could see now that the strain of execution day was on her face.

"Really, Mr. DeWolfe," she said, "this is rather awkward." Again her eyes flicked behind her in a moment of indecision. She seemed to have moved farther into the doorway.

"We may have discovered where Marcus got the money," he said.

"Oh?" Hope now brightened her face. "Mr. DeWolfe, my mother is ill this morning. I hope we can keep our voices low. Please come in."

She stepped back, opening the door.

He went inside quickly. "I'm sorry about your mother. I wouldn't like to disturb her."

"Won't you sit down?" she said.

He had often wondered what the interior of this house would look like. The parlor windows were small and the room was dark and painfully conventional. The furniture had probably come from their New York home years ago, but it was not shabby. The high-backed sofa and armchairs with carved legs seemed strangely unused. The tables were ornate and their scarves scalloped and fringed. A heavy stairway came down along the wall and turned sharply into the room. Its balustrade and newels were deeply carved.

She took the sofa and he sat in one of the armchairs.

"I thought you would be interested," he said, "to know that we have made a little progress."

"Of course I am." She glanced anxiously toward the stairway. "You said you knew where Marcus got the money?"

"We know that his father's grave was opened at about the time of the murders. There's some evidence that Marcus may have opened it."

"And money was buried there?"

"It seems probable."

"I've never heard of Indians burying money," she said. "I'm sure he's terribly ashamed if he opened his father's grave."

Her face became a study in dismay, revealing that at bottom she had believed the boy guilty. This discovery seemed to disgust her with herself.

"Then he may actually be innocent," she said.

"It seems possible."

"Mr. DeWolfe, if you told this to my father, I believe the case could be dropped."

"Your father has a Grand Jury indictment and a previous conviction to back him up."

"Whatever he thinks about you, he is honest. I've heard of indictments being quashed."

"Why don't *you* tell him, Miss Ring?"

Terror made her eyes wild. Some impulse, a little revolting as he thought about it, had caused him to want to test her.

"I couldn't do that," she said.

"Of course not."

"Please, Mr. DeWolfe, don't act as though you were sorry for me. You've no cause to be."

He rose from the armchair and she rose from the sofa in the same instant. Tears were in her eyes and she struggled to keep control.

"I waited for your letter, Janet," he said. "But Luke didn't bring it." He stepped toward her and took her elbows in his hands, feeling her body stiffen. "The other night," he said slowly, "while I was working late in my office, I had a remarkable idea. And then I dismissed it as impossible."

Presentiment brought a challenge into her eyes, warning him not to say anything ridiculous.

"I was thinking," he went on, "that I would like to take you to the Opera House some evening——"

"It *is* impossible," she said.

"I saw myself hiring a rig for the evening—a rockaway with a driver, maybe—and stepping right up to your front door. I was all dressed up in a cutaway and a stovepipe. I rapped at the door and your father admitted me. He was astounded, but there wasn't anything he could do about it, for my calling on you was inevitable and he knew it. You came down the stairway dressed beautifully and we went together to the Opera House and I was as proud as anything."

"To have defied him," she said.

"But there was more to it than that—much more."

She moved to pull away from him, but he held her arms.

"How about it, Janet?" he said. "It would be a good thing. Let's not be afraid of your father. It might even be good for him."

"It certainly would," said a voice from the landing, and they turned, startled, to see Mrs. Ring standing there in a dressing gown, leaning against the newel.

"Mother!" Janet cried, pulling free of his grasp and running toward the stairway. "You're supposed to be in bed."

"Now, now, try to relax, darling," said Mrs. Ring. She smiled at Angus. "How do you do, Mr. DeWolfe? I am Alice Ring, Janet's mother. I've heard a lot about you." She laughed as though she could not possibly have made a more appropriate joke.

Delighted and amazed, he watched her, a thin, round-faced little woman, with long gray hair flying loosely. Her eyes bore a somewhat glazed look, and as she laughed she came close to losing her balance.

He bowed in acknowledgment of the introduction.

"How do you do, Mrs. Ring. This is an unexpected pleasure."

"Mother," Janet repeated, quickly pushing her back up the stairs, "you're supposed to be in bed——"

"Yes," said Mrs. Ring. "I'm supposed to be sick, but I'm not, darling, and you know it." She braced against Janet's thrust, and pulled herself straight by holding onto the balustrade. "I am slightly intoxicated, Mr. DeWolfe," she said cheerfully. "We usually pretend that I am ill. I often drink a little on execution day. You must not ask why, for I might say things which would embarrass Janet." Now she turned to Janet, who was standing helplessly beside her. "Come, darling, let's go into the dining room. Mr. De-Wolfe might like a drink. And I'm sure I could use one."

"Mother—for heaven's sake!"

"I was eavesdropping from the upstairs landing, Mr. DeWolfe, and I thought your idea was wonderful. By all means, Janet must go with you to the Opera House."

"Splendid," said Angus, moving toward the foot of the stairs.

"Mother, please!" Janet cried.

"I would love to see the look on your father's face. I do believe I would enjoy it as much as Mr. DeWolfe." Mrs. Ring's expression turned suddenly very serious. She spoke earnestly to her daughter. "It would serve your father right if a gentleman took you somewhere in the evening. All dressed up in a stovepipe hat."

Now Mrs. Ring broke into quiet sobbing and dropped her face into her arms, leaning on the balustrade.

Awkwardly, he went to the stairway and started up. Janet's mother lifted her eyes suddenly and looked down at him. Her face was tear-streaked and she made no attempt to hide her feelings.

"Don't try to help me, Mr. DeWolfe," she said. "I'm not going to fall down."

"Of course not," he said.

"Now, Janet, I'll go back to my room. You don't need to help me, either."

"All right, Mother," Janet said uncertainly.

Mrs. Ring moved past her on the landing, then stopped again. All the crying-look had vanished.

"Go with him, Janet," she said plaintively. "Look at me, and go with him."

"Please, Mother. . . ."

"I don't want to humiliate you, my darling. I die every day you continue to live like a spinster in this bloody house. If you can't defy your father, then move away permanently—where you can have the freedom to make your own choices."

She paused, looked at her daughter harshly, then swung her gaze toward Angus.

"Mr. DeWolfe, you must not get the idea that I am disloyal to my husband. I think he is a great man. I realize that he has become a fanatic, and I fear that he may make terrible mistakes. But if you think he is evil, you are not worthy of even one evening's company with my daughter." And after a moment she turned and went on up the stairs, sobbing again as she disappeared.

He watched Janet come down from the landing.

"Well," she said with a helpless shrug, "you have now met the skeleton in the family closet."

"She's a delightful and forthright skeleton."

"I didn't intend to suggest that my mother was the skeleton, Mr. DeWolfe. Her drinking is. She doesn't do it often. You really had no right to come here today, of all days."

"I heard many years ago that your mother drank at execution time," he said. "I had forgotten."

She was surprised. "You did?"

"It was the first year your father was Judge here."

"Were you here then?" she asked.

"Just passing through."

"Somehow I hadn't realized that you were ever in the West before you came here to practice, Mr. DeWolfe." She smiled. "I thought you came just to antagonize my father."

"I have a wonderful idea," he said. "If you will call me Angus, and give me that drink your mother offered, I'll sit down and tell you the entire story of my life, complete in every boring detail."

She laughed nervously.

"You are full of ideas," she said. "I'll give you the drink. But you'd better not stay too long. My father will come home and shoot you. He keeps a loaded Double Action Army .45 in the library. It's almost as big as he is."

He followed her into the dining room. Lacy curtains brightened the windows, taking the gloom off the mahogany table and sideboard and the stiff-looking tapestry-bottomed chairs.

She brought a bottle of good whiskey from somewhere and placed it before him at the dining table. Then she put a small pitcher of water and a glass beside the bottle. Their eyes met for quick little exchanges.

"Before you begin your autobiography," she said, "I must caution you that we have only about twenty minutes. Then you'll really have to go."

"I suppose so," he said, without conviction.

"This is a trying time for my father, and I couldn't run the risk of upsetting him."

[97]

"Then perhaps we could upset him next week," he said hopefully.

She shook her head. "No. I'm sorry."

"When will we?"

"Don't you see? It wouldn't be fair to him. While you're preparing for a trial, I mean." And then she hurried to give her argument some logic. "It would be an awful shock to him, if I should ever go out publicly with you. It would seem to be taking unfair advantage just before you face each other in the courtroom."

"I'll be facing the prosecutor, not your father."

"No," she said. "You'll be facing my father. You both know it. I appreciate what you are doing for Marcus. I think I understand how you feel about your work—and your position in Ridgefield. And I admire you, Mr. DeWolfe—but I could not be sure, if I went out with you, that it was *me* you were taking, or merely the daughter of a Judge you would like to annoy."

He twisted the glass in his hand, glancing up to consider her expression.

"That would be most unflattering," he said. "I don't blame you for being skeptical."

"I didn't intend to suggest that you would deliberately do such a thing. But it might be why you're attracted to the idea."

Their eyes met. And the message she sent was clear. She would never be a party to such a scheme.

"I hope," he said slowly, "you're not so afraid of your father that you'll never go out with any man." Her eyes moistened. She looked suddenly tired. "I've offended you, Janet——"

"A little," she said. "You were going to tell me the story of your life, before we got off the subject."

"Yes. I had it all planned. I was going to have you thinking I was quite a fellow."

Soft laughter came from her throat and he was acutely conscious of her nearness.

"What had you planned?"

"It escapes me now. I never can remember the clever things I intend to say."

Self-consciously she poured him another drink. He rose from the chair and took the bottle from her hand.

"Janet . . . we're having a devil of a time getting to know each other. When will you see me?"

She looked at him steadily.

"If we could meet . . . secretly. For a while."

"Secretly?"

"Would you mind terribly, Angus?" Her voice was eager. "I just couldn't

[98]

make an issue of it with Father now. I tried, but I couldn't. I wanted to write that letter. I planned it so I'd see you that day at the livery stable. Luke told me where you'd be."

"Luke?"

"Yes. We're such a bunch of fakers, Angus. Luke told me to write that first letter to you. He even told me what to say."

"I didn't even know you knew him, Janet."

"Good heavens," she said. "I think he supplies Mother's whiskey."

They were convulsed with laughter.

"Where would we meet?" he asked suddenly.

"At Marcus's cabin."

"I wouldn't like to court a girl in another man's garden."

"At least meet me there. We can walk in the woods."

"When?"

"Could you come this afternoon?"

"Can you leave your mother?"

"I'll tell her where I'm going. She'll be delighted. It may even sober her up."

"Does your father know about her drinking?"

"She kept it hidden for years, but I think he's always known. I'm naïve —I only discovered the nature of her illnesses a few years ago."

"I have an appointment at two thirty. I can't leave my office until about three."

"I'll be waiting for you," she said. "Angus?"

"Yes?"

"I wasn't lying about the gun in the library."

"Your father isn't *that* fanatic."

"He hates you."

"I'm almost forty years old, Janet. Someone should take a gun to me if I didn't meet you somewhere."

"You're going to be a forty-year-old fool, I'm afraid."

"That's part of my plan."

"And I had thought all this time that you were just a stuffy lawyer."

"And I had thought you were a cold-fingered little old lady."

"Cold-fingered? Good heavens, Angus."

She laughed and her lips parted.

When he kissed her, she yielded warmly—eagerly. Her body trampled her fears and came toward him, shocking him with its magnificence.

"My God, Janet," he said.

CHAPTER ELEVEN

Angus circled the north side of the square behind the Courthouse and tried to approach South Street from that direction. But it was impossible.

The frenzy of the crowd seemed to him the wildest contrast to his own feeling, which was joy. He pushed through the edges of the crowd, seeking passage to his office where he would sit and delight himself with thoughts of Janet Ring, while bulging-eyed throngs enjoyed the sight of dying criminals. . . . Each to his own.

Unable to get through, he stood at last near the hitch rail in front of Tony's Tonsorial Parlor, half a block off the square, transfixed by the morbid throng.

As he watched, he remembered something he had once read by Charles Dickens after the novelist had observed the public hanging of Frederick Manning and his wife, Maria, at Horsemonger Lane. Seats had been sold in nearby upstairs windows and temporary bleachers had been erected for cash admissions to the spectacle. Dickens had written to the *Times:* "The horrors of the gibbet faded in my mind before the atrocious bearing, looks, and language of the assembled spectators. When the sun rose brightly, it gilded thousands upon thousands of upturned faces so inexpressibly odious in their brutal mirth or callousness that a man had cause to feel ashamed of the shape he wore, and to shrink from himself as fashioned in the image of the devil. . . ." Watching, Angus found himself considering the shape he wore. And looking out over the crowd, his gaze fell upon the gallows.

He had a long, slanting view of the weather-grayed structure. The huge hewn beam, silhouetted against the sky, stretched monstrously over a scaffold fourteen feet high. Beneath it ran a narrow trap floor, hinged on the sides for dropping open in the middle. After the execution, the bodies would dangle a foot off the ground below the trap.

A tall young man standing next to him motioned toward the scaffold.

"Ugly-looking contrivance, isn't it?" His intonation suggested that he was a Westerner who had been educated in the East or abroad.

"Yes, it is," Angus answered, a little surprised.

"The sight of the gibbet is a chastening experience, don't you think?"

"That's its purpose, I suppose."

The man was well dressed and neat in a black broadcloth coat and striped waistcoat. He was, perhaps, ten years younger than Angus, and his restless eyes bore a thoughtful expression behind which lay, perceptibly, the suggestion of a mischievous twinkle.

"I understand Judge Ring observes all this from his chambers," the stranger said, glancing up at the windows across the street. "Do you suppose it actually makes him cry?"

"So I've heard," Angus said. "Do you know Judge Ring?"

"I met him once," the man said cryptically.

Their eyes now searched each other in a frankly open smile, imbued on the part of each with perplexity, for they both sensed that they were in a similar way strangers to this crowd. Then the man turned his attention once more to the courtyard.

Presently Angus heard a commotion behind him and saw Colonel Beleau pushing toward him. The Colonel was flushed and breathing hard.

"Hello, Angus. I saw you come up. I thought I'd be trampled getting over here."

"Hello, Colonel," he said, making room beside him at the hitch rail. "I haven't seen you in a couple of weeks. You wanted me to attend a hanging with you, and here we are."

"I'm glad I found you," the Colonel said. And then he noticed the man Angus had just been talking to. "Floyd, my boy!" he cried. "How pleasant to see you."

"Hello, Colonel," the young man said, shaking hands.

"This is my former partner, Angus DeWolfe. Meet Floyd Green, Angus —a great young friend of mine. Floyd grew up out west of Ridgefield."

The Colonel's enthusiasm for the stranger sharpened Angus's interest in him. He learned that Green was now a journalist for a St. Louis newspaper and had indeed recently spent some time abroad, writing and studying. Angus was quickly impressed with him, but wondered at a certain aspect of his demeanor which suggested a kind of cynical Olympian laughter at the world.

"I tried to call on you earlier today, Mr. DeWolfe," Floyd Green said. "Your office appeared closed. I'm glad I found you."

"Why were you looking for me?"

"To arrange an interview, if possible. You are becoming famous as an adversary to the Judge here. And I understand you are opposed to capital punishment. I am doing some writing on the subject. During my recent visit to England I gathered data on British criminal procedures and hanging methods. Now, there's a barbaric people—the British."

"Very well, Mr. Green," Angus laughed. "How about tomorrow morning, at ten thirty?"

"Splendid. I'll come to your office."

The Colonel, who, Angus realized, had been watching and listening with an attitude of suspicion, now joined the conversation.

"Did you actually witness any executions in England, Floyd?"

"Yes, as a visiting press representative, Colonel. I've done several Sunday supplement pieces on the subject." Floyd Green grinned mischievously. "The build-up to a hanging is perfect drama. People love to read about death. And blood. Almost everybody loves blood."

"Then you've made a study of—this?" said the Colonel, waving his arm toward the tension-swollen crowd.

"Well, I've never seen public executions except here, Colonel. In England I watched private hangings in Newgate and Horsemonger Lane. They do it inside their prisons over there now." Green turned to Angus. "Hanging isn't as macabre as it once was, Mr. DeWolfe. The techniques have improved. This gallows is built to allow for a decent drop. In the old days they simply pulled a cart from under the victims, which caused slow strangulation. The drop is much more humane, if less dramatic, don't you think?"

Angus was watching the Colonel, whose face paled at the suggestion. Then he turned to the journalist, wondering just how much sarcasm had been intended.

"I have read about England's experiments with the drop," he said. "The famous hangman, Jack Berry, uses a different drop for each instance—depending on the weight of the victim, I understand."

"Yes. No one seems to know just where the long drop started over there, but Berry has experimented extensively with it. He has compiled a table of drops—according to weight and general physical structure. A very long drop sometimes decapitates, and a short drop merely chokes. Berry's formula seems to produce the ideal lesion more often than not."

"The ideal lesion?" asked the Colonel. He seemed a little sick.

"There's some disagreement about that, isn't there, Mr. Green?" Angus asked. "Depending on the position of the knot? As I understand it, quick death depends upon severing or at least crushing the spinal cord."

"That's quite right, Mr. DeWolfe. . . . Complete cervical dislocation between the atlas and the axis is considered perfect, Colonel. Few people seem to understand the significance of the knot. For generations hangmen have used what is called the subaural position—that is, with the knot resting under the ear. There is evidence now, however, that it requires much less force to produce a dislocation if the knot is placed in the submental position."

"So I understand," said Angus. He turned to Colonel Beleau to explain further. "That means under the chin, Colonel—so the head will snap straight back. Of course, the knot slips from under the chin sometimes, and works mischief. Jake Lotz strangled a man that way a few years ago, and hasn't used it since."

The Colonel was shaken.

"You certainly know a lot of ghastly detail, Angus," he said, his chin quivering.

"I've looked into the subject," Angus admitted.

"Obviously," said Floyd Green, pleased.

Angus had to suppress a chuckle. He suspected now that the Colonel's friend was laying it on for the Colonel's personal benefit, and Beleau had grown decidedly pale.

"It hasn't been too long since the English put on a much better show than this one," Floyd Green said. "They used to have a fine pageant for murderers. If found guilty by yeomen officers of maliciously striking a fellow by reason whereof blood was shed, their hands would have been stricken off before they were hanged." Angus noticed the Colonel's face slacken a bit. The journalist shrugged and continued: "The Statutes of the Bill for the King's Household directed a sergeant of the woodpile to provide a chopping block, a yeoman of the scullery to heat the searing irons, a master cook to produce a dressing knife, a sergeant of the cellar to provide spirits for enabling the victim to stay conscious, a sergeant surgeon to strike off the hand and sere the stump, and a groom of the falconry to douse the surgeon with vinegar if he should become weak at his post. Robust imagery, isn't it?" Now Floyd Green smiled benignly.

"Robust?" asked the Colonel, who had turned pale green.

Angus swallowed his own rising disgust, and stared at the satirical newspaperman in amazement.

"In our own way," he said, "we've done a robust job right here in Ridgefield, Mr. Green. Today will make eighty-one who've died on this gallows."

"Yes, I know. Look, they're bringing the prisoners now. . . ."

A sudden chorus of jeers arose from the crowd. The procession of prisoners and guards, followed by the minister and a physician, came from the side door of the Courthouse and marched in step toward the scaffold. The crowd hushed as suddenly as it had cried out. The marchers' boots and chains were loud on the wooden stairs.

Quickly, the convicted murderers were lined up underneath the nooses and the hangman prepared black hoods for their heads.

"The English use white hoods," the journalist whispered to Angus. "There must be some significance in it. I'll have to check that up—it might make a feature piece."

The chief deputy marshal held up his hands for silence, then turned to the condemned men, his words reverberating throughout the square.

"Before you are placed into the hands of almighty God, it is the court's intention that you be given the opportunity to speak a final word." He read the first two death sentences but the criminals had nothing to say. They stood in silence and shook their heads, then waited underneath the nooses, holding themselves erectly. You had to admire them, Angus thought—no matter how contemptible they might have been, you had to admire them now.

The chief deputy shrugged, then read the next sentence.

"William Peaty, you have been sentenced to die for the murder of Johnny Murdock. Have you anything to say?"

"Yes, I have," cried William Peaty.

After an instant of titter, the crowd grew even quieter than before.

The condemned criminal, nervous and hawk-eyed, somehow implausible-looking in his new suit, took a small step forward. His leg irons clanked as he leaned toward the crowd.

"I have a preachment for my fellow men," he said, his voice pitched high to carry over the courtyard. "And to all little children who are here. I never killed that man when I was sober, I done it when I was drunk! Don't ever drink, my children! Don't ever touch your mouth to a bottle of whiskey as long as you live. God bless you all. God bless my mother, and God damn whiskey!"

For a moment the silence was oppressive. Angus thought he could hear the condemned man's breathing all the way from the scaffold. Then a roar burst over the crowd as it shouted approval of the repentance. Arms waved and hats were thrown into the air.

The chief deputy turned perfunctorily to the fourth man.

"Eliot Smith"—he shouted, to be heard above the lingering noise—"you have been sentenced to die for the dual murders of Walker and Milo Williams. Have you anything to say?"

"I say get this over with as fast as you can," the man replied hotly, eyes glaring.

And the crowd gasped in admiring disbelief.

The chief deputy only shrugged, turning to the last man.

"Oak Tree Sampson, you have been sentenced to die for the murder of Marvin Smith. Have you anything to say?"

"I have," said Oak Tree Sampson.

He was a plump, round-faced man, with long hair down around his shoulders. He looked as strong, for all his plumpness, as the Biblical Sampson himself. His eyes bulged contemptuously as he stepped forward, unmindful of his irons. He raised his hand and his finger seemed to point directly at Angus.

"All of you good Christian folks," he shouted, "are just as guilty as I am, and you know it. Every God damned one of you." He paused dramatically in the silence his booming voice had created. Then he turned to face the hangman. "Please get this over with, Mr. Lotz," he added with a weary shrug. "I can't stand the sight of you, either."

Then he stepped back into position amid a thousand gasps of horrified disbelief.

Angus swallowed. He glanced at the man standing beside him at the rail, and saw him swallowing also. He wondered how the Colonel was reacting, but decided not to put him on the defensive yet. He stared straight ahead.

The hangman was placing the nooses around the necks, pulling the knots up tight behind the ears.

"The subaural position," Floyd Green whispered. "I hope he doesn't botch it."

Now the hangman walked down the line of men and pinioned their hands securely. Then he stepped back, smartly executed an about-face, and descended the stairs. He took his position at the spring below the trap and turned to look up at the chief deputy.

At the chief's signal, Jacob Lotz tripped the spring. The trap hinges flung open.

The five men plummeted, but only four of them jerked in suspension and dangled as the crowd gasped. William Peaty had somehow loosened his hands and lunged for the edge of the trap as he fell. He clung to the side, clawing desperately up, maddened in his struggling hold on life.

Jacob Lotz rushed up the stairway and kicked the man's hands loose to make him fall with the others. The crowd cried out as William Peaty convulsed on the end of the rope, choking.

Now Jacob Lotz did what he had done once before. He leaped through the trap and grabbed William Peaty around the waist with his arms. The neck stretched and broke as the flesh tore and blood spurted three feet against the back wall below the trap.

"Mother of God!" cried the journalist.

Women screamed. Even the sky seemed darkened.

Angus did not look at Floyd Green. He turned instead to face Colonel Beleau.

"Jesus Christ, Colonel," he said, "can you possibly condone a thing like——?"

He stopped speaking only because the Colonel was not there.

"He's gone, I'm afraid," said Green.

"Gone?"

"He walked away while the death sentences were being read. I believe he was ill, Mr. DeWolfe. I'm glad the Colonel didn't see this. He's a very gentle-hearted person."

"I'm sorry he didn't," Angus said, staring at the shaken look on the satirical young man's face.

They stood before each other, speechless.

The crowd, too, was transfixed. Angus could not look toward the scaffold. The bloody sight would have been too much for him. Floyd Green was not looking at the scaffold, either. He was looking up, instead, at the windows of the Federal Building.

"The Judge is a curious man," he said. "I've been told that his wife drinks during the executions."

"So I've heard."

The journalist smiled—bitterly, Angus thought.

"Until tomorrow?" he said, extending his hand.

"Goodbye," Angus said.

Floyd Green walked away, elbowing himself out of the crowd. Angus stood alone among the spectators, contemplating again the curious shape he wore.

CHAPTER TWELVE

The wonder of love took Angus for its own exclusive possession. Its mystery teased him with discovery after incredibly sweet discovery. Its delicious reality caressed him and made of each day a separate age of time.

He saw her often. Not seeing her became an itch, and he could scarcely contain himself until their next meeting. The dam that broke that morning in the dining room had admitted the warm rush of her abundant affection which spread quickly over his lonely existence.

He would hire a horse at Slattery's and ride out to the cabin, and they would walk among the cottonwoods far above the mouth of Big Creek, and he would tell her the story of his life and she would tell him the story of hers.

"You look strange, riding a horse, Angus. I had never seen you on a horse until we began coming out here."

"Miss, when I was younger, I used to stand up in the saddle and shoot the buffalo."

"What a liar you are!"

"I'll bet I could do it now, old as I am."

"You poor self-conscious quatrogenarian," she laughed. "Forty isn't old."

"How you talk. I won't be forty until the end of January."

"I took riding at Miss Gibson's Academy. Seems silly to think that any-one ever took riding lessons, doesn't it? I wish I'd been born out here, and had grown up a real Western girl."

"Like Belle Starr? Now, there's a Western girl."

"I could be a cracking good bandit, if I tried. There aren't many success-ful lady bandits."

"I'd defend you at all your trials. You know me—defender of the bad ones. I love you, Janet Ring."

"I love you, Angus DeWolfe."

"Hush, dear child. . . ."

And his kisses would tell her what he had been wanting to tell someone all his life and what she had been waiting all hers to hear.

Once he brought along a sidesaddle from Slattery's. He unhitched her horse from the buggy and put it on him.

"I've never ridden sidesaddle," she said, laughing the bubbling laugh that had changed his world.

"Didn't they teach that at Miss Gibson's?"

"I hope Tex doesn't mind this contraption. Heaven only knows when he was last ridden."

"Is that his name? Tex?"

"My father bought him when we first came here. He's getting old now."

"So are we, my love. Let's hurry. Here, give me your hand."

They rode into the hills to the north of Ridgefield. The autumn air was heady, and their new dimension of existence was intoxicating. In the drunkenness of love they rode together; sometimes they giggled, sometimes they laughed, sometimes they merely smiled their secret smiles.

"A tremendous change has come over you," he said.

"My father has noticed it, too. He keeps looking at me."

"Has he said anything?"

"No, thank heaven. . . . It's strange, Angus, remembering how lonely I was for so long. This place seemed like the very end of the earth to me. I thought I'd never have a life, except as a teacher of Indian children."

"I know the feeling. I've wondered why I was out here, myself. Now I know. I was looking for you. If you'd stayed in the East, I could have found you there without going through all this."

"You've probably had a hundred love affairs."

"Closer to a thousand, I imagine."

"Seriously, have you ever been in love before?"

"I've been in love with every respectable lady I've ever known. You're the first one who has ever felt like returning it."

"You're lying to me."

"No honest man could bear to tell the truth about his love life, Janet. . . ."

Sometimes they walked along the river and lay on mossy banks and ate the lunches she had packed and enjoyed special goodies that her mother had sent along.

"It seems incredible that they'd take you in the Army at the age of fourteen," she said once.

"I was big and dumb. The Army didn't care."

"What did your brother and father fight about?"

"My father didn't happen to like the kind of women Nat appreciated. They finally came to blows, and Nat left home. He was only nineteen."

"And already a ladies' man?"

"I used to admire him. I wanted to be a ladies' man, but I never knew what to say."

"Did your father forgive you for running away?"

"He died the summer I went home. I really didn't get to know him very well. He was glad I had decided to continue my education."

"It must have been difficult for you to go to school again after all that time. I wish I had known you then."

"I thought women were the root of all evil."

"What made you change your attitude?"

"Time," he said. "Time spent lonely and waiting for someone who turned out to be you. Janet, for God's sake, let's elope."

"Another boy wanted to elope with me once. The only boy I ever went out with. He was sure I'd have to elope if I ever got married."

"What happened to him?"

"He disappeared just when I'd made up my mind to do it."

"I won't disappear. Let's steal your father's rig and run away, out into the Cheyenne country, and get married by a medicine man and become a couple of Indians. Your father would never find us."

"He's got deputy marshals all over the world. Even in China, I think."

"I can lick him with one hand."

"Angus, don't talk that way. . . ."

"What will we do? I can't stand this secret business any longer."

"Please don't talk about it now. Please just kiss me——"

"Janet, listen. We've got to talk about it. We can't postpone our lives. We're committing no crime——"

She began to cry and held herself tight against him. She always broke into tears when he pressed this subject. And deep within him resentment began to grow.

"Stop crying," he said. He held her away, forcing her to look at him. "We'll never settle it unless we talk about it. You have a right to your life, and I have a right to——"

"I know, I know . . . but darling, darling, darling . . ."

She broke away suddenly and ran through the woods along the creek. He ran after her.

"Janet, stop," he yelled. "Don't run away!"

But she was still running. She disappeared around a clump of thick blackjacks and reappeared again on a small knoll above the creek.

"Janet!" he cried.

He ran faster, determined to catch her. He was angry, and hurt. He was going to speak harshly to her now. It was time to meet this problem head-on.

Then she tripped over a root and fell. He saw her tumble painfully through the leaves at the foot of a giant walnut tree. When he reached her she was holding her foot, and her face was tear-streaked and pale.

"Let's see it," he said, quickly removing her shoe.

"It isn't my ankle. It's my instep—I don't think it's serious."

They sat in the leaves while he massaged her foot until she was sure it was all right. She tried her weight on it and felt no pain.

"I'm well again," she said, not looking at him.

"Janet, talk to me."

"Darling," she said, "I'm no good. I have no courage."

"You've simply got to face your father with this. There's nothing he can do but accept it."

"He never would."

"Do you realize that he spies on you, Janet? He probably knows about us already. But he wants to keep you terrorized and feeling guilty about it. If it's out in the open, he couldn't."

"Angus, I hate him."

"Then stand up to him. When he quotes the Bible to you, talk back. It would probably startle him speechless if you refused to take his abuse. He isn't *God*, Janet!"

"I just couldn't hurt him. The court has been an awful responsibility to him. And Mother's drinking, and—he's crushed, Angus—that's why he's so difficult. He's had nothing but pain in his life."

He knew that pressing her now would only harden the impasse. A terrible realization reached him that things would not change. Hopelessness engulfed his mind for an instant, and then his mind rebelled. He did as she did—he stopped thinking about it.

Sighing, he took her hand and walked toward the cabin.

"How is your foot?" he asked.

"It's all right, darling," she said.

October temperatures began to touch the woods. The oaks, the elms, the walnuts suggested red and gold and brown. Coveys of quail and grouse hid low. Squirrels gathered nuts with urgent purpose. Indians danced their harvest dances and prepared for winter.

He built a fire in the cabin fireplace and they stood before it, drinking hot coffee which she made on the coals. Her cheeks and lips were rosy. Firelight danced in her eyes, and her eyes glowed when she looked at him and sipped her coffee.

"Angus, I've been thinking about Marcus. I don't believe I've been very honest with myself about him."

"In what way?"

"The whole thing may have been my fault. I was more interested in him than I've been willing to admit."

"I've thought all along that you must have been," he said, grinning at her.

"I'm sure the idea of going to the garden secretly attracted me more than

Marcus himself did. Isn't that awful? I know that it seemed romantic, to be doing something my father didn't know about."

"But he did know about it."

"I have a feeling that's one reason he's set on prosecuting Marcus again. Could that be possible?"

"I've wondered the same thing. Incidentally, the Supreme Court granted our writ. Did your father mention it at home?"

"He told my mother last night."

"The ruling ordered a new trial. Your father placed it on the November docket."

"He was bitter, Angus. He stormed and raved to my mother about it. He's preparing another attack on the Supreme Court. He worked on it all night in the library. He's going to call in Hoey Johnson again."

"The ruling was very critical of him. I'm sure he was stung."

"What's wrong?" she asked. "Why is he having so much trouble?"

"He believes he is the law."

"I've heard him say many times at home that he is only a servant of the law. He says he has never hung a man—the law hangs them."

"He says that. And then he tells the juries to convict."

"He believes that juries are composed of uneducated men."

"But not stupid, we hope. Our system depends upon the ability of juries to arrive at facts by themselves. It's not your father's function to suggest them. The Supreme Court will never permit it. He's his own worst enemy, Janet. He creates reversible errors."

"Then criminals *are* getting off on technicalities, aren't they?"

"If there were no technicalities, Marcus would now be dead."

"Do you believe my father has executed innocent men?"

"I have no idea. Certainly most of them have been plainly guilty."

"But if you'd had your way, they would have gone free?"

"I've never tried to free a man I thought guilty of a terrible crime."

"You freed Gunnysack, didn't you?"

"No, the Tribal Court freed him. I turned him over to them. I've only tried to keep men from hanging."

"Then you're setting yourself against the law, aren't you? Capital punishment is part of the law, whether you agree with it or not."

"The law gives to every man the right of every legal device for protection. I'm not *illegally* saving them from the gallows. I'm not changing any laws, and I'm not breaking any laws."

"You despise my father, don't you?"

"I might have said yes, if I had never known you. He was given too much power. Nothing seems to anger him as much as the right of appeal."

"And that's why he hates you. Because you are successful with appeals."

"If he continues criticizing the Supreme Court for overruling him, he'll be removed."

"And you think he should be?"

"Very sincerely I think that he should."

"It would kill him."

"He's doing it to himself."

They finished their coffee and sat before the fire on a buffalo robe in the falling dusk. Shadows deepened in the small room.

"This is our last afternoon together for a while. I'm going back to the reservation tomorrow."

"Without settling anything with me?"

"Darling," she said quickly, "we probably need a little time apart to find out how we feel about all this."

"I know how I feel about all this," he said. "After the Maywood trial, I'm coming for you. If you don't want to live here, we'll go somewhere else. I don't want to waste any more of my life without you."

"Oh, darling, we'll see. I'll be back for the trial."

"You're always vague about it," he said, searching her eyes. "Listen to me, Janet. I'm not going to continue seeing you secretly."

"Are you sorry, Angus?"

"I'm beginning to feel sneaky."

He kissed her fiercely, and then she lay in his arms on the buffalo robe before the fire and sobbed.

Finally he said, "Don't cry."

"Angus—run for your life, if you know what's good for you. I can't help it. I can't do anything about it."

"You can! You can do a lot about it, Janet!"

He pulled her against him again and felt the wonder of her body and knew that he must not lose her. He knew, too, that her character had been maimed. She would wear the scars of her father's abuse all her life. The extent of his sadness was not comprehensible.

"Angus," she said softly, "just love me. Don't talk."

CHAPTER THIRTEEN

Janet drove away from the cabin in her buggy. He allowed her sufficient start to reach Ridgefield ahead of him. The moon, which would later brighten the autumn night into near day, had not yet risen.

He reined the horse off the road as he approached town, circling several blocks to arrive at the livery stable from a different direction. The feeling of sneakiness that he had mentioned to her crawled through him as though his conscience were its natural habitat. He would have reached Mrs. Borden's in five minutes by walking fast if he had not been stopped by Luke Sweeley, who was sitting in his dilapidated surrey near the stable under a spread of elm trees.

"Evening, Angus," said the old man.

In the darkness he could see neither Luke, the surrey, nor the mule. But he recognized Luke's voice.

"What's on your mind at this time of night?" he asked.

He went through the shadows and leaned against the surrey. Luke kept his voice conspiratorially low, speaking from the darkness.

"They's some people waiting to see you over at Bordens. Thought you might like to know, so you wouldn't be took by surprise. Not that it's any of my business."

"Who are they, Luke?"

"Hoey Johnson and a newspaper friend of his from St. Louis. A fellow named Green that used to live around here. They're going to ask you for a statement about what the Judge said today. It's got some folks excited."

"I'm much obliged to you, Luke."

"Something else, Angus. Doc McKay was looking for you. He went up to your office this afternoon, but you was gone."

"Do you know what he wanted?"

"Didn't say. But he was looking all over. And Angus," Luke went on quickly, "I heard it gossiped that you've been meeting secretly with Miss Janet. Now, I ain't making it up just to get something out of you. I thought you'd like to know that I've heard it around town. Giddy-up, Eubanks!"

He slapped the mule sharply and wobbled off into the darkness with Angus staring after him.

So, the romance was not such a secret. He hoped that everyone in Ridgefield would soon know about it. If it became public knowledge, then the pretense would have to end. The idea appealed to him and he felt a little better. How much of Janet's fear was realistic, he couldn't be sure—but he was ready to find out. Relishing the thought, he asked himself just where his love for her ended and his desire to take her away from the Judge began.

And for that matter where exactly might he separate her love for him from her basic need to escape her father?

She believed that Maywood had been trying to free her from a kind of bondage. Now who was trying to free her? He smiled in the darkness. Perhaps Janet would be freed despite herself.

At Mrs. Borden's, he found the newsmen waiting for him on the front porch.

"Hello, Angus," said Hoey Johnson. His smile, barely visible from the lamplight inside the parlor window, at first seemed friendly enough. Angus told himself that there was no reason to view this man so personally. Hoey Johnson was a lackey to his uncle, who owned the *Monograph*, and should at worst be taken for that and dismissed. But the sight of the man revolted him.

"Good evening, Hoey," he said.

"Angus, you've met Floyd Green, of the St. Louis *Daily Light*, haven't you?"

"Yes, we've met," said Floyd Green. The St. Louis reporter was still the pleasant-looking young man Angus remembered from the recent interview. He was taller than Johnson, and larger boned. He did not appear to be anyone's lackey.

Hoey Johnson said, "I suppose you've heard about Judge Ring's statement, Angus."

"No, I haven't heard about it, Hoey."

"It's strong stuff. And it mentions you. Let me read it."

Before he could protest, Hoey had backed up near the window to read from a paper in his hand:

"Once again the Supreme Court has opposed justice. And once again a murderer is permitted to remain among civilized people under the guise of awaiting a new and presumably fairer trial. In an interview in Washington, the Attorney General stated that my explanation of the case to the Maywood jury was an excessive disquisition on the laws of homicide, drawn from medieval and otherwise out-dated sources. He got the idea, of course, from our local criminal protector Angus DeWolfe. The Attorney General and Mr. DeWolfe are legal imbeciles. My sources were recent issues of Criminal Law Magazine and Stockton's *Criminal Evidence and Homicide*.

It would seem that they and the Supreme Court are ignorant of this great basic work. If not, they must be in some kind of conspiracy. I cannot permit such lies to be disseminated among this community of my friends and neighbors without challenging them."

After reading the statement, Hoey Johnson frowned thoughtfully, stuffing the paper into his pocket.

He rocked back on his heels, watching Angus narrowly. His pose was overbearing and presumptuous: the ever-alert reporter, totally sensitive to whatever innuendo existed, poised to absorb it all so that his readers would know absolutely everything when they had finished reading his pieces. There were times when Angus wondered if the world wouldn't be better off without newspapers. Johnson was half smiling, certain that he was taking in everything.

"That's it, Angus. It'll be in tomorrow morning's edition. I'd like to run a statement from you along with it."

"No," he said slowly. "I couldn't, Hoey."

"It'll look bad for you," Hoey said, his frown lifting into what Angus imagined Hoey himself would have described as perceptive skepticism. "I'll have to say in the story that you were offered a chance to defend yourself. Floyd Green here is going to write this up for his paper, and it will be picked up all over the East."

Hoey Johnson turned to Floyd Green for support of his argument. But Green ignored him; his eyes were on Angus.

"Let me say, Mr. DeWolfe, that Hoey is speaking only for himself. I am simply going to report the Judge's statement, and statements from representative citizens of Ridgefield who will be willing to make them for publication. I'd like to include one from you."

"Thanks, Mr. Green," Angus said gratefully. "But it would seem inappropriate for me to comment, in view of the impending retrial of the defendant in question."

"Would you tell us whether you expect an acquittal this time?" Green asked.

"I'm sorry. You'll have to excuse me from any comment at all."

"Angus," Hoey Johnson insisted, stepping in front of Green, "I'll have to include that in my story, too. That you wouldn't say you expected to prove your man innocent."

"I'm sure you'll have to include it, Hoey," Angus said. "You're a very honest man. I wouldn't ask you to leave out anything. Mr. Green, after the conclusion of the Maywood case, I'll be glad to answer any questions, either personally or by mail, that you'd care to put to me. That's all I can say now."

"Fair enough," said Floyd Green with a smile.

Angus stepped around the newspapermen and went inside the boarding-house.

The usual crowd was at Mrs. Borden's table and they stopped eating when they saw him. They appeared, for a moment, as though a photographer had snapped them the instant they looked up, poised with their forks raised in attitudes of motion, frozen motionless. He had been the topic of their conversation and his presence had silenced them. He was no longer one of them. Those who were normally friendly to him, Abe Heller and Silas Hennessey and Johnny Borden, smiled at him uncomfortably. Harry Borden scowled. Billy Moss looked down at his plate; he must have been doing the talking. Sarah Borden peered over her skinny shoulder from the corner of the table where she was serving a platter of fat biscuits.

He turned quickly and went into his room, embarrassed.

He took off his coat and hat and hung them on the tree in the corner, then sat down on the edge of his bed. He felt exhausted. He was sorry he had come home, for he would be unable to face the dining room.

He would move now. After the Maywood trial, his future would be decided by Janet. Lovely, wonderful Janet—whose secret could not be kept forever. He thought for a moment of meeting her at the train tomorrow and refusing to let her leave. He could see himself slapping the daylights out of her father, when a soft rap at the door interrupted the pleasant reverie.

He rose quickly and went to the door.

It was Mrs. Borden. Her face was stiff with self-control. He knew that her confusion was agonizing.

"Will you be eating supper, Mr. DeWolfe?"

"No, I won't," he said. "Please excuse me tonight."

"I just wondered. It's getting cold."

"I'll be leaving tomorrow, Mrs. Borden."

"Moving?" she asked.

"Yes. To the hotel."

"You will be happier," she said.

"I'm sure of it. You folks will be happier, too."

"I hope we haven't been unkind to you. I respect you, Mr. DeWolfe. But it will make things simpler for us if you leave."

"I should have left long ago," he said.

She closed the door softly.

He turned to his washstand and poured the basin full of water, then washed his face and hands. He put on his coat and hat again and went out, leaving the house without looking toward the dining room. He was glad he had not waited any longer, for the rook game would be starting any minute in the parlor.

At Phil Beckett's drugstore on the south side of the square, he found Doc McKay behind the prescription counter, busily compounding liquids from sundry bottles on the shelves.

"Hello, Doc," he said.

"I was looking for you, Angus."

"Luke told me."

"Can you stick around for a few minutes? I'll be through here."

"Sure, Doc."

He leaned on the counter, watching McKay finish his task. The doctor was a stubby, balding man with a gray-brown mustache and sparse gray eyebrows. His skin was a healthy baby pink. His hands moved delicately as he measured drops from one bottle into another.

Angus had had no occasion to visit him professionally, but his casual contacts with Doc during the past year and a half had been pleasant. He felt vaguely that McKay was competent at his profession, for the simple reason that he did not seem to be a fool.

"Thanks for waiting, Angus," he said.

"What's on your mind, Doc?"

"Could we go somewhere? To your office, maybe?"

"Sure."

They left the drugstore together and walked down the street to the harness store. Angus led the way up the staircase from the street entrance to his office. He lighted the lamp, then pulled up a chair for Doc and gave him a cigar.

"Angus, I'm on the spot," Doc said. "I've been debating with myself all summer whether I should have a talk with you about it. Life would be a hell of a lot simpler if we didn't have ethical considerations, wouldn't it?"

"Simpler, and maybe duller," Angus said.

"I'm sure you're unaware of it, but Judge Ring is a sick man."

Angus felt his pulses quicken.

"I was not aware of it, Doc. I won't pretend that he's a great friend of mine, but I think I can honestly say that I'm sorry to hear he isn't well."

"You don't have to pretend, Angus. I think I know how you feel. If I were a lawyer, I'd probably hate him."

Angus looked up in surprise.

"There aren't many people who feel that way, Doc. You could get run out of town for saying that."

"Yes," McKay laughed, "I suppose so. But I'm not going to pretend, either. He's badly mixed up, and if I were a lawyer, I'd fight him the way you're fighting him. At least I like to tell myself I would. You're doing an important job, and it must feel awfully lonely to be doing it against the advice of everyone you know. I've been trying to work up enough courage to tell you that ever since the Gunnysack case. Not that it's any help to you, because I'm not going to shoot off my mouth around town."

"I certainly appreciate your saying it, anyway, Doc. There's no reason why you should get involved."

McKay's eyebrows lifted thoughtfully.

"Sometimes I wonder about that. Doctors have it pretty easy on these explosive matters. We keep on dishing out pills and thumping chests, and as long as we keep our mouths shut, everybody is on our side. Well, I want to say that I admire your stand against this wholesale execution mill the Judge has built. I've been rooting for you ever since your first murder trial. I was a witness for Ben Procter in that one, if you remember."

"That was the Wiggins case. You gave medical testimony."

"Yes. I knew when you cross-examined me that you were going to be something new in Judge Ring's life. Well—enough of that, Angus. Let's get to the point."

"All right, Doc," Angus said, smiling.

"I have a client, in a manner of speaking, whose life I am trying to save."

"Is the Judge that sick?"

"He collapsed in his office this afternoon. Twenty minutes after his harangue against the Supreme Court. When I got there he was conscious, but he wasn't making much sense. Kept quoting the Bible, saying he'd never hung an innocent man in his life. He went right out of his mind for a while."

"Has he ever done this before?"

"Twice this summer. Once when you licked him on that Foxjaw case, and again after you got involved with the Maywood thing. I never did know just what led up to it, but he started pacing the floor one day, cussing you for all he could think of, and he passed out."

"Does his family know, Doc?"

"I promised I wouldn't tell them. Maybe I shouldn't have promised."

Angus relighted his cigar and looked at it as he blew smoke.

"Let's see, Doc," he said thoughtfully, "you're telling me that I'm about to drive him mad and——"

"No, Angus. I'm telling you that he *is* a little mad. He has been for years, and is gradually getting worse. It's obvious that his heart is bad. When he gets so agitated that he could bust, then he's ripe for a heart seizure, or apoplexy. If you keep after him, in my opinion you'll kill him."

Angus frowned.

"You could have put it another way, Doc. You could have said that if he keeps after the Supreme Court of the United States he'll kill himself."

"I could have. But I'm fighting for his life. And the Supreme Court isn't pressuring him day after day. You're the one who's pressuring him."

"And you believe I should let him hang my clients, just to keep him healthy? Doc, you can't be suggesting that."

"It's not as though he were hanging innocent men, Angus. The Judge has done a great work out here. Before he came to Ridgefield, this court was a disgrace. You couldn't get an honest man to testify, because he'd be killed if he did. Willard Ring cleaned it up. He's gone off the deep end now, there's no doubt about it. But he'll retire soon. His health will force it on him. I'd hate to see you kill him just because he's wrong and you're right."

"You're sure he's that far gone?" Angus asked.

"Sure enough to come to you with it. These things are problematical, of course. But I think he'll have a stroke in one of these mad fits, if he doesn't become completely deranged and try to kill you. He's capable of it. I'm serious."

"Doc," Angus said slowly, "let me suggest a hypothetical situation. Suppose this Indian, Maywood, were innocent. What would be your advice?"

"Christ—you don't think he's innocent. Do you?"

"It's a hypothetical question."

"We can't always let hypothetical considerations guide us in practical matters. You're trying to cheat the gallows for this Indian, like you did for Wiggins and Gunnysack. Maybe life in prison is more humane, I don't know. But he's guilty, Angus. I watched that trial. I was talking to Phil Beckett about it again this afternoon. The Indian faked the alibi—surely you can't believe the Quaker was lying about it. And the money. They found it on him. The Sac and Fox Agent down there knew those people were carrying it."

"Doc—listen to me," Angus said. "I know where the boy got that money. It wasn't Jake Flower's money at all, and I'm going to prove it in court."

McKay's pink face went suddenly pale.

"Are you sure?"

"I am certain. It won't prove that he didn't kill those people—but we don't have to prove his innocence. They have to prove his guilt, and I'm going to tear their case all to hell, Doc. If you tell this to anyone before I'm ready, so help me God, I'll shoot you. I could get deranged myself, you know. There's a hell of a lot of pushing going on in this town, and I'm not doing any of it."

McKay got out of his chair. His face could not have been whiter if he'd had no blood.

"Angus," he said, "I have made your job tougher. You would never have told me how to treat a patient. Please forgive me if you can."

Doc picked up his bag and hurried toward the door. Angus sat alone and listened as he went down the stairs.

CHAPTER FOURTEEN

At Gray's barn, Janet picked up the stableboy, who delivered her to the sidewalk in front of her home, then took the buggy away. She knew, when her mother cautioned her at the door with a gesture of silence, that her father had come home ahead of her this evening.

"Where is he?" she whispered.

"Upstairs, lying down. He came home early."

"Is he ill?"

"It's nothing serious, I think. He said Doctor McKay checked him over after he felt a little exhausted in his office this afternoon. I took him some soup and a glass of milk. Did you have a good time?"

"Yes, wonderful, Mother. Angus loved the jelly biscuits you sent."

Alice Ring's eyes brightened and Janet followed her into the kitchen. "Where did you go today? What did you do?"

"We went for a long ride down the river. Then we came back to the cabin and had coffee. Angus built a fire in the fireplace."

"Are you in love with him?" her mother asked.

Am I? she asked herself. Color rose in her face, and she felt its surge of warmth.

"Yes, Mother," she said softly.

"Has he asked you to marry him?" Then her mother added quickly, "Now, don't be rude. I merely asked a civil question."

"And I'm not going to answer it."

"If it weren't for me, you wouldn't even be going out with him. Darling," she said, "marry him if you love him. Don't be afraid of what will happen."

"Do you realize what you're saying, Mother?"

"Your father will forgive you. Somehow I'll see to it. Angus seems like a wonderful boy."

"He'll be forty years old next January," Janet laughed. "He isn't exactly a boy."

"That's just the right age to have a little sense. You're almost thirty yourself." And she added accusingly: "You're getting on, you know."

"Do you remember what you once said about Marcus, Mother? You said twenty wasn't terribly young. You even pointed out that he was one of the original Americans." Then she gave her mother a little hug. "I love you, Mother, and I'm ever so grateful to you."

Alice Ring pulled away. "Thank you," she said, beginning to cry. "I'm sorry, darling. I'm worse than a child."

"It's all right, Mother."

"Sit down with me, Janet. I want to tell you something."

They sat beside each other at the kitchen table. Alice Ring dabbed at her eyes with a handkerchief. She had never looked particularly old to Janet before. And Janet could easily have wept.

"Did you know that before we came out here your father was ambitious to become President of the United States?"

"Father?"

"He was close to President Lincoln and a personal friend of General Grant. It isn't as farfetched as you might think."

Amazed, Janet listened to her mother describe the early career of her father who had left the farm in New Hampshire against his own family's wishes in order to continue his education at a Literary Institute in Rhode Island.

He had not been inclined toward undue fanaticism as a young man, but had studied the Bible quietly as he absorbed the classics at the Institute and read law, while supporting himself by hiring out variously in a salt-works, a blacksmith shop, and occasionally on fishing boats. His only romance had been with Janet's mother—who was Miss Alice Pettiwood of Brooklyn, New York, whom he met after he moved to New York City to apprentice law at the age of twenty-four. She had been the only single daughter of a prosperous importer, who was one of his first important clients. He learned later, as Alice herself learned, that his father-in-law had retained him and invited him to Brooklyn because he was considered a good marriage possibility for Alice, who was believed to be backward. That accounted also for the sizable dowry, Alice Ring said.

Bitter at having been in a sense bought for his wife, Willard Ring refused to associate with the Pettiwood family any longer, and threw himself, with the help of the dowry, into a political career. He was elected to Congress and achieved a successful record. But by the time Janet was ten years old, their social life in Washington had become tedious. The Congressman could have been both popular and highly respected in the inner circles of important political figures; but Alice Ring did not relish the social aspect of their profession and was quite incapable of coping with it. She found herself taking a couple of bolstering drinks of whiskey from time to time, and, fearful that it would become a more serious problem, if not a scandal, her husband withdrew from politics and accepted an appointment to the bench. He could have been a Senator from New York, with limitless possibilities, if things had gone differently.

"He had a very bright future, Janet. But I ruined it for him. He told me once that he would have rather had a more adroit wife than the dowry. It was as though I'd died and gone to hell. Your father took the appointment here because he was ashamed of me. He wanted me out of sight. And I've been living here in hell ever since."

"Good heavens," Janet said, horrified that her mother would say such things.

"I love him, Janet. His life has been difficult and I haven't known how to help him very much. He doesn't really care for me any more—he's only interested in you."

"Sometimes I think he hates me, Mother."

"No. He lets you teach on the reservation only because he's afraid he'd lose you completely if you didn't have that." She stared at Janet and said, "This horrible court has brutalized him. He feels terribly guilty for having kept you single. Defy him, Janet. Go away. When you're at school, he's much better. He relaxes more and sleeps better. When you're at home, you remind him of his selfishness, and he becomes cruel, bent on bending the world to prove that he's not wrong."

"Oh, Mother. . . ."

"You have a splendid young man, and marvelous opportunities ahead of you. And I want what's left of your father for myself. He's become too fanatic to live, unless something happens." She lowered her voice, but it was charged with urgency. "I'll find a way to comfort him, Janet. Please go with Angus."

"My God, Mother. I don't know what to say."

"Would you like some coffee? You know, I haven't even cooked supper."

"I guess I'm not really very hungry."

"Try to eat. How about a jelly biscuit? I didn't send them all to your young man. Janet, I love him. I absolutely adore him. You must be out of your head, not to have grabbed him already."

Alice left the table and was reaching into the cabinet for the coffee jar. Janet turned and saw her father standing in the kitchen doorway, clad in a long night robe, holding in his hand a tray with the empty soup plate and glass. She realized now that her mother had seen him, too, and had backed up against the cabinet.

His massive eyebrows were arched high, and his eyes were large. He stared at her and said in a low, Biblical intonation: "'A foolish woman is a clamorous thing—she is simple, and knoweth nothing. To him who is simple, she whispers: stolen waters are sweet; bread eaten in secret is pleasant.'"

He came into the kitchen and put the tray on the table.

"Have you a young man who loves jelly biscuits, Janet?" he asked.

She could not answer, and he turned to her mother.

"Alice," he said, "who is this gentleman you absolutely adore?"

Janet said quickly, "We're not going to tell you, Father. I've had a couple of perfectly casual encounters with a certain person recently, and it's only natural that Mother would think it might be something serious. But it isn't, and the less said the better."

"That's very sensible of you, Janet. It must have been awkward, having your mother send jelly biscuits to a perfectly casual encounter." He turned to Alice Ring. "I'm feeling much better now. Could I have one of the biscuits in question, and another glass of milk?"

"Good," said Janet. "I'd like one, too. Shall I make the coffee, Mother?"

"Never mind," said her mother. "I'll make it."

Janet decided to stand her ground at the table.

"Please sit down, Father," she said. "I'm glad you're feeling better. I hope you're not working too hard—you seldom get a good rest."

He sat opposite her, his face quivering. "I'm perfectly willing to turn the subject away from your casual acquaintance," he said, "so you needn't be so concerned over my health. It sounds fatuous, and doesn't become you, my dear." He sighed tiredly. "After the Maywood trial next month, I think I'll take a short vacation. Perhaps your mother would like to go to St. Louis, or even to Chicago, and take in a few entertainments."

"Splendid!" she cried, so eagerly that she startled herself.

"I'll be sorry to have you leave us again tomorrow," he said. "Are you all ready?"

"Yes. I sent my trunk several days ago."

"The Society of Friends is doing important work out here. I'm gratified that you're having the opportunity to be a part of it. It's some compensation, at least, for having given up a normal life to live in this country."

"I love my work," she said. "The Sparkmans are wonderful to me."

"Have you ever thought of compiling a study of the Quaker activities among the Indians?" he asked. "I've been intending to suggest it to you for some time. Publishers in the East would welcome it, I'm sure."

"I don't think I could ever write anything, Father."

"Have you tried, my dear?"

"No," she laughed. "Schoolgirl poetry is the best I could ever do."

Her father said, " 'He becometh poor that dealeth with a slack hand: but the hand of the diligent maketh rich.' " Then he smiled tolerantly. "You should have something to occupy your idle time, Janet. I am reminded of the Apostle Paul's admonition to the Thessalonians: 'For we hear that there are some which walk among you disorderly, working not at all, but are

[123]

busybodies.' You do have several weeks of idleness each year, and I hope you'll consider involving yourself in some worthwhile activity."

"Oh," she said, "I would love to write something—but that's as far as I ever get." Then to humor his mood, she added, "Perhaps I should try my hand at poetry again. I haven't tried in four or five years."

" 'The soul of the sluggard desireth, and hath nothing: but the soul of the diligent shall be fat,' " he said.

"Perhaps my first new poem will be an 'Ode to a Fatted Soul.' "

He stiffened and glared at her.

"Are you mocking me, Janet?"

"Of course not, Father."

"The Scriptures are not ridiculous. And I don't believe it is ridiculous of me to suggest that you do something better with your idleness than have perfectly casual encounters with adorable young men who love jelly biscuits."

She bridled, her dignity outraged.

"You have no right to say such a thing to me," she heard herself reply.

"Are you disputing my duty to offer you guidance?" He got up and walked around the table toward her.

She rose quickly from her chair and faced him.

"I've done nothing wrong," she said.

"Haven't you?" He reached out and flicked her hair, which was tied down with a ribbon. "Don't you think hair ribbons are wrong for a woman your age? I've been noticing you lately. Hair flying brazenly, loud dresses, bright shawls like squaw-girls wear. Can't you entice a man with your natural looks? Is that why you're doing this to yourself—so some jelly eater will notice you and sneak around to see you?"

"Please, Willard," her mother protested. "It isn't fair——"

"Hush, Alice. You're in conspiracy with this thing. If Janet wants a man so badly, I think it could be arranged for her to have someone respectable." He turned to face her again. "Would you like to go back East, where you'll have a better chance? I'd give you the money——"

"She doesn't have to go husband-hunting, Willard!"

"Alice," he snapped, "I asked you to hush. Go upstairs and drink yourself stupid if you must, but for God's sake be quiet."

Her mother ran crying from the kitchen.

Janet stepped back from her father, but he came toward her and she wanted to hit him.

"How can you do that to her, Father?"

" 'Even a fool, when he holdeth his peace, is counted wise.' But your mother has never had even that much judgment."

"She's the only person in the world who really loves you."

His face reddened and his cheeks became puffy. His voice rose shrilly, the way it always did when he was threatened.

"There are ten thousand people in Ridgefield who love me. It will be a pity if I can't include my daughter among them."

"Yes, Father," she said, "it will."

She found, miraculously, that standing up to him was giving her strength. Some mystical force had suddenly sent power into her body and her heart. She stared steadily at her father.

He was silent. Then he held out his hands in a small gesture.

"My dear, I've been deeply disturbed that you haven't had the opportunity to marry. I realize that every woman wants a husband and a family."

"Do I seem so bad off to you?" she asked.

His eyes flashed. She knew that he was uncertain how far to go with her. It was the first time she could ever remember having made him uncertain.

"You must feel some desperation," he said bitterly, "to be seeing someone you're ashamed of. Perhaps we could all go East together, after the trial, and look up our old friends. Your mother and I could get you established, and I'm sure you'd have invitations to stay on for a while. You have aunts in New York City whom you hardly know. You could get acquainted with them." He paused. "I have a little money. I could give you enough for a generous dot, my dear, with which you could bargain for civilized coverture——"

"How dare you pretend to be a father!" she gasped. "What a horrible thing to say!"

"It would be better than flaunting yourself on the streets of Ridgefield," he cried. "I shall not permit you to keep company with men in this barbaric place."

"All places are barbaric, Father."

"I shall not permit it. Do you understand me, child?"

"Yes, I understand you," she said, somehow commanding control of her voice. "May I quote from Isaiah, Father? 'Woe unto them that call evil good, and good evil; that put darkness for light, and light for darkness; that put bitter for sweet, and sweet for bitter! Woe unto them that are wise in their own eyes, and prudent in their own sight!'"

He stared at her, his eyes bulging.

She said, "I'm going upstairs now. Good night. . . ."

She turned quickly and left him standing alone in the kitchen. She ran upstairs, deeply hurt, but strengthened. . . . Thank you, Angus, for giving me strength. . . .

When she reached her room she found her mother sitting on the bed, glass in hand, bottle on the floor, eyes glazed.

"Hello, my darling," said Alice Ring. "I'm going to spend the night with you, if you don't mind. Your father, who art in Ridgefield, dost not like me very much when I am drinking. God bless my poor husband." She smiled absurdly. "God bless God. That's curious blessing, isn't it, Janet?"

Morning came bursting upon her through the undrawn blinds in her room. Before going to bed she had opened the blinds so that she might watch the moonlight, and now it was morning and her day would be full. Her mother had already left the room and could be heard downstairs in the kitchen. She thought of her father and lay still for a moment, urging her thoughts and feelings to clarify—to speak to her in a united voice, humane and realistic, both fair to her parents and to herself. But her feeling was all hate. Pity for her mother; hate for her father.

And then she thought of Angus and remembered with a smile that she had been dreaming about him just before awakening. She tried to sort out the dream and realized frantically that it was disappearing almost before her eyes. Only snatches remained. He had ridden up to the depot on a fine horse, ridiculously standing upright in the saddle, wearing fringed buckskins and carrying an enormous buffalo gun. She remembered that she was already aboard the train. The train was pulling away from the station . . . what had he done then? She had already forgotten. She closed her eyes tightly to remember. She could almost recapture it—but it was gone.

Still smiling, she got up from the bed. I'll have to leave you standing there in the saddle, Angus, she mused. I'll bet you got me off that train somehow. And then she thought: I'm sure you did. After all, it was my dream. . . . I wonder if you got me off the train in your dream, Angus? And she said aloud, "My darling buffalo hunter."

Amused at herself, she stood before her dressing mirror. She pointed a wagging finger at herself and said, "This is what happens when you sleep with your face in the moonlight, Janet Ring."

She poured water into her basin and washed. Then she pulled on a robe and went downstairs.

"Good morning," said her mother cheerfully.

"Where's Father?" Janet asked.

"He's already had his breakfast. He wanted to go to his office for a while before train time. He said he'd have the buggy here by ten o'clock."

"Did he say anything, Mother? About last night?"

"No. He never does."

"It's amazing."

"Beneath the surface there's goodness in him, Janet. I know you don't think so. But I'm going to bring it out again. After you leave. I think he'll have to retire from the bench before there's much chance."

"He won't retire, Mother."

"Yes he will. One way or another. . . . I was glad he criticized the Supreme Court again. The more he does it, the sooner he'll be retired."

"Wouldn't it hurt him terribly, Mother? Wouldn't it just about destroy him?"

Her mother whirled around in anger, and Janet learned something about her that she had not quite known. Her mother's face was red and her eyes flashed.

"Whatever you mean by that, you must remember this," she said. "Your father is all I've got—and as long as he's alive, I'm going to try. If you believe I'm doomed to failure, please be kind enough to keep it to yourself. . . ."

When Janet returned to her room upstairs after breakfast, she took out her stationery box and her pen. Before dressing to go to the depot, she sat down at her writing table and wrote a letter to Angus. She wrote carefully, making three drafts before she was satisfied. The only thing she did not alter in the successive drafts was the salutation:

My Dearest:

At last I am writing the letter you wanted. I love you.

You were a buffalo hunter in my dream last night. You were the most magnificent buffalo hunter who ever turned up in a girl's wild dream. You were dressed beautifully in buckskins. I love you, I love you.

Darling, you are right. It is time I faced my father with the truth. Honestly, he treated mother and me as though we were low animals last night. He had been ill in his office during the afternoon, and was at home when I returned. He knew I'd been out with a man, but I refused to tell him who. I'm not going to tell him until our plans are definite, and then I have decided I don't care what he says or does.

I'm glad I did not defy him before, as I was not sure of my feelings toward him; but now I am sure. Thank you for being so patient with me. You are a wonderful person and I shall try never to make you feel sneaky again.

Please write immediately. I'll die waiting for your letter. I doubt if Paul Sparkman can arrange to replace me until after the end of this term, but I shall try to be relieved by the time the trial is over if you want it that way.

All my love,
Janet

CHAPTER FIFTEEN

Angus was more comfortable living at the New Ridge, where he took a room on a weekly basis. It was a large, open room and he soon rather appreciated the impersonal feel of it—the anonymity. The carpet was quiet under his feet and his washbowl was happily almost big enough to climb into. He wondered why he had waited so long to leave the Bordens.

A week before the trial, he persuaded Colonel Beleau to call a conference in his office. He was grateful for the Colonel's help, and a little surprised. Ever since the public hangings in September, when Angus and the newspaper chap from St. Louis had talked him into nausea, Colonel Beleau had felt a trifle hurt.

Angus offered cigars to Ben Procter and Red Molloy after they had gathered in the Colonel's private office behind the little reception room.

"We'll smoke the Colonel out of here," said Procter with a chuckle. He knew, of course, that a deal was about to be proposed. And it could be assumed that he would commit himself to nothing until he had spoken to Judge Ring.

"I've tried to smoke the Colonel out many times," Angus said, "and I can tell you, gents, that it can't be done. He's got a constitution like a boiler factory."

"Stop kidding me," said the Colonel with a shrug of his big shoulders. "I may not live longer for not smoking, but I'll go to my grave with a better taste in my mouth."

Red Molloy laughed effusively. He was plainly glad to be included in this meeting. He was poised to learn whatever he could. He intended to become a first-rate prosecutor someday himself—after his mentor had moved on up the ladder to—where? The bench, perhaps? Not likely, unless Judge Ring died suddenly and Procter fell heir to an emergency appointment. Ben had been careful not to associate himself with the Judge's criticism of the Supreme Court. Red Molloy was ready to step into Ben's shoes, and he did not pretend otherwise.

"We're waiting for Doc McKay," Angus said.

"Here he is now," said the Colonel, who rose and admitted Doc to his inner office, helping him off with his coat.

Doc was a little out of breath and his normally pink face was quite flushed. His expression was grave, and gravity in Doc McKay's bearing commanded respect.

"Sorry I kept you waiting, Angus," he said.

"That's all right, Doc. Have a cigar?"

"No, thanks. I have several patients to see this afternoon and I'd like to get away as quickly as possible."

"Of course, Doc. We could do this later if you'd like."

"I can spare a few minutes, so we might as well proceed since we're here. Are you expecting anyone else, Colonel?"

"No, I think not," said Colonel Beleau. "Do you want to begin, Angus?"

"Yes, I will." He turned to face the others. Procter and Molloy were standing together near a window opposite the desk, behind which the Colonel sat in a swivel chair, rocking thoughtfully. "Ben, I'll start by telling you and Red that both the Colonel and Doc have agreed with me on the importance of a problem that's facing us all. The Colonel was good enough to call this meeting in his office to give it a semblance of objectivity. It's in connection with the Maywood trial, but it's even more vitally connected with Judge Ring." He added, to Beleau: "Is that a fair way to put it, Colonel?"

"It is, indeed," said Colonel Beleau. "As you know, gentlemen, I have no interest in the Maywood prosecution, other than that of an ordinary citizen. As a matter of fact, I advised Angus last summer to stay away from it. We might still be partners if he'd listened to me. . . . But I have a great concern for the problem Angus is talking about."

Ben Procter and Red Molloy were paying close attention. Angus drew on his cigar, watching them.

"It's about the Judge's health," he said. He turned to McKay. "Would you tell them what you told me, Doc?"

"Certainly, Angus." Doc pursed his lips, then pinched the bridge of his nose, obviously weary and in need of sleep. "My position is uncomfortable to me, Ben," he said. "The Judge is dangerously unwell. I have examined him several times recently and I'm alarmed. I won't go into details, but I'm sure you'll want to know that in my opinion he won't be able to tolerate the burden of his office much longer. I have advised him to retire, and I have discovered that a specialist in St. Louis gave him the same advice last year. His temper fits are gravely dangerous. One of them could easily precipitate a blood-stroke, or even a fatal heart seizure. I told this to Angus after Willard became unconscious while excoriating the Supreme Court. And I told it to the Colonel earlier this week. They both urged me to come here and tell it to you."

Doc paused, indicating that he felt he'd said enough.

"Doc has work to do," Angus said, "so I suggest that we continue without him, if he'd like us to. I wanted him to tell you this himself."

"Thanks," said Doc. "Have you any questions, Ben? I don't like discussing my patients with their friends—but there isn't much I can do for Willard except try to lessen the turmoil of his life. We believe that prolonged emotional tremor is one of the contributing causes of blood-stroke."

"Do you think," asked Ben Procter, "that he shouldn't preside at the Maywood trial? Is he that sick?"

"I feel," said Doc, "that his condition may be critical. He shouldn't be doing anything that would greatly agitate him."

"Christ," said Red Molloy, "everything agitates him. Doesn't it, Ben?"

"He's fairly worked up over this case," Procter admitted. He glanced bitterly at Angus. "The reversal stung him—especially the remarks about his medieval sources."

"I'd like to be excused now, if you don't mind," Doc said. "I regard the rest of your conference as no affair of mine. I'll be glad to talk to you later, Ben, if you want more information."

"Thanks, Doc. That will be fine."

"We appreciate your coming," said Colonel Beleau. "I hope we haven't kept you too long."

"Not at all. But I must ask that what I have told you be kept in confidence. My patients' problems are not public information—and I've had to argue with myself whether I should tell this."

"Does his family know about it?" Ben Procter asked.

"His wife does. I had to tell her since I talked to you, Angus. I don't think his daughter knows."

"I'm sure we're all grateful that you told us," said Colonel Beleau, and the feeling was quickly affirmed by Procter and Molloy.

"Goodbye, then. . . ." Doc smiled and left.

Angus studied Procter's reaction. Whatever could be discerned from quick glances while Doc McKay's footsteps receded out of hearing would have to guide his next move. He wished he didn't care whether Procter could be convinced or not. He would enjoy fighting it out. This case offered the first opportunity he'd had to face the Judge at trial with favorable odds. He breathed deeply—a little regretfully.

"Ben, I'm not going to try to add anything to what Doc has said about the Judge's health. You'll probably talk to him privately, anyway. I'm looking for a way to obviate this trial. . . ."

He paused. Before he could continue, Red Molloy began chuckling in amusement and Ben Procter rose about a foot in height—an act of physical magic which he had learned to perform in court when pouncing upon a suddenly culpable witness.

"I've no doubt in this world that's what you're looking for," he cried. "You can't possibly believe that Judge Ring's health would——"

But the Colonel cut him off.

"Wait a moment, Ben." Beleau was red-faced, at once embarrassed and stricken with anger. "Let Angus finish what he's trying to say. He isn't ass enough to think he can arrange a plea simply because Willard is a sick man." The Colonel's inflection was as caustic as Angus had ever heard, and he had to grin.

"Here's my position, Ben," he said. "It will surprise you, I'm sure, to learn that I have a case for Maywood. That boy is innocent, and I'd love to go to trial. If I'm right, the Judge is way out on a limb. And frankly, there's nothing I'd enjoy more than chopping it off."

"Go ahead," Ben Procter said. He ran his fingers through his hair, letting his hand come to rest on the back of his neck. He was not relaxed now. "You must have more to say, Angus."

"The Colonel has seen my evidence and he knows what my testimony will be. Ask him if I have a case, Ben."

Procter and Molloy flicked glances at each other.

"I think we'd rather hear about it from you," Red Molloy said. "Wouldn't we, Ben?"

"You misunderstood me," Angus replied. "I didn't say ask *about* it, Red. I said ask him if I *have* one. I don't expect you to take my word for it." He knew they would be impressed with anything the Colonel told them. Colonel Beleau was not a man readily associated with chicanery.

Procter turned slowly to Beleau.

"You know about it, Colonel?"

"Yes, Ben. Angus has gone over it with me."

"And you believe he has a case?"

"The evidence is unassailable. You'll believe it yourself."

Procter waited a moment before continuing. He looked doubtful.

"What are you proposing, Angus?"

"I can see three possibilities. The first is that we go to trial as docketed. If it works out that way, I'm ready. The second is for a change of venue. I don't know if you could possibly sell that to the Judge—he's determined on this case, and he's got a lot of people looking down his throat. He knows that Washington will be watching closely. But I'd be willing to have it tried in another court, and I'm prepared to ask for a change if you think you can arrange it." He watched them. Molloy seemed to be restraining a sneer, and Procter's face bore only disbelief.

"What's your third possibility, Angus? I'm sure it's the one you're really interested in."

"Reopen the Grand Jury inquiry. I'll make my case available to it. I'm confident the indictment would be withdrawn."

"For Christ's sweet sake, DeWolfe!" Procter was astounded that such a thing would be proposed. "Do I have to remind you that Maywood has already been convicted once? And——"

"It was upset on appeal," Angus said heavily.

"Not a chance, Angus. Never."

"It could be done, Ben. If you thought it was important."

"Why should I think it would be important? What new evidence can you show me?"

"I said I'd make it available to the Grand Jury."

"There'd have to be a reason to reopen it. An overwhelming reason connected with the merits of the case."

"Ask the Colonel——"

"You'll have to tell me, Angus, if you expect——"

"Cut it out," Angus said. "You know I won't tell you."

"Why not, if you're so certain?"

"I remember Mike Hall's testimony in the Gunnysack trial."

Procter stiffened, ever so slightly, but it was noticeable.

"Are you insinuating anything?"

"Not if you don't force me to."

"Hall wasn't tampered with."

"My people are not going to be, either. I'm not revealing a word that's not before a jury. That's the only way I can see it."

"Angus," Ben Procter said suddenly, "this isn't going down right. Do you know what I think is wrong?"

"What's wrong, Ben?"

"You don't give a damn about the Judge's health. That's what's wrong."

"Are you sure of that?"

"I've watched you slash him to ribbons. If he's as bad off as Doc fears, it's more your fault than anyone's."

"Maybe Angus feels his conscience, and wants to atone," Red Molloy suggested sarcastically.

"Shoot straight with me, Angus," Procter went on. "I should think you'd like to humiliate him if you could. Why're you doing this?"

"Ben—let me put it this way. If Doc's fears should become a reality, and the Judge collapsed and died—who would stand to benefit the most. You or I?"

They were silent. Colonel Beleau twisted miserably in his chair. Angus relighted his cigar, drawing on it deliberately and watching Ben Procter through the smoke. Procter had an obedient face, and it was now serving him well. Red Molloy's face, however, had not yet learned. Red was obviously stung; but he was waiting for his boss to make the next move.

"Your insinuations are pretty rough, Angus," Procter said at last.

"Let's admit that we've both been rough and let it go at that."

"I don't think the Judge would consider either of your alternatives for a minute. Unless, of course, I could tell him more about your argument of innocence."

"I'd be gambling with the boy's life if I did that. I'd rather gamble with the Judge's."

"If I went around him to the Grand Jury he would explode with anger. And I gather that's what we're trying to avoid."

"The Colonel and I have discussed that. And I think it would rile him less than being defeated in court. It would also save face for him—which is important, I suppose."

"If your man is innocent, you mean."

"He's innocent," Angus said. "You don't need to tell the Judge I talked to you. Tell him the Colonel put you wise as a favor. He could be made to look like the zealous protector of the innocent that he claims to be."

"I'd give him a stroke just trying it. He's much too deeply committed to this case."

"Talk it over with the Colonel. He'd go with you to the Judge, wouldn't you, Colonel?"

"If Ben would like me to," said the Colonel miserably.

"Angus. . . ." Procter said with a sudden new urgency. "Tell me the truth—why are you trying so hard to protect him if you have a defense?"

"You believe he's dangerously ill, don't you?"

"Yes—Doc wouldn't make that up. But I need to know why you care enough to do this."

"Fair enough, Ben. I'll tell you, if you'll give me your word that it will go no further until after this thing is settled."

"I'll give you my word."

"And you, Red?"

"Of course, Angus. If it's important."

"I'm going to marry Janet Ring. That's why I'd like to protect the Judge and give him a chance to retire."

"Angus, my boy!" cried the Colonel. He jumped from his chair.

"Jesus!" said Ben Procter, totally astounded. "That's what would kill him, Angus, as sure as Christ died on the cross."

After Procter and Molloy had departed to determine what, if anything, could possibly be arranged, the Colonel sat in his swivel chair and chuckled and looked at Angus happily and shook his big blond head.

"You were so contemptuous of her last summer," he said, relishing his role of being right. "You really made me angry with that letter she wrote you about Maywood."

"We live and learn," said Angus. "Like you always told me."

Beleau clouded a bit.

"I'm sure you wouldn't admit you'd learned anything from me, Angus. Don't start pulling my leg."

"I wouldn't dream of it, Colonel."

Now the Colonel was beaming happily again. "I remember you asked me if she could have been having a secret love for the Indian. I thought it was absurd, and now she's been having one for you. If anyone had asked me, I'd have said that was absurd, too." He burst into hearty laughter. "Shows you what a good judge of character I am. Mrs. Beleau will want to have you both to supper soon. She'll be excited when she hears this. She believes unlikely couples make the best marriages."

"Are we such an unlikely couple? Janet was raised in an environment of the law. She grew up in the East, as I did, and was transplanted out here. You'd be surprised how many interests we have in common. We even take the same view of her father."

"You're doing the right thing, trying to prevent this trial. I'm praying that Willard will listen."

"I'm not sure how Janet will be able to handle it if he doesn't. She's ready to confront him with our plans now—but if she learns of his condition . . . I don't know. The little bastard had better listen to Ben."

"You shouldn't speak of him that way, Angus."

"It just comes out. He's hurt her terribly, Colonel. I don't think I'm greatly concerned about what may happen to him—but I could still lose her if I'm not careful. Do you think Ben can convince him?"

"Let's not predict," said the Colonel. "I just don't know."

Angus paused at the corner of the square. November's bright cool sun spread brilliance over the town. Nothing exciting had happened since the September executions, and Ridgefield was keyed to periodic excitement. Conditions were right for an emotionally charged atmosphere to engulf the trial if Willard Ring could not be persuaded.

Angus stood for a moment, looking up the avenue toward the Judge's home. And he thought of Janet's mother. He had never spoken to her except that day she had appeared on the stair landing, disheveled in her dressing gown, less drunken, perhaps, than desperate. "If you can't defy your father," she had said to Janet, "then move away permanently, where you can have the freedom to make your own choices." Now, at last, Janet was making choices. Should he try to force her to go back home during the trial? Or should he let her stay at the hotel with the Sparkmans and the other witnesses? She had told him she wanted never to go home again. Could any reason for sending her back into her father's house be justified?

"Go with him," Alice Ring had said. "Look at me and go with him." The burden of fidelity to the conflicting forces in her family had been in her heart—had shaped her cry to her daughter, and then her lame defense of her husband. "He has the most difficult job in this country. I realize that he has become a fanatic, Mr. DeWolfe, and I fear that he may make terrible mistakes. But if you think he is evil . . ."

Do I? he wondered.

Gentlemen of the jury, I ask you to look at this defendant, reflect upon the evidence against him, then answer the questions put before you. He has threatened the life of an innocent boy in order to inhibit his daughter's natural desire for romance. Is he therefore morally corrupt? He has repeatedly staged barbarous execution carnivals for mass public consumption. Has he impaired the sensibility of his community? He has denied the validity of legal justice. Has he undermined our concept of due process? Is he evil?

Am I the jury? Angus asked himself. Could such questions be answered with certainty? And if the answers could reasonably be *yes*, could it be established that the fanatical man had knowingly, willfully and maliciously committed the deeds ascribed to him? If he were a criminal, would his crime equate with murder, or with manslaughter? Or was he merely insane?

Angus began walking along the avenue, drawn toward the Rings' home by a feeling that some part of his action was answerable to Janet's mother.

Alice Ring received him warmly, and without apparent surprise. She did not pretend to wonder why he had come. She was not as tall as Janet; and it struck him that, despite its singular roundness, her face reminded him greatly of Janet's face. Through soft, anxious eyes, she looked at him hopefully.

"I thought you might come to see me," she said.

"Did you, Mrs. Ring?"

"Doctor McKay told me that you knew about my husband's health. The poor doctor is quite upset that he has felt obliged to talk about it."

"I know. Doc is in a difficult position."

"Won't you sit down, Mr. DeWolfe? Could I give you some tea? Or perhaps some whiskey?" She smiled at him uncertainly. "We have some good Irish whiskey in the house, I believe."

Restraining a smile, he assumed a sober detachment and sat opposite her on the high-backed sofa.

"No, thank you, Mrs. Ring. I shouldn't stay more than a few minutes."

He marveled again at the room. Its darkness cast malevolence upon everything he knew about Janet. He wanted to haul the blinds to the ceiling and let the light in. He wanted to open the doors and windows wide, permitting the breeze to ripple through, bringing the smell of fallen leaves and the sounds of life. He said, "I have come to see if you can possibly help me with something."

"I'll be glad to if I can." Now she smiled, and it was Janet's smile. He was astounded at the feeling it gave him.

"I have just come from a conference in the office of Colonel Beleau, with Mr. Procter and Mr. Molloy, concerning the trial next week."

"So I imagined," she said. "Mr. Procter told my husband yesterday that Colonel Beleau had asked him to come."

"He spoke to you about it?"

"Yes. Last night."

"I'm sure he knew we were going to propose something."

She nodded, clasping her hands tightly, in expectation.

"What happened, Angus? I mean, Mr. DeWolfe," she quickly corrected. "I'm sorry—I have spoken to you so often with Janet that——"

"Please call me Angus," he said.

"Thank you." Alice Ring smiled. "You were telling me about the conference."

"Yes. I'm proposing that the indictment be reconsidered by the Grand Jury. It would be an unusual circumstance, in view of Marcus's previous conviction, but if Judge Ring gave his consent, it could be handled that way. I think this trial could be avoided. I have substantial proof that Marcus is innocent. Mr. Procter won't return the case to the Grand Jury without your husband's approval. I wonder if there is any way you could possibly help persuade him."

Pitiful resignation settled over her face.

"I'm sure there isn't. I can have no effect——" Then she caught herself, obviously choosing to refrain from criticism.

"Do you think Procter will be able to persuade him?"

"No, he won't be able to."

"The Judge is looking forward to this trial, isn't he?"

"More's the pity," she said. "It's all he thinks about." She added in a dazed voice, "He told me this would be his greatest triumph, Angus. He hopes it will be observed by the people in Washington. He says he is going to send this man to the gallows, and then retire."

"He spoke of retiring?"

"Last night, for the first time. He knows he isn't well."

She looked at him with a strangely uncontrolled countenance. Her clasped hands trembled, but her voice was clear: "I know you are doing everything you can to protect Janet's father from himself. But you must not think of that at the expense of your client—not even inadvertently."

He did not reply, but watched her. She stared at her hands, breaking them free of each other.

He rose from the sofa.

"Thank you for talking to me, Mrs. Ring. I'm sure this has been painful for you."

"That's all right."

"I haven't told Janet about your husband's condition," he said.

"So I have gathered from her letters. I'm not going to tell her, either. She wrote me that you didn't want her to stay at the hotel during the trial. She is a little hurt, I think, because she doesn't understand. But I hope you won't press her. It will be better if she stays there."

"Do you think so?"

"If Marcus is acquitted, her father simply wouldn't be able to face her. I hope, for his sake, that he won't have to."

"Goodbye, Mrs. Ring," he said.

"Goodbye." She followed him to the door. "Angus—Janet loves you very much. Thank you."

He grinned uncomfortably. "We don't thank people for love," he said. "We return it."

He stooped over and planted a kiss on her forehead, then went through the door quickly and hurried down the walk, believing, with a crushing conviction, that the weakest condition of man was sentimentality. And the curse of it was that it could sneak up on almost anyone.

CHAPTER SIXTEEN

The Monday morning edition of the Ridgefield *Monograph* carried an editorial in a box on the front page:

> At nine o'clock this morning, Judge Willard Ring's mighty gavel will again bring to order the Federal District and Circuit Court to try the Shawnee Indian, Marcus Maywood, for the crime of murder. This man has already been tried and convicted by a jury of his Ridgefield peers. That conviction was callously set aside by the Supreme Court of the United States in an arrogant opinion which maligned the character and qualifications of the only courageous Judge the Ridgefield court has ever known. We have no doubt that Judge Ring will be vindicated by the outcome of this second trial. It only remains to be seen whether the *high* court in Washington can possibly tend to the business it knows something about and leave Judge Ring to finish the job of cleaning up this country which he has so gloriously begun.

Janet said, "I wonder how newspapers feel they can be so sure of themselves."

"Freedom of the press, it's called," Angus laughed. He tossed the paper aside and prepared to leave the New Ridge suite he had engaged for her.

"I'd better go," he said. "I don't know whether I'll have a chance to see you at noon."

"That's all right. I won't go away. How long do you think the trial will last?"

"Two days at the most, if Procter moves along. Your father will probably hold evening sessions until it's finished."

"Darling," she said, "I love you."

He stood before the affectionate warmth of her gaze.

"Wait till you get my bill. That will test your love. Don't forget that you retained me for this case."

"I'm not paying any more bills until after I'm married," she said. "Then my husband will take care of them."

"Is that why women get married—to get their bills paid?"

"Why else?" she asked; and her lips parted a little when she smiled. He kissed her, then went to his own room to get his hat and coat.

On his way to the courtroom, he saw Red Molloy, who was already coming across the square toward the Federal Building, and his mood changed quickly. Molloy stopped to let him catch up.

"Ben did his best, Angus," the assistant prosecutor said.

"And I did mine. There's no need for this trial, Red."

"If you'd given us your evidence, we might have gotten further with the Judge."

Angus swore contemptuously.

"You know why I didn't."

"Judge Ring gave Ben a royal cussing for his trouble. I heard it myself, standing outside in the hall."

"Well, at least I tried."

"Ben asked me to speak to you, Angus. He said to make it perfectly clear that he would present this case to the jury just as vigorously as if you'd never called that meeting in Beleau's office."

"Spoken like an honest public servant, too," he retorted, surprised at his own cynical excess. "You also have a duty to keep your office free from intimidation by the Court. Tell Ben I said that, will you?"

Red Molloy tried to grin.

"There's no reason for hard feelings between you and me. Is there?"

"There's no reason for feelings of any particular kind, that I know of."

"Ben asked me to tell you something else, Angus. He doesn't think for a minute that you honestly believe that Indian is innocent. He thinks you're desperate."

"Then give him this honest message for me, Red. Tell him we'll see who is desperate before this trial is over."

"All right. But I don't see any reason for you and me not to be friends. Do you?"

"No reason at all. It's just a matter of whether we can possibly do it, Red," Angus said.

He pushed through the crowded entrance and went up the stairway. The corridor and courtroom were packed except for a section roped off for the prospective jurors. Two deputy marshals had been assigned the special job of keeping order around the door. He was conscious of the stares he attracted as he passed up the center aisle toward the well of the court. Ben Procter was not yet in sight.

He went immediately to the defense table which sat below the L-shaped palisade of hand-turned pickets that separated the well from the raised platform where the two rows of jury seats ran at right angles to the bench and witness chair. He stood for a moment, surveying the empty platform.

Colonel Beleau spoke to him from behind.

"Good morning," the Colonel said with forced cheerfulness. His face bore its inevitable intimation of discomfort. Someone who didn't know him might have surmised that his shoes were too tight. It was Colonel Beleau's lot to walk through life in tight shoes, wearing whenever possible a pleasant expression.

"Hello, Colonel."

"I want to sit at the table with you, Angus."

"You what?"

"You heard correctly, my boy." A sheepish smile formed faintly beneath the surface of the Colonel's face. "I doubt if I can be of any real assistance— I don't pretend to be sharp on criminal proceeding. But I'd like to associate myself with you at this late date, if you'll let me."

"Well . . . of course, if you want to, Colonel."

Beleau flushed in acute embarrassment.

"It may be worth something to have me sitting here—it will be a surprise to the jury, anyway. But I'm asking this selfishly. I've been feeling pretty bad about this case for several days. I was wrong, Angus; I'd like to turn around and be right."

"The effect on the jury will be terrific," Angus said, extending his hand. "Colonel, I love you."

He understood anew why Colonel Beleau had been important to him. How many people could ever bring themselves to say unequivocally, *I've been wrong?* Could I say it? he wondered.

"I had thought," the Colonel whispered from the side of his mouth, "that you were in love with a certain schoolteacher." Then he looked away as unconcernedly as if he'd been Luke Sweeley.

Ben Procter appeared at the opposite table, then came over immediately to speak to him.

"Red gave me your message," he said. Procter showed no trace of annoyance. He was already performing before an audience. Any display of feeling, from now until the trial was concluded, would be calculated for the exact effect he desired to produce. "My opening will be brief," he said. "And my witnesses are ready."

"Good."

"I'm surprised to see you here, Colonel. I thought you had no interest in this case."

"I'm not a visitor, Ben," said the Colonel. "Angus has engaged me to assist him."

"Well, that's a new wrinkle." Procter shook his head with only a touch of surprise—perhaps, Angus thought, deliberately suggesting that nothing could surprise him greatly. "Maybe you don't have the case completely in your pocket at that. . . . Your client is in the prisoner's room, Angus."

"Thanks."

Procter turned away, hunching his shoulders as he reached his own table and bent over it with Red Molloy.

"I'd better go get the boy, Colonel. It's five minutes to nine," Angus said.

He went through the door into the back hallway behind the stair well. The guards admitted him to the prisoner's room where Marcus was sitting in a chair. The boy rose immediately.

"You look great," Angus said. "Just great."

Marcus tried to smile.

"I feel very strange, Mr. DeWolfe." His brown face was charged with vitality—his eyes snapped with intelligence as he spoke. He had on the new suit of clothes Angus had bought for the trial. His black hair was perfectly groomed.

"Strange? In what way, Marcus?"

"I'm not sure. Getting dressed up like this, for one thing."

"It's always important to make a good impression in court. Don't look at the jury too much. Concentrate on the testimony. The jurors will be watching you, and it's better not to make them self-conscious."

"I'll do my best."

"We have a break already," Angus told him. "Colonel Beleau is going to assist us."

"He is?"

"He's convinced that you're innocent, and his presence at your side will have a strong effect on the jury. He has never taken criminal cases—and he's a highly respected man."

"Is my mother here?" Marcus asked.

"She's over at the hotel."

"Did she ask to see me?"

"Yes."

"Wouldn't they let you bring her?"

"I'm going to tell you the truth, Marcus. I didn't want you to talk to her."

"Why not?"

Angus looked at him. "I was afraid you might change your mind and tell her not to testify about the money." He grinned at the boy. "I had a hard enough time convincing you to co-operate with me."

Marcus frowned. "But I promised you."

"Nevertheless, I don't want any emotional flare-up at this point. There'll be plenty of time to talk to your mother later."

"How did you convince her?"

"Miss Ring did it. She's over at the hotel with your mother now. Da-ni-mah is there, too."

Marcus stared at him steadily. Then he said, "I'm ready, Mr. DeWolfe."

"Good. Keep your spirits up. Remember what I told you last night. Let everybody in the courtroom know you're confident just by the way you carry yourself."

Marcus straightened up and went through the door ahead of him, walking erectly. As they reached the courtroom a hush fell over the spectators. Scarcely a murmur could be heard.

They proceeded to the defense table, their footsteps conspicuously loud on the floor. The silence was making Marcus uncomfortable, and Angus was gratified when the Colonel rose to let the courtroom see him warmly shake hands with the boy. The Colonel pulled out Marcus's chair for him.

Then Sam Doolan, the crier, came into the courtroom.

"Order in the court! Please rise!"

Everyone stood up as Judge Ring strode in, mounting the platform briskly, looking refreshed and determined. He stood for a moment behind his desk, peering out over the crowded room.

"The United States District and Circuit Court of Ridgefield is now in session," Sam Doolan cried loudly. "Judge Willard P. Ring presiding, be seated."

The Judge sat in his huge chair, gavel in hand, waiting for the noise to subside. He rapped sharply.

"The Government of the United States versus Marcus Maywood," he said. His voice was clear and controlled—at its baritone best. His face was serene. He appeared to have had a good night's sleep. His countenance seemed revitalized since Angus had last seen him.

Ben Procter stood up, making as always a fine dramatic figure in the courtroom.

"The case for the Government is ready, your Honor."

Judge Ring nodded, then turned his gaze toward the defense table coolly. Angus was not prepared for the stoutness of the Judge's bearing. The little man didn't look as though he'd been sick a day in his life. He wondered if the Judge had noticed the Colonel yet. If so, it was not apparent.

He rose to face the Judge, and the courtroom behind him was as silent as death.

"If it please the Court," he began, "I am compelled, in fairness to the defendant, to ask for a continuance and a change of venue."

The Judge shot back his question:

"What are your reasons, Mr. DeWolfe?"

Angus said quickly, "The inflammatory discussion of this case in the local newspaper, even on this very day, has created an atmosphere of prejudice against my client. It will be impossible to select a jury that has not already formed an opinion. My request is doubly urgent, your Honor, because the previous trial of my client, and the public controversy surrounding its appeal, has rendered this entire community incapable of objective judgment."

Judge Ring leaned forward in his chair.

"It is my opinion, Counselor, that newspapers do not necessarily make up people's minds for them. I will state, however, that discussions of the merits of a criminal case in newspapers, both before and during a trial, are highly improper and in absolute disfavor with this court. I urge newspaper editors and journalists—and I note that we have several present today—to employ the most scrupulous care in their manner of reportage. It is quite out of keeping with the cherished traditions of our nation to in any way prejudice the case of a defendant, and I trust that we can rely upon our great fourth estate to use discretion during this trial." He glanced at the section reserved for the press, then turned again toward Angus. "Now, Counselor, I will rule on your motion. Because you can determine by personal interrogation of each juror whether he has already formed an opinion, I will deny your request."

"Respectfully, your Honor," said Angus, "we except."

The Judge nodded pleasantly.

"Your exception shall be noted."

Angus sat down and Sam Doolan disappeared through the back door to bring in the prospective jurors.

"Colonel," said Angus, leaning over and covering his mouth in order to converse as privately as possible, "does the Judge surprise you at all today?"

"Incredibly," said the Colonel.

"I've never heard him talk this way before."

"He is most alert, Angus. I think he's determined not to hand you an error this time."

"It looks that way, doesn't it?"

"Perhaps he's learned something. He isn't a stupid man—you must know that."

"I have an idea, Colonel. The sooner the jurors have you identified with the case, the better. Many of them will know who you are, I'm sure. Will you examine them for me?"

"If you'd like," the Colonel said, through lips drawn suddenly tight. "I am absolutely at your service, Angus. It would seem to me that the most important factors are to pick a fairly young jury that is free of prejudice against Indians."

"Good enough," Angus replied, turning back toward the Judge. Judge Ring was still looking at him with a pleasant smile on his face. But it was not a genuine smile. Only the mouth and lower half of his face contributed to it. The Judge was not smiling with his eyes at all. He was glaring, and Angus stared back at him close to wonder.

Ben Procter strode before the first twelve jurors called to the box. Angus watched him declaim the importance of being fair to the Government as well as to the defendant. He was aware, as always, of Procter's impressive courtroom appearance. He did not want to underestimate the man, and sharpened himself against the inclination. Procter spoke to each juror in turn, asking perfectly routine questions in a voice highly charged with imputations of significance. He succeeded in getting two of them excused by the Judge for cause, then challenged a third peremptorily.

He was satisfied at last with five farmers, two retail merchants, a cattle trader, a blacksmith, a clerk, a carpenter and a foreman at the foundry. He stepped back and bowed to them in respect, then faced the bench.

"Satisfactory to the Government, your Honor."

Judge Ring nodded and instructed the defense to examine.

Colonel Beleau leaned over and whispered:

"These look pretty good to me, as a whole, Angus."

"I think so, too."

"Any twelve people in Ridgefield will believe the boy is guilty, at least in the beginning. We both know that."

"So do Procter and the Judge," he said. "We probably can't do any better than these. Use your best judgment."

The Colonel rose and walked slowly to the jury box. The crowded room tittered its first acknowledgment of Beleau's presence. Judge Ring did not betray surprise. His procedural attitude bespoke an avid concern for the ritual that was taking place: he appeared, Angus thought, to be transfixed by the proprieties he was jealously guarding.

"Gentlemen," said the Colonel, "some of you probably know who I am. For those who don't, my name is John Beleau. During this trial, I will act as assistant to the defense counsel, who is Mr. Angus DeWolfe. He is the dark-haired man sitting over there at the table beside our client, Mr. Maywood." He gave them time to look in Angus's direction before continuing. "Now, Gentlemen," the Colonel went on, "I want to inquire if there is any one among you who does not feel at this very moment that Mr. Maywood is innocent. According to law, he is guilty of absolutely nothing unless, after listening with open minds to the testimony and seeing with impartial eyes the evidence in this trial, you shall then find him guilty beyond a reasonable doubt."

Again the Colonel paused.

The courtroom was hushed.

"I ask each of you," said the Colonel, stepping back two paces from the jury box, "to look at me. According to traditional justice every defendant reaches the bar, before a jury of his peers, clothed in a presumption of innocence. Is there any one of you who will admit that he does not right now consider Mr. Maywood innocent?"

The jurors' faces were entirely sober, and they looked at the Colonel intently, saying nothing. He went on:

"It is public knowledge, of course, that Mr. Maywood was convicted in error five months ago by a well-meaning jury sitting where you now sit. Is there any one of you who does not believe that, despite the erroneous conviction last June, Mr. Maywood stands before you at this very moment absolutely innocent? Do you understand that there can be no justice unless he remains innocent in your eyes, regardless of the prosecution's evidence, until you have heard every last word of testimony that Mr. DeWolfe will present to you on behalf of Mr. Maywood?"

So urgent was his question that the jurors nodded in return.

The Colonel looked at them, searching their faces. Then he turned deliberately to the bench.

"Your Honor," he said, "this jury is entirely satisfactory to us."

As he returned to the defense table there was no sound in the room.

"Members of the jury will stand and raise their right hands," said Sam Doolan, swearing them in.

Now a wave of excited murmurs swelled over the courtroom and Angus whispered to his friend: "Magnificent, Colonel."

The Colonel's face colored slightly.

"Of course, they're all prejudiced against the boy. I tried to make them ashamed of it."

"You did it, too."

"I'm somewhat astonished at myself, Angus. I hadn't thought of a word of that until I heard myself saying it. . . ."

"You're going to make a damned good criminal lawyer," Angus said, smiling broadly.

Ben Procter's opening to the jury began as a simple, factual statement. As he went along with the story he expected to prove, the tempo of his words increased and the emotional tone of the narrative became ugly. Angus was poised, waiting.

Procter had affected a peculiar set of dramatic posturings with which he emphasized his trial points. One of his tricks was to begin a sequence in a low voice, let it rise perceptibly toward its inevitable denouement, then suddenly turn his back on the witness and complete his thrust with eyes raised toward the ceiling. It was questionable, Angus thought, whether such theatrics helped or hindered Ben Procter's cases, but his own view was unequivocal: the technique was embarrassingly shallow, and did injustice to the dignity of the law. . . . Another trick, which the prosecutor was now employing, was to turn from the jury and walk swiftly away, as though he had forgotten to bring something to the courtroom and had remembered to go after it in a hurry, then stop abruptly, swing around again, and deliver his punch line:

"And you will see, gentlemen, that *after he had killed all four of them, he brutally—callously—dragged the——*"

"Objection, your Honor," Angus said bitterly, jumping to his feet. "The Government's allegation is murder—nothing else. Mr. Procter can only be trying to inflame the passions of the jury."

Judge Ring nodded coldly.

"Sustained." Then he spoke to the prosecutor, his words mechanically precise: "The Court will not tolerate excesses of emotion, Mr. Procter. Now you may proceed with your opening statement."

Shaken with surprise, Procter stared unbelievingly toward the bench, then briefly at Angus before continuing. That he felt betrayed was manifest. Angus could understand why, for inflammatory descriptions of the defendant's depravity had long been his choice weapon in this court. It had been objected to many times, but never before sustained.

And Angus was quite as surprised as Ben Procter. He exchanged glances with Judge Ring again. The Judge was sitting so stiffly in his chair that he looked unreal: a properly attired clothing-store dummy would in that moment have shown no less animation behind the great maple desk.

"There's something definitely wrong, Angus," Beleau whispered.

"What do you think, Colonel?"

"He's bent on giving you every latitude—that's obvious. And not characteristic of him."

"He feels certain of another conviction, and he wants to demonstrate to the world how fair he is."

"There's more to it than that. Don't look now—he's still watching us—but notice his face carefully. His eyes."

"I have noticed."

"Willard is sick——"

Ben Procter's voice roared to the conclusion of his opening to the jury:

"*And the Government will then ask you to find this man guilty of murder in the first degree. You consciences will give you no other choice!*"

All eyes shifted quickly to the Judge, who turned his own gaze upon the defense table.

"You may now deliver your opening remarks, Mr. DeWolfe."

"If your Honor please," said Angus, rising slowly, "in fairness to my client's defense, I would like to reserve my opening until the prosecution's evidence is concluded."

Ben Procter was on his feet with an objection, but the Judge denied him before he got it out.

"You may reserve your opening if you care to; proceed for the Government, Mr. Procter. Call your first witness."

Feet shuffled, bodies shifted in the seats, throats cleared, muffled conjecturing filled the close air.

Judge Ring's hand brought down the gavel.

"Order in the courtroom!"

Angus watched him.

The case for the prosecution began.

CHAPTER SEVENTEEN

Before the first witness had left the stand, Angus knew the pattern that would be developed. Judge Ring was so intent upon the form of the trial, that he appeared to be largely oblivious to its substance. His conduct was a complete reversal. Heretofore he had cared little for form and technicality; the heart of the matter had always been the crime itself, and the subsequent punishment for its perpetrator.

Angus and the Colonel discussed this unexpected development with each other in whispered snatches as Ben Procter, ponderously loud and embarrassingly ponderous, paraded his drama of circumstantial evidence before the jury and the little man in the high-backed chair. Angus sharply felt the responsibility he had assumed. More than merely the legal axis of Marcus Maywood's world, he was (he could not scold it away) the focal center of a moral crisis.

He watched the witness stand.

Hubert Scouten told of coming upon the murder scene in the woods while riding barebacked mules with his sister from a gristmill up on Owl Creek. Hubert was a skinny boy, probably two years younger than Marcus. He did not seem dishonest; his slowness of mind lent him an air of perfect plausibility. Angus rose to cross-examine.

"I have only a few questions, Hubert," he said. "I believe every word you have told the jury, and I only want to clarify a couple of points."

Hubert seemed reassured. He moistened his lips and waited.

Angus said, "You saw the man riding the brown and white paint before you came upon the burning wagon and the brush fire. Is that right?"

"Yes, sir."

"Which direction were you traveling when you saw the man?"

"Direction? I was going just about north, I guess."

"Can you be sure?"

"Of what?"

"That you were going north?"

"Sure I'm sure. We'd been to old Green's gristmill——"

"All right. Now tell us, in which direction was the man on the brown and white paint traveling when you saw him? Can you remember?"

"Sure. He was angling from the other way. Toward us. Kind of southwest."

"And you didn't speak to him?"

"No. He was riding fast."

"Did he see you?"

"Not that I know of."

"After you saw him, how far did you travel before you came upon the burning wagon?"

"Oh . . . three, four hundred yards I guess. I saw the smoke over to the right."

"I want you to think about the next question very carefully before you answer it, Hubert." He paced his words deliberately. "From what you saw of the man on the brown and white paint, would you say it was quite possible that he could have merely been riding by, as you were, and might not even have seen the smoke from the burning wagon?"

"I don't know," Hubert said slowly. "I saw the smoke, I know that."

"But the man on the paint could have been riding in a circle, for all you know, couldn't he?"

Hubert grinned and shook his head awkwardly.

"I guess he could have—if he wanted to."

The courtroom laughed and Judge Ring quickly brought down the gavel.

"Now let me get this point perfectly clear, Hubert," Angus went on. "As you approached, when you saw the man riding toward you on the brown and white paint, the smoke was to your right. Is that correct?"

"Yes, sir."

"And the man who came toward you was over to your left, wasn't he?"

"Yes, he was a bit to the left."

"How far?"

"Oh, not far. Just a little piece."

"And you stopped and watched him come on past you?"

"Yes, sir."

"If he was to your left, we can assume that he was actually further from the fire than you were. Isn't that right?"

"Well, I don't know about that," Hubert said, pondering the question. "Me and Mary thought he had been coming from just about the direction of the burning wagon."

"But you hadn't yet seen the wagon, had you?"

"I mean *after* we saw it, we thought that."

"But you could be very wrong, couldn't you? You don't really know that he was *ever* any closer to the burning wagon than he was at the time you saw him. Isn't that true, Hubert?"

"I guess so."

"You *know* so, don't you?"

"Yes, sir."

"And you have no idea whether he even saw the smoke, do you?"

"I just know that I saw it."

"But you haven't the vaguest idea whether *he* saw it, have you?"

"No, sir."

"I have no further questions," Angus said.

Hubert Scouten had no time to relax. Ben Procter was on his feet instantly.

"Just a moment, Hubert. I have one more question." He stood before the witness, hands on hips, rearing back slightly. "Look again at the defendant. And tell the jury if you are certain that he's the man you saw riding the brown and white paint from the direction of the burning wagon."

Hubert complied by looking Marcus over again.

"He's the man, all right."

"You're *sure* of that, aren't you?" Ben Procter's demand was loud and vulgar.

"Sure I'm sure," said Hubert Scouten.

Angus rose quickly.

"We're not disputing that this witness saw Mr. Maywood riding through the woods that day, your Honor."

"Very well, very well," said the Judge, rapping with the gavel.

Procter glared in turn at the defendant, at Angus, and at the jury. Then he dismissed Hubert and called the next witness.

Mary Scouten took the stand and told the same story that her brother had told. Angus declined to cross-examine her.

He said, "We have no reason to disbelieve this young lady, Judge. No questions."

Then Albert Maple, the Sac and Fox Indian Agent, testified for the prosecution, establishing the corpus delicti and the money. He had been entertaining two deputy marshals from Ridgefield in his home when Hubert and Mary came riding their mules into the yard, excitedly describing the scene of multiple death that they had come upon in the woods. They had ridden eight miles, and they were at first incoherent from fright and fatigue. After going to the scene, Maple had identified the bodies as those of the Jake Flower family from Taney County, Missouri.

Angus began cross-examining the Agent in the same manner he had used with Hubert Scouten.

"Mr. Maple, I want to say first that I am sure you have been telling the truth to the best of your ability. My questions will not be for the purpose of tricking you, or crossing you up in any way."

"Very well, sir," Albert Maple said, nodding appreciatively.

He was a forthright, friendly man of forty-five. Because he spent a great deal of time outdoors, he was lean and muscular, tending to be wiry in physique. His skin was as dark as an Indian's during the summer, and here in November it still bore a substantial tan. It could reasonably be assumed that, as a professional liaison official between the Indians and the United States Government, Albert Maple would not be unduly eager to support the prosecution: even though he was Ben Procter's witness, he would answer responsibly any questions put to him by either side.

"Let me ask you," Angus said, "how many times you had seen Jake Flower in your life before you saw him dead."

"That's easy to remember, Mr. DeWolfe. Three times. That is, he had visited my Agency three times."

"How can you remember so accurately?"

"Well, he came through on his way to the run for the opening of the Un-assigned Lands. He was excited, talking about the farm he'd have after he'd claimed a homestead. He was wondering about how was the best way to make the run, whether to ride, or what. I told him I'd heard some were going in on the train, hoping to get into the interior faster. Jake thought that was a good idea. I must have talked to him two or three hours that night. He stayed over with us, then he set out the next morning after breakfast. We wished him luck as he rode away, and I had the fever myself. I wanted to go make that run the worst way."

"Tell us about the second time you saw him," Angus said.

"Well, after he had staked his claim, he came back through the reservation, happy as a jay bird. He said he decided to try entering the Lands by train from the south, and it had worked. He had jumped off the moving train and run three miles until he found his spot. Then he had staked his claim. He stayed with us again and told us all about the people he'd met up with out there. He said the government made them run the train slow so as to be fair to the other folks going in. It was interesting to talk to him, and we invited him to stop with us when he brought his family to the Territory."

"And that was the occasion of his third visit?"

"Yes, sir. About four weeks later, the Flowers camped overnight in a walnut grove just below my house. And we had another nice visit with them."

"I see." Angus went on quickly, without changing his casual tone: "And during that visit, while he was sitting on your front porch at dusk, he told you he was carrying some money with him?"

"Yes, sir."

"About three hundred dollars, I believe you said."

"That's right, Mr. DeWolfe."

"Can you remember exactly what he said about the three hundred dollars?"

"I think I can. He said he'd made up a list of materials he'd need to start framing a house. He wasn't going to build out of logs, because he'd always lived in a log house and he didn't want another one. And sod houses didn't last long enough, he said. He was going to frame one room, and then add to it as he could. He and his wife had also calculated how much they'd need for shoes, food and bolt goods the first season. I remember Jake telling me about this list of stuff, and he said, 'If I can buy a couple of shoats and grain ain't too high until I can grow me some, and if I can get my cow freshened, I'm going to make out all right. I've got three hundred bucks in cold cash in my poke, and that ought to put me over.' That's just about what he said."

"You're sure he said three hundred bucks?"

"Yes—I'm sure about that, all right."

"But you didn't see it, did you?"

"No. He said he had it in his poke."

"Do you know where his poke was at that time?"

"No. I supposed it was in his wagon."

"You didn't think it was on his person?"

"I didn't consider it much, to tell you the truth."

"Do you think he might have been saying 'in my poke' just as an expression—and might not have actually intended that the money was in a real poke?"

Albert Maple shrugged. "I wouldn't know, Mr. DeWolfe. I just remember that he said, 'I've got three hundred bucks in cold cash in my poke.'"

"Did he mention anything about the denomination of the money? Any way you could characterize it?"

"No. Not at all."

"Then it could have been in gold, silver, paper—anything, couldn't it?"

"Yes, sir. I've no idea about that."

"Then it's possible, for all you know, that Jake Flower had no money at all, isn't it?"

The agent seemed surprised at the question. He said, "I suppose so, Mr. DeWolfe. I know what he told me."

"Mr. Maple, if we could prove to you that Jake Flower was traveling without any money at all, would it surprise you greatly?"

"Yes, sir. It certainly would."

"But for all you know, it might be possible, mightn't it? Because you don't know that Jake Flower actually had any money, do you?"

"No, sir. I only know what he said."

"Why did you *suppose* the poke he mentioned was in his wagon?"

"Well, no good reason. I don't know why. It just entered my mind at the time."

"Mr. Maple, when Jake Flower came back through your agency after he had staked his claim, you said you had a nice visit with him, didn't you?"

"That's right."

"Did he mention anything about money then? Did he say he had had any trouble over money down in the Lands?"

"Come to think about it, he said some folks only wanted silver. Paper money wasn't trusted everywhere. That's all he said that I remember."

"Now let me ask you this: *if* Jake Flower was traveling with three hundred dollars," (Angus greatly emphasized the word if) "and *if* it had been three hundred *silver* dollars, he'd almost have to have had it in his wagon, wouldn't he?"

"Objection, your Honor," Ben Procter said. "This silly speculation is highly irrelevant and immaterial. Mr. Maple has said that he didn't see the money—he only knows what Jake Flower told him."

The Judge brought down his gavel and spoke to Angus, his mouth still grinning tightly.

"Objection sustained. Keep to the point, Counselor."

Angus hesitated. Then he asked, "Mr. Maple, you said it entered your head that the poke might have been in his wagon. Could it be that you remembered what he'd said about silver money——"

"Your Honor, I object to this speculation——"

"Sustained, sustained!"

"I have no further questions," Angus said, grinning broadly. "Thank you, Mr. Maple."

"I have a question," said Ben Procter, striding quickly to the witness stand. The courtroom strained to hear him. "Mr. Maple, you just now indicated that for all you know the money Jake Flower was carrying could have been gold, silver, paper—anything. It couldn't have been *Confederate* money, could it?"

"I wouldn't think so," Albert Maple replied, and the courtroom rocked with laughter. Judge Ring brought down the gavel hard. Ben Procter stepped back to emphasize his next question.

"In other words, Mr. Maple, it was good, United States spending money, the kind of money that a bandit would like to get his hands on?"

"Your Honor, I object——" Angus said quickly, but Judge Ring drowned him out with the gavel.

"Sustained. Mr. Procter, that kind of question is highly improper and you know it. Proceed to the point, or I shall dismiss this witness."

"That's all, your Honor," Ben Procter said.

But Angus remained on his feet.

"If it please the Court," he said, in a tone less merely indignant than morally shocked, "I should like to offer a vital correction to the record."

"And what is that?" Judge Ring asked.

"Mr. Procter just referred to the money Jake Flower was carrying, when in reality there is no proof that Jake Flower was carrying any money at all. I respectfully request that the prosecutor's question be corrected, or else stricken entirely from the record."

"It shall be stricken from the record," said the Judge, "and the jury will disregard any reference to it as an established fact. Step down, Mr. Maple."

Judge Ring drew his watch from his waistcoat pocket and frowned at it. He wound it with the gold key which dangled from the chain, then replaced the watch. He said, "We will stand in recess for one hour. The jurors are reminded of the rules of the court: they must not speak to each other or to anyone else about this case while they are away from the courtroom. This includes members of their families, friends, neighbors, townspeople, or newspaper people. Anyone trying to discuss the case with them will be in contempt of court and will be dealt with accordingly."

The Judge did not look at the jury while delivering his admonition: he looked at Angus. Then he brought down the gavel and strode from the platform through the back exit.

Ridgefield's noonday mealtime had been delayed all over town to coincide with the court's twelve-thirty recess. Many people remained in their seats in the courtroom, unwilling to take a chance on losing them; but talk of the trial quickly filled every eating establishment in the vicinity of the square. Colonel Beleau's connection with the case had been the most impressive development thus far.

"I'll bet that Indian is innocent," said a man in the Catfish Café. "The Colonel wouldn't be up there defending him if he wasn't."

"Maybe DeWolfe has got him fooled."

"I'll bet they're going to prove that Jake Flower wasn't carrying any money. That's what they're leading up to."

Newspaper reporters converged on Angus and the Colonel as they left the Federal Building.

"I'm sorry, gentlemen," Angus said. "I can't talk about a trial until it's over. See me in a couple of days."

Hoey Johnson, the *Monograph's* simpering star, was having a marvelous time being the center of attention. Every visiting reporter was invited to be his guest at the New Ridge dining room. Now he stepped out in front of them.

"Angus, Ben Procter says he expects another conviction. Can't you at least tell us whether you expect to get an acquittal?"

Angus didn't bother to answer, but Hoey's question caused him to remember Floyd Green. He glanced around, but Green was not in sight.

Disengaging himself from the crowd, he walked with the Colonel toward the hotel.

"Did you see Doc this morning?" he asked.

"He said he'd stop by the hotel for a minute. We'll have a chance to speak to him."

"I think Marcus looks fine, don't you?"

"It won't be hard for people to see him as an innocent man when the story starts coming out."

"Especially with you sitting beside him, Colonel."

Beleau cleared his throat in embarrassment.

"Colonel," Angus said as they walked together, "tell me about your friend, Floyd Green." The Colonel frowned and Angus went on hastily: "Janet told me last night about her romance with him ten or twelve years ago. She thinks her father ran him out of town. He doesn't look like the type who could be chased easily. Do you know anything about it?"

"It's better not to dig up the past, Angus."

He knew already that he'd hit on the truth.

"If you won't tell me, I'll ask Green himself. After all, Colonel, a former suitor of Janet's could turn into a rival. I need to know about him, don't I?" Angus tried to smile casually, but found it difficult. Because he'd hit on another truth?

"Floyd is a fine fellow. Doesn't Janet know why he left Ridgefield?"

"She suspects that the Judge had something to do with it." He paused, then decided to press the Colonel for more. "She told me she tore her dress while catching a bouquet at a wedding party and her father believed Floyd had torn it. We can conclude, I suppose, that the Judge thought Floyd had been molesting her. Or something of that nature." He found that his pulses pounded as he spoke of it.

The Colonel frowned, walking briskly. "Floyd and his father came to my home the next day. It was on Christmas, as I remember. They wanted to engage me as Floyd's counsel. Hanson Green was mad as a wild horse. He didn't believe his boy had mistreated the girl. Floyd said he hadn't, and I believed him, too. But after I looked into the situation, I could understand how the Judge might view it. I convinced them that it would be a good opportunity for Floyd to go to St. Louis or somewhere and learn a trade or a profession. He was interested in newspaper work even then. I helped him get a job on the *Express*. He learned about galleys, slugs and sticks in a hurry. He was printer's devil for less than a year before he started gathering personals and writing occasional bits for the paper. The *Light* hired him as a by-line reporter and he did so well that they sent him abroad." Then

Colonel Beleau added, "The best thing that ever happened to him was leaving Ridgefield."

"It certainly sounds like it."

"He's married now, and has two little girls. He brought them to see me."

"I'll be damned." Angus noticed that he felt a little better. Safer? he asked himself. "That's a happy story, isn't it, Colonel?"

"Very. For Floyd, anyway. I guess now we can say it's a happy story for Janet, too."

They reached the corner and turned down South Street.

"What did the Judge do?"

"Damn it, Angus, it doesn't matter now. It's past and forgotten."

"Janet hasn't forgotten."

"She will. And the sooner the better."

"I'll bet I know, Colonel. I'll bet the little sonofabitch charged that boy with attempted rape."

The Colonel flushed, terribly embarrassed.

"There wasn't a charge of any kind."

"But he *threatened* it?"

"Willard thought that was what had happened. But there was never a charge made against Floyd."

"Because he left town in a hurry."

"At my advice and insistence," the Colonel said quickly. "He told me that Janet didn't love him anyway—that she went out with him because she was lonely. I thought it was probably true, and I didn't see any sense in having a mess stirred up. So I convinced him and his father. Every young fellow has to leave home if he is going to fulfill his dream. I did it. You did it. The Judge did it—he left home when he was seventeen because he wanted to go to school. It's only natural—and those are probably lucky who have some additional force to propel them. They go sooner."

"Did you help Floyd financially, Colonel?"

"He paid back every cent. I'm proud of him. Floyd is one of my favorite people." Beleau cleared his throat. "I have always thought of you as being in his class, Angus. Except that he has more respect for his elders." Red-faced, the Colonel stepped up his pace.

"He's younger than I am," said Angus with an innocent shrug. "He should have."

Reaching the New Ridge, they went inside the lobby and stood for a moment at the entrance to the dining room.

"I'm going upstairs to get Janet. If I don't tell her what's going on, she may decide not to marry me. You know how women are."

"I'll excuse myself, Angus——"

"No you won't. I insist."

"I wouldn't like to intrude."

"You couldn't if you tried. Select a table for us, won't you?"

He left the Colonel at the dining-room door and crossed the lobby alone, trying to appear oblivious to the attention he attracted. He was uncomfortable in the public spotlight. He did not mind standing in the well of the court with all eyes on him; but the stares he drew in public places threatened the sense of anonymity with which he believed personal conduct should be privileged. He hurried up to the suite where Janet was acting as hostess for the witnesses he had brought from the Shawnee country.

Luke Sweeley met him at the door, wearing a new suit and looking every bit as splendid in his own way as Marcus Maywood. Indeed, Luke's bouncy manner suggested that he might break into a jig out of sheer exuberance.

"She ain't here, Angus," he said. "I'm staying with the old folks while she's gone."

"Where is she?"

"Said to tell you she was going to meet Floyd Green in the dining room." Luke gazed casually at the ceiling in the corner above Angus's head.

A small ugly bolt of anger shot through him. There was no denying it, he resented Floyd Green's intrusion; and his pulses were pounding again. . . .

Then he took himself in hand, and spoke to Marcus's mother, with Luke's assistance as interpreter, reassuring her that the trial was progressing as he had anticipated. Although the Shawnee woman was probably ten or twelve years younger than Luke, she looked much older. Sitting in a chair with a blanket drawn around her, she might have been older than the sky itself. Her face showed no emotion, but her eyes, half hidden in their wrinkled sockets, told him that she was alert.

When he returned to the dining room, he saw Janet at a table with Floyd Green. He went toward them, and Green rose to shake hands warmly.

"No doubt you're acquainted with Miss Ring?" the young man said, turning the statement into a question in mid-air. He found that he insisted on thinking of Floyd as a young man.

He said, "Yes, Miss Ring and I have met, as it happens."

He thought for a moment that Janet would giggle. He did not like giggling women.

"It would be a pleasure," Floyd Green said, "to have you join us, Mr. DeWolfe."

"No, thank you. I'd offend the other newsmen if I did. Hoey Johnson wouldn't tolerate it."

Floyd laughed. He was indeed a handsome young man. His face was strong in countenance. It was difficult to believe that he could ever have been what Janet called a "country boy."

"I understand, of course," he said.

Janet looked at Angus searchingly. He was certain that she was enjoying herself. He remembered some folklore about keeping women ignorant, pregnant and barefooted, for a happy, uncomplicated life. It seemed like a good idea.

He bowed and turned away from their table to look for Colonel Beleau. And when at last his eyes focused sufficiently to find the Colonel, he saw that Doc was also at the table.

He pulled out a chair and sat down with them.

"Were you in court, Doc?" he asked.

"Yes. I was there all morning."

"What did you think of the Judge?"

"The Colonel and I have just been talking about him. I'm amazed, Angus."

"He's under control, don't you think?"

"But he's not quite himself," Doc said. "I can't make it out."

"Will you be there this afternoon?"

"I've got to visit a couple of patients first—then I'll come back to the courtroom."

"I hope you will," Angus said.

A waiter appeared at their table and took their orders. Angus did not care what he ate. He glanced across the dining room at Janet and Floyd Green. He turned back to his own companions, noticing that both Doc and the Colonel were watching him with amusement.

He tried to appear unconcerned, but he wasn't fooling them. Chuckling merrily, the Colonel cleared his throat.

"I have heard," he said, "that green wood makes the hottest fire because it's so full of sap."

"Is that an old Chinese proverb, Colonel?" he asked bitterly.

"No," Colonel Beleau replied. "I don't think so. It's just a saying that I picked up while traipsing around the world gathering data on the barbaric rituals of various primitive tribes. . . . But it's robust imagery, don't you think?"

Before he could fully appreciate his fun, however, Beleau was embarrassed. His constitution simply had no tolerance for another man's discomfort.

"Forgive me, Angus," he said, flushing tomato-red. "I'm afraid I've made an ass of myself." The Colonel's misery put Angus in good humor again.

CHAPTER EIGHTEEN

"Order in the court. Please rise."

At the sound of Sam Doolan's voice in the courtroom, people shuffled noisily to their feet. Judge Ring came in, swinging his short arms in cadence with his strides. He brought down the gavel and sat in the high-backed chair behind the huge desk. Angus watched him.

The smile still clung to the lower half of his face, and his eyes bored into the courtroom.

"Call your next witness, Mr. Procter," he said.

Deputy marshal Dave Matthews testified.

He had been, along with deputy marshal Soby Walker, visiting the Sac and Fox Agent when Hubert and Mary Scouten rode their mules into the yard. He related the same story Albert Maple had told about going to the scene of the crime. Ben Procter loudly took him through every detail of that afternoon, producing the blood-caked quilt that had been wrapped around the body of Jake Flower's wife. Often his questions could have been objected to as leading the witness, but Angus kept his seat. He believed that juries were antagonized by constant objections and this story was not only well established, it was essentially harmless.

Procter finished examining Dave Matthews, whirling toward the defense table, his head high, his arms outstretched, pointing emphatically.

"You may cross-examine!" he shouted, at once demonstrating to the jury his moral outrage and theatrically embodying his condemnation of murder with total belief in the case he was building.

Angus's smile was broad. He rose from his chair.

"I have no questions, your Honor," he said in an easy voice, throwing in the slightest hint of amusement. "I'm sure Dave Matthews has told us nothing but the truth."

The courtroom laughed and Judge Ring instantly brought down his gavel.

"Step down, Mr. Matthews. Call your next witness, Mr. Procter."

The Judge pressed on, never permitting the tension to relax for a moment. He sat behind his desk, a relentless machine—grinding out the process of justice with technical precision, suffering the crowded room neither pathos, wrath, nor humor. And all the while he watched the defense table. Whatever feeling lay behind his frozen face was his own inscrutable secret. Angus marveled at him.

Soby Walker took the stand and repeated the story of the murder scene for the third time. The jury and spectators stretched and squirmed in their seats. Angus knew that Procter had sensed the ennui, for he left the Indian country abruptly and brought the narrative back to Ridgefield.

"And then what did you do?" he asked ponderously.

"I came back here to the Indian Office downstairs to see if Maywood was missing from work."

"You had thought of Maywood when Hubert and Mary Scouten described the man they saw riding from the murder scene?"

"Yes, sir——"

"Your Honor," Angus said, rising quickly, "Mr. Procter knows that Hubert and Mary Scouten didn't see that man riding from the murder scene——"

"Sustained," said the Judge. "The jury will disregard it. Mr. Procter, I am persuaded that you deliberately phrased that question to confuse the jury. Don't do it again. Proceed."

Ben Procter swallowed his angry surprise. Angus had to hide his own grin. He could not have counted the number of times he had seen Procter get away with such a tactic; he could understand the man's abysmal confusion now.

"Marshal," the prosecutor said, turning to face his witness again, "we want to be absolutely fair, don't we? Now . . . from the description the Scoutens gave you of a man they had seen riding in the woods *near* the murder scene, you thought immediately of Maywood. Isn't that what you said?"

"Yes, sir. Especially from their description of the brown and white paint."

"And you came straight to the Indian Office to check up on him?"

"That's right."

"Who did you talk to?"

"Roy Davenport."

"And what did you learn about Maywood?"

"He had been missing for almost a week. Roy didn't know where he was."

"Then what did you do?"

"Dave and I started looking for him. We went out to his cabin east of town on Luke Sweeley's place, but we couldn't find him. Luke didn't know where he was, either."

"How long did it take you to find him?"

"About a week. We took turns going to the cabin to see if there was any sign he'd been there."

"And after about a week you found him?"

"Yes, sir."

"What did you do?"

"Asked him some questions. He said he'd been down in the Nations, all right. Said he'd been staying with the Quaker schoolteacher during the time the murders were committed."

"That was his alibi?" Ben Procter shouted. He strode swiftly away from the witness stand, then looked back over his shoulder. "He told you that he had been staying with Paul Sparkman during the time the murders were committed?"

"Yes, sir."

Procter whirled around to face the witness stand. His tone inferred great cunning on Maywood's part.

"How long did he claim he'd been with the Quaker?"

"Three days. He said Tuesday, Wednesday and Thursday of the week in question. The killings took place on Wednesday."

Ben Procter now crept closer to the stand, significantly lowering his voice, stalking his denouement.

"And then what did you do, Marshal?"

"We searched his cabin."

"Did you find anything of interest when you searched the cabin?"

"Yes, sir. We found some money."

"How much money did you find?"

"Three hundred dollars. In the feather mattress on his bed. A rip in the seam had been sewed up."

"Did you ask him where he got the money?"

"Yes, sir. But he wouldn't tell me. He just refused to talk any more."

"Refused—completely?"

"He shut his mouth tight."

"Then what did you do?"

"We arrested him on suspicion, and brought him in."

"I have one more question to ask you, Marshal." Procter started walking away from the stand again, beginning the question as he went. "When you examined the money you found in Maywood's mattress, you looked it over very carefully, I presume."

"That's right, I did."

"Tell us," said the prosecutor, stopping and staring up at the ceiling of the courtroom, "was it *Confederate* money?"

"No, sir, it was legal tender, all right."

"Your witness!" Ben Procter cried triumphantly in the direction of the defense table. He waited until the courtroom had tittered and the Judge had vigorously brought down his gavel before returning to his own table, glaring at Maywood as he passed.

One thing could clearly be deduced about the prosecutor, Angus reflected wryly: the man wanted it plain to everyone how deeply he hated sin.

Angus waited until Procter had taken his seat before rising. Then he leaned over and spoke to Marcus in the hope of offsetting some of Ben Procter's loud contempt of the boy.

"How do you feel?" he whispered.

"All right, I guess," Marcus said, a smile quavering on his mouth.

"We're doing fine. Keep up your look of confidence."

"I'll try," Marcus replied.

Angus rose and spoke from where he stood.

"May I ask, Marshal," he said, shaping his words crisply, "if it was three hundred *silver* dollars that you found in Mr. Maywood's mattress?"

"No, sir," the Marshal answered, amid a ripple of laughter which was instantly squelched by the Judge's gavel.

"What kind of money was it? Do you remember?"

"Yes, sir. It was ten-dollar silver certificates."

"United States Government silver certificates?"

"That's right."

"How many were there?"

The witness grinned, realizing that he would look pretty silly if he couldn't count.

"Thirty," he said, as the courtroom snickered in amusement.

"Did you notice the condition of them?"

"What do you mean?"

"Well, if they'd been in somebody's pocket when he turned over in a boat and got wet, they might show they'd been wet. Or if they were old, and had been passed around a lot, they might have been very dirty. Or they might have been scorched in a fire. Did you notice anything of that nature about them? Think carefully," he cautioned.

The deputy marshal considered for a moment, stroking his chin with a big rough hand.

"I believe they were dirty, Mr. DeWolfe."

"*Worn* dirty?"

"I really don't remember very well. I just seem to recall that they were maybe a little dirty."

"What did you do with them?"

"I turned them over to the district attorney's office."

"To Mr. Procter?"

"No, I gave them to Red Molloy, I believe."

"And you are certain that there were three hundred dollars' worth of ten-dollar bills? All silver certificates?"

"Yes, I'm sure of that."

"Thank you, Marshal. I have no further questions, your Honor."

For the next hour, Ben Procter swirled and cavorted in the well of the court, propelling his case against Marcus Maywood toward its damning conclusion. Angus helped him keep up his pace by declining to cross-examine whenever possible. The big moment of the prosecution would come, he knew, when Procter called Paul Sparkman to the stand.

It went fast.

Roy Davenport, the Area Supervisor of Indian Affairs, for whom Marcus had worked in the Ridgefield office, told about the boy suddenly leaving his job. No, they hadn't given him any time off, and he hadn't said anything about leaving. He had merely "turned up missing" one morning. He had never returned because he had been arrested about ten days later.

Angus rose to ask a single question. Had Marcus been a satisfactory employee prior to his disappearance? Oh, yes, said the Area Supervisor; Marcus had been an excellent worker on the census lists—no complaint on that score.

"No further questions," he said.

"Step down, Mr. Davenport," the Judge intoned. "Call your next witness, Mr. Procter."

Ben Procter stood and stared at the jury for a long, speculative moment. Then he addressed the bench.

"Your Honor, the Government desires to call only one more witness. That will be Paul Sparkman."

Angus felt the courtroom react. Everyone knew that the Quaker's testimony in the first trial had been the essential evidence against Marcus. He watched Paul Sparkman, immaculate in black, cross the well, turn around the open end of the palisade, and proceed to the witness stand. He affirmed his honesty before the eyes of God and everyone waited intently.

Ben Procter's voice, as he asked the witness's name, assumed a tone of reverential solicitude.

"And your occupation?"

"I am a teacher in a private school on the Shawnee Indian reservation."

"May I ask under whose auspices?"

"The Society of Friends."

Sparkman was sitting erectly. His voice was calm and assured. Angus noted that he never took his eyes off the prosecutor.

"Should I not call you *Reverend* Sparkman?"

"Thee may call me Friend," replied Paul Sparkman, smiling pleasantly as the courtroom laughed.

Now Procter came from his table and stood in the center of the well, his feet apart and his hands clasped behind him. He asked a barrage of questions designed to show how long the witness had been conducting the school and the nature of his work. Yes, one of his pupils had been Marcus Maywood.

"Can you tell us whether any unusual incident occurred during the last week of May, with respect to this defendant?"

"The lad paid me a visit," said Sparkman, sitting stiffly in his black clothes, his large shoulders bulging.

"He came from Ridgefield down to your home on the Shawnee reservation?"

"Thee's quite correct."

"Will you tell the court and the jury about that visit?"

Paul Sparkman hunched his shoulders, trying to relax in the chair, and told his story: Marcus had ridden his pony (the brown and white paint, Ben Procter interjected) into the Sparkmans' yard that afternoon, and had inquired if Sparkman would be willing to do him a great and urgent favor. There was a rumor in Ridgefield that an Indian was being sought for questioning with regard to something that Marcus didn't know anything about, and since he had recently been visiting his mother over near Bundy's Gap, he would have no one to verify his whereabouts for the preceding few days. He wondered if Sparkman would be good enough to say that Marcus had been with him during the past week.

"And what did you tell him?"

"I'm afraid I may have let the lad believe I'd do it." The Quaker's sober face was deeply concerned. "I was trying to ease his mind without directly saying no. Thee must understand that the lad was always——"

"We're only concerned with what he is *now*," Procter cut in. "Would you tell us whether you asked him the nature of the trouble he was in?"

Sparkman frowned.

"Naturally, I asked him why he thought they might be searching for him. He said he was not certain that he was being sought, but *feared* he might be. He felt an Indian wouldn't be believed by the deputy marshals unless a white man verified his story——"

"Now, Friend," Ben Procter said quickly, reddening a bit, "just answer my questions, please."

Angus noticed that Sparkman could not restrain a tight smile.

"Ask thy questions," he said gravely.

"Can you tell us exactly the date of the defendant's visit to your home when he asked you to alibi for him?"

"I would not like to call it an alibi——"

"Can you give us a definition of the word 'alibi'?" the prosecutor snapped.

"Very well, call it an alibi, if thee desire," said Sparkman wearily.

Procter moved toward the stand.

"I don't wish to characterize it falsely. If it wasn't an alibi, what was it that this defendant asked you for?"

Paul Sparkman stiffened again in the chair.

"It was an alibi. And the date was twenty-third of May, this year of our Lord."

"And he asked you to alibi for the entire previous week? Is that correct?"

"Thee's correct again."

"If I tell you that four people were murdered near Bundy's Gap on May nineteenth, would you agree that the alibi you were asked for would cover that date very nicely?"

"It would cover that date, yes."

Ben Procter turned his back on the witness and gazed abruptly at the ceiling.

"Is it fair to say that you had always considered yourself a friend of the defendant prior to that time?"

"It is fair for thee to say that, if thee also add that I am still his friend."

Procter blew his cheeks full of air, then let it out slowly.

"Is it fair to say that, as a believing Quaker, you are a friend of *all* people, whether they be innocent citizens, or depraved felons, or something in between?—just answer my question, please."

"Thee can say that, most certainly."

"Did you collect funds to retain counsel for this defendant at his first trial?"

"I did."

"And you contributed to those funds out of your own pocket?"

"Thee's quite correct."

"You would have done as much for any former student who happened to be in trouble, wouldn't you?"

"Thee can be most assured I would."

"And are you helping pay the cost of his defense in this proceeding also?"

"I am," Paul Sparkman said.

Ben Procter whirled around.

"And you are testifying against the defendant because your Christian conscience requires that you tell the truth? Isn't that the simple fact of the case?"

"No," said the Quaker evenly.

Procter was taken aback. He glared at the witness.

"Do you mean that you're *not* testifying to the truth?"

"Thee must not put words into my mouth. I mean that it is not the *simple* fact of the case. It is indeed a complex fact."

"But you have been telling the truth, haven't you?"

"God is my witness."

"Even though it has been painful to you?"

"Truth is not painful to me."

"You didn't like it when you were subpoenaed, did you?"

"I was sorry to have to come."

"But your Christian conscience required you to come here and tell the truth?"

"If the point must be labored."

Procter whirled toward the defense table.

"You may cross-examine," he said grimly.

The courtroom was again as silent as death. Angus felt all eyes slowly turn on him. This is your challenge, the silence seemed to be saying: let's see what you can do about it. . . . He rose from his chair.

"I have no questions, your Honor," he said politely. Then he sat down again.

He had taken the courtroom by surprise. Ben Procter, the jury, and even the Judge, had clearly expected him to seize upon the demonstrated friendliness of the Quaker in an attempt to draw divergent inferences, at least, from the alibi request. He was pleased to believe that he had brought the surprise off well. The attention and consequently the imagination of the jury had been diverted to it, thus dampening the effect of Ben Procter's big gun.

"That's the case for the Government, your Honor," Procter said, still flustered.

The Judge rapped sharply for silence.

"Are you ready for the defense, Mr. DeWolfe?"

Angus rose with calculated deliberateness.

"Your Honor, I move for a dismissal of the indictment on the grounds that the Government has offered nothing but conjecture and speculation against my client."

The cold half-smile did not alter on the Judge's face. He said, "That's a matter for the jury to decide, Counselor."

"Respectfully," Angus said grimly, "I urge you to——"

"Your motion is denied," the Judge replied, equally grim. "You may now deliver your opening statement to the jury, and then proceed with your witnesses."

"It is half past four, your Honor. Could we have a brief recess? My witnesses will be brought immediately to the witness room. They are over at the New Ridge."

"Will twenty minutes be enough time, Counselor?"

"Yes, I think so."

"Then we will resume at ten minutes to five," said the Judge. He gave a cursory rap with his gavel and strode from the platform. The spectators rose to their feet to stretch, and waves of gabbled speculation cascaded over the courtroom.

Angus spoke quickly to the Colonel.

"Will you go to the hotel after them?" he asked.

"Yes. Do you think the Judge will try to push on through tonight, Angus?"

"I hope so. I've seen him take testimony until midnight. My guess is that he'll call a supper recess and continue." He added in a very low voice, "Suggest to Janet that she might go visit her mother while the other people are up here."

"Very well," Beleau replied, leaving in a hurry.

Angus went with Marcus to the prisoner's room. He was pleased with the boy's strong attitude. They sat side-by-side on a bench in the tiny cubicle behind the main stair well.

"Now how do you feel?" he asked.

Marcus moistened his dry lips and clenched his jaws. "A little nervous, I guess."

"Are you ready to tell your story?"

"Yes."

"I've decided to lead off with you, if you're sure you're up to it."

"I'm ready."

"I'm going to set a trap for Procter, Marcus. We can knock him off balance in the very beginning, if he falls for it. You've got to talk straight to him, with plenty of guts. Can you do it?"

"I think so."

"All you have to do is tell exactly what happened; but tell it right out, without hesitating. Take your time when you need to—you don't need to rush your answers. But speak right up, all the time."

"Do you think they'll ask me why I went down to get the money, Mr. DeWolfe?"

He said quickly, "I don't know. Maybe not. But if Procter asks you, I'll object and force the Judge to rule on it. He knows why you needed money."

"Will he make me tell it?"

"I don't know. He'll have a perfectly easy way out, if he wants it. Janet doesn't mind if you tell."

"That's the only part I don't like. I'd hate to do that."

"You'll have to if the Judge demands it."

Marcus swallowed.

"All right."

Angus paused for a moment, then said, "I told you I'd write to a friend in Washington about you—remember? Well, I did . . . and I have already received an answer."

The boy's face perked up.

"You have?"

"I've been waiting to tell you—I thought it would give you a lift. Mr. McCordle has spoken to someone he knows in the Department of Indian Affairs. He is sure you can get employment. Now all we have to do is finish this business, and get your money back. You are going to need some traveling funds. Are you ready?"

Marcus grinned.

"I'm ready," he said. "And thanks a lot, Mr. DeWolfe."

"Don't let Procter's loud blustering upset you. He's a ham actor—everybody knows he's just creating dramatic effects. You can handle him if you simply stick to your story. If he asks you a question that implies an answer you don't want to give, tell him so. I'll watch for that, and protect you with objections. You don't have to answer any question until the Judge directs you to, so don't let Procter bully you."

"Mr. DeWolfe," the boy said, "did Janet promise my mother she wouldn't ever have anything to do with me?"

"Yes," Angus said.

"I hope we can leave her name out of this. I wouldn't want to embarrass her. She's been good to me."

"That will be up to the Judge. You must tell the truth."

A sardonic smile gathered on the boy's face. He said, "Everyone is supposed to tell the truth in your court except the lawyers."

"Lawyers don't testify. If they did, they'd tell the truth."

"They should anyway," Marcus Maywood said.

CHAPTER NINETEEN

The witnesses for the defense were closeted by Sam Doolan in the witness room and guarded by a special deputy marshal.

Angus returned to the courtroom with Colonel Beleau. The Colonel handed him an envelope.

"Janet sent you this," he said.

While they waited for the Judge to emerge through the back entrance, Angus read the note. It had been hastily scrawled on hotel stationery.

Dearest:

I went to see Mother for a few minutes this morning. She told me about my father, and the handicap you are working under. You mustn't let it influence your fight for Marcus. (I hope my concern that you might doesn't demean you.) My father is capable of feigning ill health. He may actually have Doctor McKay more upset than is realistic.

Darling, I think you were jealous in the dining room. It gave me a wonderful feeling. I really am a terrible person. I'm so glad Floyd is happy. He told me all about his family.

My father is treacherous. Mother believes he knows about us. Don't let him bully you because of me.

All my love,
Janet

Judge Ring brought down his gavel.

Angus stayed on his feet. The inevitable hush came over the courtroom quickly.

"Proceed, Mr. DeWolfe," said the Judge.

Angus wondered, as he observed the little man who would become his father-in-law if fate should properly conspire with human forces already in motion, whether the oddly frozen smile had not almost disappeared. His memory of it throughout the tedious day was sufficiently indelible to suggest the smile upon the Judge's face even if it was not quite there. But the eyes showed specific emotion, which was a change.

Angus stood before the jury, facing the twelve solemn finders of the facts.

"Gentlemen," he said, "my associate, Colonel Beleau, reminded you before you were impaneled that traditional justice required an open mind on your part until the conclusion of all the testimony. I am sure your minds are still open." They nodded as though they believed it themselves.

And after a pause: "Marcus Maywood is innocent of the terrible charge against him. You will know, when we have concluded, that he is innocent. You won't have to worry about reasonable doubt. You will have no doubt at all. I shall not give you any flowery oratory because, frankly, it disgusts me. We do not dispute any of the testimony you have already heard. But we will show you that this case of circumstantial evidence is treacherous and misleading. I will now begin by calling Mr. Maywood to the stand, to let him tell you himself that he is innocent."

The Judge impatiently gaveled the room into silence.

Marcus took the stand, raised his right hand, and swore on the white man's Bible to tell the truth.

Angus stood in the center of the well before him.

"Mr. Davenport has told his Honor and the jury, Marcus, that you did not come to work one day last May. It was May seventeenth to be exact. Is that the truth?"

"Yes, it is, Mr. DeWolfe."

"Where did you go that day?"

"Down to the Shawnee country to see my mother," Marcus said.

"How long did it take you to get there?"

"Well, I got there on Wednesday. I left Ridgefield on Monday night."

"Did you pass near Bundy's Gap on your way to visit your mother?"

"Yes, sir. I was thinking, as I passed the Gap, that my father had been killed there several years before."

"What did you do while you were down there?"

"I asked my mother to come to Ridgefield to live with me."

"Is that all?"

"She gave me some money, but she wouldn't come to live with me. She didn't want to live in the white man's world."

"Then what did you do?"

"I returned to Ridgefield."

"Tell us about your arrival back in Ridgefield."

Marcus swallowed and shifted himself in the chair, sitting erectly, his young brown face sober and responsive. Angus thought he was doing splendidly.

"I rode in at night, through the woods behind Big Creek, and left my pony in Luke Sweeley's barn, where I always keep him. After I brushed him down, I started to my own place, through a path that comes in from the back along the creek. I heard some men talking, and I stopped to listen. They were the deputy marshals, and they were looking for me. I didn't know exactly what had happened, but I could tell they thought I had killed somebody. I hid until they went away. Then I went inside and put the money in my mattress. I was afraid they might come back before I got it sewed up."

"Go on," Angus said. "What did you do then, Marcus?"

"I went back and got my pony and headed for the Nations again. To see Paul Sparkman."

"Why did you want to see him?"

"To ask him to say that I'd been with him the past few days."

"Why did you do that?"

"Because I knew the marshals thought I'd killed somebody, and they wouldn't believe me unless a white man could tell them where I had been."

"You were really *that* frightened, Marcus?"

"Many of my people have been killed by white men, Mr. DeWolfe. My father was killed," he said bitterly, "and no one was ever prosecuted for it."

"Then what did you do?" Angus asked, gently pushing him away from the emotional consideration of his father.

"I went home again to Ridgefield. And right away they arrested me."

Angus paused in his questioning. He mopped his face with his handkerchief, then returned it to his pocket. He pointed his finger, not accusingly, but for emphasis.

"Marcus, answer me truthfully. Did you ever in your life see Jake Flower or any member of his family?"

"No, sir," Marcus said.

The courtroom was so quiet that Angus could hear his own breath. He said, "*Never,* Marcus? Not even after they were dead?"

"No, sir."

"And you tried to fake the alibi only because you feared nobody would believe you?"

"Yes, sir."

"Then you must be wholly innocent of this awful charge against you, aren't you, Marcus?"

"Yes, Mr. DeWolfe. I am."

Angus turned toward Ben Procter.

"Your witness, Mr. Prosecutor," he said with contempt, and sat down, thus quietly tossing the ball to his adversary.

For a moment, he feared that Procter wouldn't catch it. The man was quite off his guard, however, sitting dumbly in his chair beside Red Molloy. He leaped to his feet and scrambled toward the witness, fearful, as Angus had hoped, that the jury might believe him reluctant to cross-examine. But he was not reluctant; his burst of action now proved that.

And it proved also, Angus was thinking, that the man's egotism was able to deceive him completely. Procter was intelligent enough to have seen the trap if he had called upon his intellect; and he was experienced enough to know when not to cross-examine. But some overwhelming force in him needed desperately to make a spectacular show: some blind quality in him obscured the possibility that others might also have brains—even cunning.

He drew himself up large before the witness stand.

"Maywood," he said, "let's talk about that money. Shall we?"

"All right," Marcus said soberly.

"That is just about the most interesting thing we could talk about, don't you think?" Procter asked.

"I guess so," Marcus replied.

Angus choked back a smile. His pulses were pounding. Procter thrust his face forward.

"Did you say your *mother* gave you that money?"

"Yes, sir."

"That's not true, is it?"

"Yes, sir. It is true."

Procter nodded his head in satiric disbelief.

"Let's go back to that Monday night in Ridgefield. You saddled your paint in Luke Sweeley's barn and started riding toward the Nations. Is that right?"

"Yes, sir."

"Where did you sleep that night?"

"I rode all night."

"And all the next day?"

"Yes, sir."

"Where did you spend the next night? That would be Tuesday night."

"Near the Cimarron," Marcus said. "On the edge of the Sac and Fox."

"Did you sleep there?"

"For a while."

"And then you went on south?"

"Yes, sir. To my own people in the Shawnee village."

"You passed by Bundy's Gap?"

"Yes, sir."

"Did you see a fire in the woods? With a burning wagon?"

"No, sir."

"You started the fire yourself, didn't you?"

"No, sir."

"Did you see a wagon with a man, woman and two children in it?"

"No, sir."

"You didn't see anything like that?"

"No, sir."

"And you went to your mother's home?"

"Yes, sir."

"You were riding fast, weren't you?"

"Yes, sir."

"Why were you in such a hurry?"

"I wanted to see my mother."

"How long had it been since you had seen your mother?"

"About two years."

"Why did you want to see her in such a hurry?"

"To ask her for some money."

"You needed money for something?"

"Yes, sir."

Procter lowered his voice significantly.

"What for?"

Marcus moistened his lips and glanced at Angus, who nodded to him.

"I had decided to ask a girl to marry me. And I needed some money." Marcus looked down at his lap.

Ben Procter backed away two steps, raising his shoulders again.

"You wanted to get married? Were you courting a girl?"

"Yes, sir." Now Marcus looked up at the prosecutor, and added, "I was trying to, anyway."

"Could you tell us who the girl is, so that we can——?"

Angus was on his feet. He had been watching the Judge who had leaned forward in his chair.

"Your Honor," he said, "I object to this line of questioning. It is highly immaterial and irrelevant. It does not——"

"Sustained," the Judge said brusquely.

Ben Procter whirled toward the bench, astonished.

"But your Honor——"

"Sustained, Mr. Procter! This defendant is not on trial for trying to court some girl. Proceed with your cross-examination."

Angus settled back, exchanging glances with Marcus. The boy was relieved.

"All right, Maywood," Ben Procter went on, his manner scalded by the rebuff. "You needed some money, and you rode all the way to the Shawnee village to ask your mother to give it to you. But you hadn't seen her in two years. Did you know she had money?"

"Well, I knew that——"

"Answer my question. Did you know that she had money?"

"She didn't exactly have it."

"Oh, she didn't exactly have it? Are we supposed to believe that you rode for two days to ask her for some money that she didn't exactly have? Is that what you want us to believe?"

Angus rose again.

"Your Honor, I must object to this. Mr. Procter is arguing with the witness."

"Sustained," said the Judge. And Angus noticed that, so intent was he upon Marcus's answers to the questions, Judge Ring was leaning almost out of his chair. "Cross-examine, Mr. Procter. Don't argue with the witness. Proceed, proceed!"

"Very well, Judge," Procter said, flushing angrily. "So your mother didn't exactly have the money you asked for. Please explain that to the jury. If she didn't exactly have it, where was it?"

Marcus swallowed again, glanced fleetingly at Angus, then said, "It was in my father's grave near Owl Creek, Mr. Procter."

"What?" cried the prosecutor. A wave of murmurs rose from the courtroom and the Judge furiously pounded the gavel for silence.

"That is right," said Marcus. "I went down to ask my mother if I could have it."

Ben Procter turned his back on the witness stand and stroked his chin. He was looking up thoughtfully at the ceiling, or perhaps, Angus thought, at God. And he would need God's help if he went much further—for it was clear that he did not yet perceive that he was defeating himself.

"So now you claim to have gotten the money out of your father's grave? You never claimed that before, did you?"

"No, sir."

"But it seems like a good story to you now? Is that what you think?"

"No, sir."

Procter whirled toward him.

"You *don't* think it's a good story?"

"No, sir. I think it is a disgusting story, and I'm very sorry I did it."

The courtroom tittered excitedly, and the sound had a different quality than it had had all during the day. Angus was as excited as anyone. The crowd was already moving its sympathy over to Marcus's side. The extra something in the whispers—the touch of a new sweep of interest—told him.

Procter was floundering now, like a buffalo with a shot in its shoulder.

"Where is this grave you claim to have robbed?" he demanded.

Marcus was silent.

"Did you hear my question?"

"Yes, sir."

"There *is* such a grave, isn't there?"

"Yes, sir."

"Where is it? Answer my question."

"I didn't claim to have robbed it," Marcus said evenly.

"You took the money out of it, didn't you?"

"But my mother had given it to me."

"Was it hers to give to you?"

"Yes, sir."

"Did she put it in the grave?"

"No, sir. Da-ni-mah put it there."

"Da-ni-mah? Well, well—who is Da-ni-mah?"

"The wise elder of our clan. He conducted my father's burial. He is going to testify later——"

"I didn't ask you who would testify later!"

Ben Procter knew now that he had lost. Angus could see it on his face as he glared at the defense table, scowling in bitter, frustrated rage. Procter then turned toward the bench, a helpless supplicant before the altar of the little Judge's madness.

Angus's gaze followed him and fell upon the Judge. Judge Ring didn't know it yet. His eyes were wide like fishes' eyes, his face as white as plaster behind the bushy brows and whiskers; but he was still determined. He was staring at Marcus, ignoring Ben Procter.

Colonel Beleau tugged at Angus's coat.

"Ben knows," the Colonel whispered.

"He won't go much further," Angus said. "He's getting in deeper every step he takes."

"That was a dastardly trap you set for him, Angus."

"I offered him a way out last week," Angus said, unable to conceal his disgust. "It will make a stronger impression on the jury to let him tear his own case apart. I've been watching the Judge. He isn't convinced yet."

"I hope Doc is in the courtroom," the Colonel replied, looking around.

Procter decided, apparently, to make one more effort to find a spot that would hold him up. He hunched his shoulders, brought himself to all his height, and assumed a giant attitude.

"Maywood," he said, imperiously feigning the preparation of a knockout blow, "if your mother gave some money to a wise elder to put into the grave, perhaps you can tell us where she got it. Do you know where she got that much money?"

"Yes, sir."

Marcus's confident answer was like a shot into the heart. Procter visibly stumbled.

"Where?" he asked, with no power behind his question.

"From a drover by the name of Clayt Mosley who bought some horses from our people at the time my father was killed by two white men. I heard the shots myself. I was riding alongside him, and they yelled, 'Injuns!' —and opened fire. I can still see the flames, Mr. Procter. Those men were never arrested. I can describe them to you and give you their names if you are interested. Mr. Mosley is here to testify, and he can tell you even more about them."

Now Marcus stopped abruptly. He was fighting tears. He sat rigidly in the witness chair, looking straight ahead, his nostrils flared, his eyes moist.

Ben Procter shrugged and turned toward the bench.

"No further questions, your Honor," he said, and walked to his table, his shoulders slumping.

Angus got to his feet.

"Your Honor, I need only a moment of redirect examination."

Judge Ring did not take his eyes off Marcus.

"Proceed," he said.

Angus remained at his table, speaking across the well, not loudly, for there was no sound to distract him.

"You told us, Marcus," he said, "that your mother gave you permission to take the money from your father's grave. Is that correct?"

"Well, she didn't at first, Mr. DeWolfe. When I first asked her, she said no. She even told me that I was not her son if I took it."

"Why did she feel so strongly?"

"She thought it would be a disgrace for me to open the grave. But I told her I was going to take it anyway. She followed me to the burial ground on Owl Creek and talked to me about it again. Then she told me it would be all right."

"So you did actually have her permission to take it?"

"Yes, sir."

"And when she testified in the first trial that she gave it to you, she was telling the truth?"

"Yes, sir."

"And you dug it out of the grave?"

"Yes, sir."

"What condition was the money in, Marcus?"

"It was a little mouldy, Mr. DeWolfe. Da-ni-mah had buried it in the sacred tobacco pouch, and that protected it some, I guess."

"How much money was in the pouch?"

"Three hundred and twenty dollars."

"In what denominations, Marcus?"

"All ten-dollar bills."

"And you later sewed them into your mattress in Ridgefield?"

"I sewed three hundred dollars in the mattress. I kept out twenty dollars

[176]

because I was going back to see Paul Sparkman, and I thought I might need some of it."

"Two ten-dollar bills?"

"Yes, sir."

"What did you do with them?"

"After I got home, before I was arrested, I put them up on a beam in Luke Sweeley's barn, with a rock on top so they wouldn't blow away."

"Did you ever tell anyone you had put two ten-dollar bills up there in Luke Sweeley's barn?"

"No one except you, Mr. DeWolfe."

Angus drew two ten-dollar silver certificates from his coat pocket and walked around to the witness stand.

"Will you examine these, Marcus, and tell us if they look like the same ones you put up there?"

"Yes—they do," he said after a moment. "They still look mouldy."

"Your Honor," said Angus, "I would like to place these in evidence for the defense."

"Let me see them," said the Judge.

Angus took them to the bench and handed them up. Judge Ring looked them over carefully.

"They *are* mouldy," he said. "Very well—we'll mark them defense exhibit number one. Hand them to the clerk, and proceed, Mr. DeWolfe."

Angus returned to his table.

"Now, Marcus, will you describe the pouch the money was buried in?"

"It was a buckskin pouch, about this big," he said, holding out his hands.

"About nine inches across, would you say?"

"Yes, sir. It had a drawstring running through it."

"A buckskin string?"

"Yes, sir. Sacred tobacco is always sprinkled into a grave from a pouch like that."

Angus drew the pouch from his portfolio, held it up for a moment, then took it to the stand.

"Is this the pouch the money was buried in, Marcus?"

The boy looked over the pouch, which was in turn passed up to the bench for the Judge's inspection. He identified it, and marked it defense exhibit number two.

Angus returned to the center of the well and stood facing Marcus quietly.

Then he said, raising his voice for emphasis, "Tell the jury, Marcus May-wood, why you did not reveal this story before."

The boy moistened his dry lips again, and took a grasp on the arms of the witness chair. "I didn't think anyone would believe me, for one thing.

And I was ashamed of it until you talked to me. My mother believed the money was evil. She shamed me for wanting it."

"You were so ashamed that you risked being hanged?"

"I thought they'd hang me anyway."

"That is all from this witness, your Honor," Angus said.

The Judge was transfixed. Slowly he forced himself to turn from the stand to Ben Procter.

"Have you any more questions, Mr. Prosecutor?" he asked trenchantly.

"No, Judge," Procter said without getting up.

Now the Judge peered at Marcus again, studying the boy's face and countenance. Angus watched him.

"The Court has one question to ask before you leave the stand." Judge Ring rose from his high-backed chair to ask it. "Are you telling the truth," he asked, fairly shouting, startling Marcus and the entire courtroom, "or is this all a pack of lies cooked up between you and your attorney?"

"I'm telling the truth," Marcus said bitterly.

Still standing, the Judge cried, "Step down!"

His gaze followed the boy all the way around the palisade of pickets and across the well to his seat beside Colonel Beleau. Then it descended upon Angus and the eyes were those of a fish that had been hooked, but somehow did not seem to perceive it yet.

"Mr. DeWolfe," he said, "if I discover any evidence of subornation, I will not only cite you for contempt, I will submit it to the Grand Jury."

"I am prepared to offer corroborating testimony to this boy's story, Judge. I have no fear that you will discover anything except the truth."

"Then call your next witness!"

Angus felt his blood pounding. He held himself carefully under control. And he breathed an inward sigh: he had feared the Judge would declare a recess, and he wanted to keep going without interruption. It was now after six o'clock. He knew he had given his case the proper momentum and he wanted no distraction at this time.

"The defense calls Silas Hennessey," he said.

The courtroom became noisy, for almost everyone knew Silas Hennessey, but no one knew what connection he might have with the case. Judge Ring viciously pounded the gavel again and again.

"Silence!" he ordered. "This is a courtroom, not a bawdy house. Light the lamps, Marshal—all of them. Bring in the witness, Mr. Doolan!"

His voice now bore the sound of desperation.

CHAPTER TWENTY

Trials, after they reached a certain point, Angus had often noticed, had a way of leaning forward, headed for home, as it were, with intractable wills of their own. This trial was no exception. He found himself bracing against its forward thrust, trying to check its momentum sufficiently to tighten the simple strands of Marcus's story.

The courtroom, he knew, was deeply impressed. The jury would now be watching the Judge, waiting to take its cue from him: the jurors' minds would be free and objective as soon as his was. Angus watched him, too.

Silas Hennessey reached the stand and identified himself as a teller in the Farmers' Bank of Ridgefield. He was a mild and genial man of thirty-one who, with Abe Heller, had often been a friendly adversary of Angus and Billy Moss at the rook table. He sat in the witness chair as easily as if he were dealing the cards in Mrs. Borden's living room.

"Silas," Angus asked, after preliminaries had been established, "do you remember taking an unusual deposit at the bank during the last week of May?"

"Yes, I do," said Silas Hennessey. "Red Molloy deposited three hundred dollars in ten-dollar bills to the district attorney's special account."

"Do you remember the deposit distinctly?"

"Yes, as it happens, I do."

"Why do you remember it so well, Silas?"

"Because Red told me it was the money that had been found in connection with the Flower murders."

"Was there anything unusual about the ten-dollar bills?"

"They were mouldy. I kept them out of my drawer for a while, wondering if I should retire them from circulation. We often do that with paper money that is torn or damaged."

"You remember distinctly that it was moulded?"

"Yes. Red and I were laughing about it. Red said it looked like it'd been buried somewhere."

Judge Ring gaveled furiously against the burst of excitement throughout the room.

"Silence, silence!"

Angus glanced at Red Molloy who was looking ruefully at his boss, the prosecutor.

He began again, after a long moment of thoughtful silence, "Did you take the money out of circulation, Silas?"

"No, I decided it wasn't that bad. I put it in my drawer and it went into general circulation again."

"But you remember it well, don't you?"

"Yes, I do."

Angus picked up defense exhibit number one, the two ten-dollar silver certificates that had come from Luke Sweeley's barn. He showed them to the bank teller.

"Can you tell us whether these are in a similar condition to the bills Red Molloy deposited? The ones," Angus added with a grin, "that Red thought might have been buried?"

Silas Hennessey looked them over carefully.

"These are dried out," he said. "That would be a difference. Those others seemed a little damp when I saw them."

"Aside from that, can you see any resemblance in their condition?"

"Yes, they're discolored. They look like they've been wet. Or at least damp. They're a little mouldy, the same as Red's deposit."

"Silas, were you subpoenaed to the court today?"

"Subpoenaed? No, of course not."

"Why did you come?"

"Because you said the jury ought to hear what I knew about the condition of that money, for whatever it's worth."

"Thank you." He turned to Ben Procter. "You may cross-examine."

Procter was leaning on an elbow, his chin resting languorously in his palm. "No questions," he said, without looking at the bench.

Angus was watching the Judge, who now turned with a visible sneer from Ben Procter to Silas Hennessey.

"The Court has a few questions, Mr. Hennessey," he said.

"Yes, sir?" Silas said.

"You testified that you put the three hundred dollars back into general circulation, didn't you?" The Judge's voice was rising into its shrill register. Until now he had been able to maintain his resonant baritone.

"Yes, that's right, Judge. When I put it into my drawer, it automatically went back into circulation."

"Then these two bills we have here could have passed right through your hands, into that drawer, and back into circulation, couldn't they?"

"Yes, that's quite possible, Judge. I could check it for you to make certain, if you'd like."

"Check it?" The Judge was obviously stunned. Angus knew that he was no longer looking for the truth; he was looking for a way out. "How could you check it, Mr. Hennessey?"

"I have the numbers of those bills Red Molloy deposited that day." Silas put his hand into his pocket and drew out a piece of paper. "I wrote the numbers down, just as a precaution—in case anything ever came up. We keep lots of money lists, you know, looking for stolen money and that sort of thing. Since Red thought that money might have been buried, I decided to jot down the numbers."

"Yes, yes, I understand," the Judge said impatiently. "Well, go ahead and compare them. Are these numbers on your list?"

While Silas compared them, Colonel Beleau leaned over and whispered, "That's an unconscionable trick, Angus——"

"I loaded it for the prosecutor, Colonel. But the Judge has taken over his case."

Angus refused to look at the Colonel; and he noticed that Ben Procter was hiding a fiendish grin with the palm of his hand.

Silas Hennessey shrugged on the witness stand, then offered the piece of paper and the two bills to the Judge.

"No, these weren't among those deposited, your Honor. Do you want to check them?"

The Judge ignored his offer. He leaned toward the stand, steadying himself by grasping the edge of his big desk.

"Mr. Hennessey," he said, "do you know what the word 'perjury' means?"

"Yes, of course I do, Judge." Silas Hennessey blinked at him.

"Do you know what the penalty for perjury is?"

"No, not exactly."

"Perjury is a felony, Mr. Hennessey. You can get from one to twelve years in the federal penitentiary for it. Now I'm going to give you a chance to change any of your testimony that you might care to change before I dismiss you from the stand."

Silas Hennessey sat for a moment, still blinking at the scowling man in the high-backed chair.

"Do you mean you think I've been lying under oath, Judge?" he asked finally.

"You are not here to ask questions, Mr. Hennessey. You are here to answer them. My question is, do you want to change any of your testimony before you are excused?"

"Judge," Silas Hennessey said, drawing back in his chair with visible contempt and admirably little intimidation, "if you can prove that I've been lying, I'll be glad to go to jail."

"Silence in the court! . . . Step down. Call your next witness, Mr. De-Wolfe."

Judge Ring brought down his gavel hard.

Angus called Luke Sweeley. He had to grin when the old man came limping through the back entrance with Sam Doolan, strutting a little in his new clothes.

Luke's transformation bordered on the fantastic. The spectators were audibly astounded and even the Judge gaped at him for a moment. A shiny pair of ankle-length Jefferson shoes had replaced his old mule-eared boots (which were, in fact, in a package underneath the defense table). His old overalls, habitually worn and sometimes tobacco-stained at the bib, were strikingly absent. Luke Sweeley now appeared before the crowded room in new Nankeens, dark and still smelling of Weymond's Department Store; a linen shirt with high-winged paper collar and cuffs; a single-breasted sack coat matching the color of the Nankeens; and a gray vest with brown spots and trim. He crossed around the palisade and paraded to the stand, as happy as he had ever been.

Sam Doolan swore him in. When asked his name and occupation, he said, "Lucius Cornwall Sweeley. Drayman and mail carrier. American citizen. Born in Lamptonville, Kaintuk, eighteen-eighteen."

The courtroom roared with laughter. People always laughed at Luke. But not for long this time: Judge Ring pounded the gavel hard enough to have broken its handle if it hadn't been made of hickory.

"One more outburst and I'll clear the room!" He stood up, devoured with rage. "This is a Court of Law, and spectators are here as guests of the Court. They may not interrupt it under any circumstances!" And then he said, "Proceed, Mr. DeWolfe."

It was here that Angus saw clearly what had happened. The Judge's self-control had left him, and with it his judgment and his normally disciplined sense of courtroom propriety, as he had begun to realize that the case against Marcus had collapsed. Angus could almost feel sorry for him: the shock of recognizing himself as having been dedicated to hanging an innocent man would be enough to derange a moderately normal mind—what would it do to a Bible-pounding judicial zealot who had already sent eighty-one men through Jacob Lotz's high trap door?

But the discovery, Angus thought, was probably coming in stages. The Judge was now in the stage of knowing that Marcus was not guilty; and being not guilty could almost be a crime in itself at this point. Presently the Judge would enter another stage of recognition, and know that Marcus was not only not-guilty, but innocent. . . . Angus shuddered as he considered the man's predicament.

He turned slowly and questioned Luke about the visit to Marcus's cabin last July when the boy's things were gathered up and taken to his home for safekeeping. Luke told about spreading certain objects out on his sofa and thinking about them until finally he understood why the buckskin pouch always caught his eye. He told of his hunch that the pouch had been buried and he described his trip down to the Shawnee country. He described the grave that had been opened on Owl Creek, and he identified both pairs of boots with the clay on their heels, one pair as his own, the other as having come from the floor of Marcus Maywood's cabin. The dried clay on the two sets of boot heels were unmistakably the same, and unlike any clay around Ridgefield.

Angus offered the boots in evidence; they were marked defense exhibits three and four.

"Now," he said, "some time last month, Luke, toward the end of October, did you find anything unusual in your barn?"

"Yep," Luke answered.

"What did you find?"

"Two ten-dollar bills underneath a rock on top of a beam in my hayloft."

"And what did you do with them?"

"I gave them to you, didn't I?" Luke seemed alarmed that they might have been lost.

"Yes, you did." The courtroom started a laugh that was choked off by the Judge's gavel before it got very far. Angus said, smiling, "Your witness, Mr. Procter."

"No questions," Ben Procter said.

Judge Ring turned a scowl upon Luke Sweeley: a scowl that would have withered the soul of any average citizen. But the courtroom knew that Luke wasn't average. Luke was just a silly old man. Anyone could have figured out about that sacred tobacco bag if he'd been around Indians as much as Luke had. But who, besides Luke, would get that involved with Indians?

"Don't try to hurry away, Mr. Witness. The Court has a few questions for you."

"I wasn't leaving, Mr. Judge," Luke said pleasantly. "You're welcome to ask me anything you want to."

"You know, of course, that you *have* to answer my questions, don't you? Or can you understand that?"

"Sure, I know. Angus explained it to me." It was curious, Angus thought, the pleasure Luke got from playing the role of clown. He was having the time of his life. If he could leave the stand with everyone grinning, shaking their heads at what an old fool he was, he'd be amply paid for the trouble he'd gone to.

"Did he tell you what to say to me?" the Judge asked.

"No, he just said I'd have to tell the truth to you and Mr. Procter."

"Did he also say you should tell *him* the truth under oath?"

"Angus knows I wouldn't lie to him."

"Silence!" cried the Judge. He banged the gavel as the courtroom rocked with laughter. "Now, Mr. Witness," he went on, his voice fairly squeaking, "do you know what the word 'perjury' means?"

"Well . . . let's see." Luke pondered it for a moment. "It means lying, don't it?"

"It means lying under oath," the Judge said. "And it's a very serious crime. You could get up to twelve years in prison for lying under oath. Are you aware that you're under oath right now?"

"But I'm not lying," Luke said with a casual shrug, "so it don't matter."

"How much were you paid to tell that story about taking the ten-dollar bills off the beam in your barn?" Could the Judge expect to take Luke by surprise, Angus wondered, and uncover subornation as easily as that?

"Paid?" Luke asked.

"Where did you get those new clothes?"

"In Weymond's——"

Angus was on his feet. "Your Honor," he said, "I wonder if we couldn't——"

"Overruled," the Judge said without looking up. He brought down his gavel. "Order in the court. . . . Now, Mr. Witness, let's get to the bottom of your interest in this case. Why were you rummaging through the defendant's cabin, as you claim to have been?"

"You mean when I found the tobacco bag?"

"Yes, that's when I mean."

"I thought maybe I could turn up something that would help him, Judge. I always liked the boy while he was living out there. I knew he was courting a girl when he got into trouble." Luke paused, then blandly looked the Judge in the eye. "I was sort of rooting for the kid, I guess. With the girl, I mean. I never really believed he was a killer, and the girl was very nice. Her daddy was mean to her, and I felt sorry for them both. I'm just an old fool when it comes to love, Judge. . . ." Luke's face lighted up in a modestly self-conscious smile. He looked across the well of the court at Angus, and Angus thought he wiggled his ears before turning back.

Judge Ring's face trembled. He was speechless: swallowed by his own insufferableness.

Ben Procter rose quickly.

"If your Honor please," he said. But the Judge was deaf. Procter repeated loudly: "*If your Honor please!* The Government urges a ten-minute recess."

Angus marveled at the inappropriateness of words. This affair now had but little to do with government, and nothing whatever to do with honor.

The Judge turned from Luke Sweeley, surveying everything before him in a wide sweep around to Ben Procter's table. He might have been surveying a fat and abundant kingdom, or a jealous household rich with tapestries and gold. But he was fooling no one in the courtroom—not even, Angus suspected, himself.

He said, "Why does the Government want a recess, Mr. Procter?"

"May I approach the bench, your Honor?"

"Please do," he said laconically.

Procter crossed to the well, motioning for Angus to join him. Angus leaned toward the Colonel.

"Ben is ready to capitulate," he said.

"It will be a favor to Willard if he does. The poor man is on the verge of making a sorry spectacle of himself."

"The Judge has gone crazy, Colonel. You go to the bench with Ben. It will be easier for the Judge to accept Ben's advice if I'm not up there. Don't you think?"

Angus waited, pondering the ordeal some men suffered in the act of discovering they were wrong. The issue now before the court of human fates was whether Willard Ring could make that terrible discovery and still remain in touch with himself and the reality of his world. Angus didn't believe the man was going to collapse; Janet was probably right about him. If his physical structure had been so weak, he would already have succumbed, wouldn't he? The busy fates were doubtless dealing with his mind—which was vast and sick; not with his body—which was small but adequately strong.

Ben Procter and the Colonel returned after a brief conference at the bench.

The Judge leaned forward, grasping his desk with both hands, his face bitterly contorted as he looked out upon the sea of spectators who, it now appeared, were observing something more poignant than the prosecution of a criminal: the torture of self-destruction.

"The Court will stand in recess for ten minutes," the Judge said. "You're not dismissed yet, Mr. Witness." He got up and strode with palpably affected dignity through the back exit toward his chambers.

Ben Procter pulled Angus aside in the hall behind the main stair well, closing the door to milling spectators and newsmen alike.

"I had to stop him, Angus."

"It was time."

"Can you suggest anything?"

He paused, considering Procter skeptically. The man appeared to be in earnest.

"It's your move, Ben," he said. "I have no bright ideas."

"I'm convinced your boy is innocent. The Judge knows it, too."

"What do you propose?"

"I can't let him break up in public. I could kill the little sonofabitch for not listening to me before the trial." Procter's face plainly mirrored the anguish of his contradictory feelings. He said, "I wish you'd told me this whole story the other day, Angus."

"You know why I couldn't, Ben."

"You mean Mike Hall's testimony?"

"That's what I mean."

"But Gunnysack was guilty as hell. You don't really doubt that, do you?"

"No, he was guilty—but Mike Hall lied about him. And you knew it."

"I didn't ask him to lie, Angus."

"You *let* him do it, though—and he got a suspended sentence for his trouble."

"It would have been different if Gunnysack was innocent."

"Maywood *is* innocent."

Ben Procter said, "If you'll go back in and rest your case, I'll move for a directed acquittal."

"And if he refuses?"

"The jury will acquit. I'll urge them myself. If he fights me and some-how gets a conviction—which I'm sure he wouldn't try—I'll join you on appeal."

"He might declare a mistrial."

"Then I'll take it back to the Grand Jury tomorrow."

"All right. That's fair enough, Ben."

"I'm going inside and talk to him. I'll persuade him somehow, or kick his God damned impudent little ass."

"I'll wait for you here. The Colonel will represent me in chambers."

"Angus—it's only fair to the Judge to tell you this. He didn't have any-thing to do with the Mike Hall business. Red didn't know about it, either. I'm the only one who knew anything about it."

"I had wondered if the Judge knew," Angus said. "If you need me, I'll be right outside the door. Here comes the Colonel now."

Angus waited in the hallway alone.

Whatever exultation he felt was swept up in a surge of pity for the Judge, who was plainly beaten and at the end of his own rope.

He thought again of the outlaw Jim Drogan. He had been commissioned by the Territorial Governor to bring the man in: for Drogan had been an implacable foe of law and order—he had been robber, killer, cattle rustler, horse thief, and finally, to his own disaster, murderer of Nathan DeWolfe. Without batting an eyelash, Judge Ring would have put Jim Drogan up there on Jake Lotz's scaffold to struggle as best he could with the hand-

[186]

oiled noose—subaural, or submental. But Angus DeWolfe shot him off a cliff alongside a brimming pool, beneath a lovely waterfall where the green and brown reflections of the pine, the aspen, the tall reddening sumac shimmered peacefully.

He remembered . . . and he felt sick, as he had that day in the court-yard when he had seen the ugly scaffold for the first time. The Courthouse had been new then, glistening in the sun. His mind began projecting: Janet would have been eighteen. He was glad he hadn't known her. She would have been revolted by the weary, heartsick hero who had brought in big Jim Drogan, not alive. Perhaps the Colonel was partially right. "Are you trying to square something with your conscience, Angus?"

Well: have you succeeded? he asked himself. . . .

Ben Procter's head appeared at the door, motioning for him to come inside.

He went into the Judge's chambers. The Colonel quickly nodded to him confidently.

Judge Ring was sitting at his desk before the gray-draped wall and windows. He might have been presiding at a lodge meeting. Or he might have been sitting before the fates, not the Judge, but the judged.

Procter said, "I've told his Honor about my proposition to you, Angus. Do you mind if we ask you for a summary of the rest of your case?"

"I thought you'd better give it to them, Angus," said the Colonel.

"No, I don't mind, Ben," Angus said, watching the Judge closely.

"We don't have too much confidence in Sweeley's testimony. We wonder if you're going to offer any proof that the twenty dollars on exhibit are the same bills Luke took from the beam in his barn."

Procter winked at him to indicate that he was humoring the Judge.

"Yes," Angus said, suppressing an urge to laugh at them. "I plan to swear myself in, and state that they are the bills Luke handed me. You'll then have Marcus's testimony that he put the bills up there, Luke's that he took them down, and mine that they reached court. That's the best I can do on that score."

The Judge sat in suspicious silence. Ben Procter nodded.

"And the rest, Angus?"

"Clayt Mosley is here to testify that he gave the Shawnee clan three hundred and twenty dollars, in tens, for some horses at the time Marcus's father was killed. He came up from Austin to testify. The old man, Da-ni-mah, will tell you that the money was given to the widow and that he put it into the grave at her request. The widow believed it to be evil, since it came into her possession in connection with her husband's death. And, finally, I have a storekeeper, by the name of Dan Kelso, from the Shawnee country, who'll testify that he talked to Jake Flower after he left the Sac and Fox Agent. Flower told him that he was carrying hard money because he'd had trouble getting greenbacks accepted out in the Unassigned Lands when he'd made the run. And the boy's mother is here—but I had decided I wouldn't need to put her on the stand. She's crushed that this story had to be told. She's terribly sensitive about that grave."

"Mr. DeWolfe," said the Judge suddenly, "why are you keeping my daughter at the hotel?"

Angus bridled with surprise, wondering how much, if any, the Judge had been hearing. He said, "Judge, I didn't think she should come to the courtroom during the trial. I wanted to keep extraneous emotions out of this if possible."

"She didn't even come home."

"That was her desire, not mine."

"Are you going to marry her?"

"Yes."

"Do you believe it is possible for a child to live a happy life in defiance of its parents?"

"Janet isn't a child," he said.

The Judge stared at him blankly, then looked down at his desk and clasped his hands together.

"Our ten minutes are up long since, Mr. Procter. I'll be in as soon as you've returned to the courtroom."

Angus turned and went through the door with the Colonel and Procter following him.

Fifteen minutes later, Judge Willard P. Ring dismissed Luke Sweeley from the stand and sat behind his bench, erect in the high-backed chair, gavel still in hand, smiling the half-smile of his ego's personal secret. He leaned forward, the Justicer:

"Gentlemen of the jury, as you know, the Judge of any court decides upon the law and the jury decides upon the facts. Judgment, therefore, is a twofold consideration: the wisdom of a mind presumably trained and experienced in the history and significance of law, on the one hand, and the wisdom of twelve minds schooled to distinguish between the probable and the improbable circumstances of life, on the other. Among the duties of the presiding Judge, however, is the burden of deciding whether there are indeed any facts to be decided. Instances occur which produce no facts significantly in dispute. Such is the case we have heard today. Justice decrees that where the facts are not in dispute but, undisputed, remain plausibly consistent with the assumption of the defendant's innocence, no case may lie before a jury for decision. Justice therefore requires that this defendant be set free, and you are directed to retire to the jury room and bring in a verdict of not guilty."

The Judge paused, turned to face the courtroom more directly:

"It is with humility that we close this case against Marcus Maywood. He has gone through an ordeal which might easily have been obviated had he not been irrationally fearful of the processes of justice. It is written in the proverbs of Solomon, son of David, king of Israel: 'The wicked flee when no man pursueth: but the righteous are as bold as a lion.'"

Now the Judge's eyes came to rest on Angus, who watched in amazement, fascinated to see large tears streaming down the man's face, across the enigmatic smile, onto the black lapels.

He said, "Marcus Maywood fled, but his crime, we now know, was not murder. It was filial transgression. And we may rejoice in the knowledge that his disrespect for his father produced in him a panic of remorse. For we know that when the children of Israel came into the wilderness of Sinai, Moses went up unto God and the Lord called to him, saying: Honor thy father and thy mother, that thy days may be long upon the land which the Lord thy God giveth thee. And it is written that he who turneth away his ear from the law, even his prayer shall be abomination. . . ."

The Judge stared at the gaping courtroom. Deliberately, he brought down the gavel a final time. Then he pushed back from the massive maple desk. His face was deathly pale. He opened his mouth as if to speak again, but remained silent.

He strode from behind the desk and around the jury box to the well of the court where he stared at Angus in passing. Then he walked unsteadily up the center aisle and out through the front corridor, disappearing from sight.

The spectators rose from their seats in a scramble of excitement.

Ben Procter came over to Angus.

"Where's Doc?"

"He was standing near the front door a few minutes ago."

"I'll go find him. We'd better see that Willard gets home all right, don't you think?"

"Yes, I do. I'm going to the hotel, Ben. I'll be with Janet. Will you let us know if anything is wrong?"

"Sure, Angus."

Ben Procter pushed through the crowd toward the front.

But it was Luke who came to the hotel after them. Janet was in Angus's room where she had been listening to his description of her father's behavior at the end of the trial.

"When I seen Doc and Ben Procter following him from the court, Angus,

I decided to mosey along that way myself." Luke shifted his weight uncomfortably from his game leg to his good one. "Just my everlasting curiosity, I guess."

"What happened?" Janet asked.

"Well, your daddy went right on past your house, Miss."

"Past?" Angus asked.

"Just like he wasn't going home at all. Doc and Ben hurried to catch up with him, but he collapsed before they reached him." Luke turned to Janet. "They carried him back to the house."

"Did you talk to Doc, Luke?" she asked.

"No, he stayed upstairs with your daddy."

"Did you see my mother?"

"For a minute."

"Does she want me there?"

"Yes. Said tell you and Angus to wait downstairs for her. I brought your daddy's rig over for you. It's outside."

Janet went for her coat and Angus waited with Luke in the hall, wondering if in reality Janet would be able to forgive him, and herself.

"How was he when they carried him inside, Luke?"

"Doc was worried," Luke said.

"Did he look pretty bad?"

"He didn't look good."

"How did Mrs. Ring seem to take it?"

"She ain't no weakling, Angus."

"This will be tough on Janet. I'm afraid she's going to blame herself to some extent. Will you go over with us?"

"You take her alone," Luke said, "so she can talk easier. Women need to talk when they feel bad. I'll come and wait outside in case there's anything I can do. My rig is over by the square."

"There's no reason for you to wait outside."

"I've been nosy enough, Angus."

Janet came out and they hurried downstairs through the lobby. He helped her into the buggy, then sat beside her and took the reins, trying to sort out his feelings. He realized that he had little feeling of any kind for the Judge—that would come later, perhaps, when time and the settling of circumstance would have provided a basis for evaluation—but he was concerned for Janet. He had not yet been able to read anything on her face. In the dark he couldn't see her clearly. But it would be impossible for her completely to escape her father's misfortune, whatever it was going to be.

"Darling," she said softly from the darkness beside him, "I think my father may die."

"Maybe not. Maybe it's nature's way of adjusting him to the shock he's had."

"The shock of being so wrong?"

"Of having had an innocent man practically on the gallows."

"Angus, it seems important for me to say this. I hate him. I hope he doesn't die—for my mother's sake. If he dies and I have to try to comfort her, I'll keep my tongue. But I've got to remember that I hate him, whether he lives or not."

"What you have to remember," he said, "is that you're free from him. The rest isn't important now—is it?"

"It's important for me to be honest about it."

"Haven't you always been? You have lied to him at times—you had to, I think. But you haven't lied *about* him. Not to me, anyway. And I don't think you have to your mother."

She was silent, and he said, "If you've been hating him, then keep on hating him. There's no reason to change just because he's ill. That would be hypocritical. If you haven't actually hated him—then there's no reason to hate him now."

"Angus," she said, "sometimes I wonder how you can be so calculated all the time. Didn't you ever lose your wits in your life and fly off the handle? Didn't you ever just *do* something, and then think about it later?"

"Yes."

"What did you ever do without thinking about it?" He could detect a mischievous note in her voice. And he was reassured, for that would indicate stability.

"I killed a man one time," he said. "If I had thought it out beforehand, I might have done exactly what I did, I don't know. I've certainly thought about it ever since."

Again she was silent for a moment, and then she said, "We have so much to learn about each other. It doesn't seem possible, but I love you more every time I see you."

"Janet," he said, "you know how to make a man feel pretty good."

She laughed softly.

"I didn't make you feel very good at noon today."

"No, you didn't," he admitted.

"I was sure you'd be too busy to bother with me. And it was wonderful to see Floyd again. I thought I had ruined that boy's life. Did you know I was egotistical enough to think a thing like that?"

"I can see how you might have worried about it."

He noticed that his pulses pounded again. He could hardly believe the capacity for jealousy that lived in him. "What did you talk about?"

"Oh, not much, really. We have nothing in common. He's much too worldly for me now. It's simply amazing. He wants to work on a New York paper. He thinks you're a great man, Angus. I like him for that."

"Did you tell him about us?"

"No. I wanted to hear his objective opinion of you."

"Trying to evaluate me at this late date?" he asked.

"No—evaluating Floyd," she said. And somehow he knew that he needn't fear for her any longer. Whatever was going to happen to her father would be, in its proper sense, her mother's misfortune. He felt, with some apprehension to be sure, and with a knowledge that he was better off than he had ever been before, that Janet was now free of her father because she had a man of her own.

He drew up before her house and leaped from the seat, then took her hand and helped her down.

They walked up the steps and she went through the door ahead of him. Ben Procter and Colonel Beleau were sitting beside each other on the sofa. The Colonel's face was total misery, and Angus knew immediately that Janet's father was dead.

Ben Procter started to speak, but footsteps on the landing above interrupted him. Angus looked up to see Alice Ring coming down with Doc holding her arm. The little round-faced woman was crying, but not hysterically. She was managing to contain herself greatly, he thought.

When she saw him, she pulled free from Doc's hand and came on down the stairs quickly.

He went to meet her.

"I'm sorry, Mrs. Ring," he said.

"Oh, Angus—you didn't do it," she cried. "The law killed him. . . ."